A Cottage in the Plotlands

DAWN KNOX

ISBN: 9798378843756

This edition is published by An Affair of the Heart Formatting and Cover © Publishingbuddy.co.uk Editing – Wendy Ogilvie Editorial Services

To my mum and dad.
Thank you for believing in me

Other books by Dawn Knox:

The Great War – 100 Stories of 100 Words Honouring Those Who Lived and Died 100 Years Ago

Historical Romance: 18th and 19th Century

The Duchess of Sydney
The Finding of Eden
The Other Place
The Dolphin's Kiss
The Pearl of Aphrodite
The Wooden Tokens

Historical Romance: 20th Century

A Plotland Cottage
A Touch of the Exotic
Between Two Wars
Wild Spirit
With All My Heart
Heart of Ice
Fearless Heart
Bletchley Secrets

Humorous Quirky Stories:

The Basilwade Chronicles
The Macaroon Chronicles
The Crispin Chronicles

Other books by Dawn Knox:

Sci-Fi and Speculative Fiction:

The Future Brokers (As DN Knox with Colin Payn)
Extraordinary

Short Horror Stories in Anthologies

Shrouded by Darkness – Tales of Terror
Greed
666 Dark Drabbles
Hate Dark Drabbles
Ancients Dark Drabbles
Oceans Dark Drabbles
The Female Complaint
Body-Smith 401
The Least He Could Do
Things You Can Create

Chapter One

1930 – Aylward Street, Stepney, East End of London:

Home.

And yet not home in the sense that Joanna Marshall felt any attachment to the place. It was merely the street where she and her mother were staying with Aunt Ivy.

Nasty, vindictive Aunt Ivy.

Joanna stopped as she turned onto Aylward Street. Even after a hectic day at work, she paused on the corner, as if her feet were reluctant to carry her across the road to number 10.

She took the key out of her pocket and looked along the row of terraced houses. Scruffy children sat on scrubbed doorsteps, chased each other across the cobbled road, and played hopscotch on a chalked grid. A small girl with scuffed knees skipped along the pavement towards number 10, her mouth moving silently as if in conversation with an imaginary friend. She stopped abruptly, and, with wide eyes, looked up at the houses. Then, after jabbing a finger at number 10, she reached for her pretend companion's hand and together they ran across the road. The girl threw an anxious glance over her shoulder as if satisfying herself she and her friend were safe.

Joanna smiled. She knew why none of the neighbourhood children went near number 10. Many of them had experienced the bristle end of Aunt Ivy's broom as well as her sharp tongue.

The house belonged to Joanna's Uncle John, but he spent little time there. No one wanted to be anywhere near number 10, including the owner.

Well, there was no point lingering in the hot, dusty street. Joanna's feet were sore after the long walk, and her shoulders ached after a day in the typing pool. She wanted to take off her shoes and put her bag down – if only for a few minutes – before she had to help Aunt Ivy make supper. She crossed the road, and her step lightened at the thought Ma might already have arrived home.

Joanna sighed as she approached the pristine doorstep and shiny black door. Number 10 was identical to all the other houses in Aylward Street – a front door and parlour window on the ground floor and two-bedroom windows upstairs. The same, but completely different. It was smarter than its tired neighbours, whose doors were scuffed and scraped by the frequent comings and goings. A bone china cup and saucer on a shelf of chipped and well-used mugs.

Joanna turned her key in the lock. No one else in the street bothered to lock their doors, but Aunt Ivy liked her privacy. Anyone wandering in, even with a friendly greeting, would not be welcome.

Not that anyone would have dared. Or wanted to.

Once in the hall, Joanna took off her suit jacket and hung it up. Only four coats or jackets ever hung there – her uncle's and aunt's, her mother's and hers. But today, Uncle's was missing. Aunt Ivy would have preferred it had there only been two coats hanging in the passage. It was a matter of pride to her that in number 10 there was no need to take in lodgers, unlike many of her neighbours. Neither did Aunt Ivy have needy family members who wanted a home – well, not until Joanna and her mother, Rose, had moved in after Pa had died.

At the memory of her father's death, Joanna forced back tears. Several months had passed. The pain was still acute. Sadness for her loss, for Ma's anguish and loneliness, and for the broken man her father had become on the battlefields of the Somme in 1916. She wiped away a tear and stroked Ma's jacket. At least she was home from work. "John, is that you?" It was her aunt's voice coming from the kitchen at the end of the dingy passage. A tall, gaunt woman with sharp features opened the door and her expression dropped when she saw her niece. "Oh, it's you. You're late." She turned and went back into the kitchen, slamming the door behind her before Joanna could explain. Not that Aunt Ivy wanted an explanation, nor that she owed her aunt one. But Joanna had been brought up to respect adults.

However, having reached the age of eighteen, she was now realising not all adults deserved her respect.

Aunt Ivy was one.

Miss Bartle, the office supervisor, was another. It was she who'd kept Joanna late at work after she'd changed her mind about a document and insisted Joanna re-type it. She'd claimed it had been Joanna's mistake, which wasn't true, but it had been pointless to argue. However, it meant Joanna had been late and missed her usual bus. She'd tried to be positive and think of the money she'd saved on the fare, but recently, it was becoming harder to see the bright side of things.

It had been a hot and sultry late August day – not the sort of weather in which to rush. Joanna was sticky and uncomfortable. She was about to go upstairs to brush her hair and splash her face with cold water when her aunt opened the door again. A gust of air belched into the hall, carrying the tell-tale aroma of dinner. Stew again.

"Well, don't just stand there, girl. Come and help. I'm not here for your pleasure. And where's your mother? She got home ages ago. The least she could do for your bed and board is help me. This isn't a hotel, you know."

"Here I am, Ivy." Ma appeared at the top of the stairs, and Joanna noticed how puffy her ankles were. Worse than they'd been that morning. She spent most of the day on her feet in the laundry where she worked, and recently, by the evening, she'd been in great discomfort.

Ma smiled at her daughter. "Evening, Joey. You're late, darling. Have you had a good day?" Joanna nodded. "Yes, thank you, Ma. I just had to finish some work before I came home."

"That's my girl." Her mother's face lit up with pride. Joanna had seen photographs of Ma taken years before, and people had often remarked on the similarity between mother and daughter. The same heart-shaped face. The same curly hair, although during the last year, Ma's had turned from the rich chestnut colour they'd shared to dull grey. Joanna frowned. Today, more than ever, Ma seemed older. Dark smudges lay beneath her eyes and the lines between her brows were deeper than usual, suggesting she was in pain. Or perhaps it was just the gloom of the stairwell casting shadows.

"I'm coming, Ivy," Ma said as she slowly descended the stairs, gripping the banister. Joanna could hear she was trying to keep the weariness out of her voice. Not something her aunt would have noticed. Nor cared about if she had.

"Why don't you rest, Ma? I'll set the table and help Aunt Ivy." Joanna stood back, allowing her mother to pass.

Aunt Ivy sniffed to show what she thought about her niece's suggestion as she went back in the kitchen.

While Joanna put the cloth on the table, her aunt went back to the range and stirred the stew, releasing clouds of steam that wafted the smell of overcooked vegetables and fatty lamb around the room. Aunt Ivy had already brought the polished oak canteen of cutlery into the kitchen and Joanna raised the lid. She winced, not wanting to ask how many places to set.

"Three!" Aunt Ivy snapped before Joanna could open her mouth. "Three tonight. Your uncle's been delayed. He'll be home tomorrow. His company work him too hard. I've told him to complain, but you know your uncle … he never stands up for himself." She slammed the lid back on the stew pot.

Yes, Joanna knew her uncle would be unlikely to complain. Not that there was any need to discuss the hours he worked with his boss. Joanna knew Uncle John used his job as an excuse to stay away from home so he could avoid conflict with his wife. He was a travelling salesman and often worked in Sussex, staying with his cousin in Brighton. Joanna was unaware if her aunt knew Uncle John didn't work all the hours he claimed – but suspected she did – hence the irritation in her voice. Each night Joanna dreaded asking how many places to lay for supper because when it was only three, it emphasised his absence and fuelled Aunt Ivy's resentment.

The meal was eaten in silence, other than requests

to pass the salt or to comment on the unusually sticky, stifling weather. Ma always praised the meal Aunt Ivy had cooked, however dull and unappetising.

"Delicious, Ivy. Cooked to perfection as usual."

Aunt Ivy fanned herself with a napkin and smoothed a few grey hairs back into place, checking the usually immaculate bun at the back of her head. It was too hot for conversation. Her sniff was the only reply. It conveyed the often-voiced complaint that she worked hard to produce such a fine supper while everyone else was out. It was as if she thought they were enjoying themselves all day, not working full time. Often, she'd sneer at her neighbours who she claimed thought themselves lucky to have bread and dripping. In her house, the evening meal was always cooked. Joanna doubted any of the neighbours had ever discussed what they ate with Aunt Ivy, so how would she know? Anyway, in such heat, Joanna would have preferred bread and dripping.

She wanted to groan aloud. Ma was so kind and gentle. How had their lives come to this? Having to tiptoe around unpleasant Aunt Ivy to keep a roof over their heads.

When Pa had died, he'd left their finances in such a muddle, even loyal Ma had been surprised. It hadn't been his fault, of course. Joanna remembered little about him before he'd gone to France to fight in the Great War.

Her memories, however, were vivid from when he'd come back. He'd been wounded on the Somme in 1916. After his return, nights had been filled with his screams and days with his tears. And then, gradually, Pa gave up as if his mind had simply switched off the terror and anguish.

At least, at the end, he'd been at peace. Joanna had loved him dearly, but sometimes it had appeared he'd been the child, and she the adult. After he'd died, regret had weighed her down. Could she have done more? Been kinder? More understanding? Helped him or Ma to make things better ...? If only she'd known he'd be taken from them so soon.

It had rapidly become obvious Ma and Joanna couldn't afford to live in their house in Wimbledon, and Uncle John had taken them in while they saved enough to afford their own place. Ma had found a job in a laundry and saved every penny she earned. Joanna's job in the typing pool of a solicitor's firm earned slightly more, and she handed her wage packet to Ma each week so they could pay Aunt Ivy for their keep. What remained of their shared wages was saved for their new home.

A new home.

How Joanna longed for that. Away from Aunt Ivy's critical eyes and hurtful remarks. To be a family, once again – even if Pa would never be part of it.

Finally, the uncomfortable meal was over. Aunt Ivy

insisted on washing the dishes so the utmost care was taken with her china and cutlery. Ma and Jo dried up and put everything away. Once the knives, forks and spoons had been carefully replaced in the canteen, Aunt Ivy complained her wrist hurt and suggested that for once, Joanna could carry the prized possession into the parlour and put it away.

Joanna suppressed her giggles as Aunt Ivy led her down the hall as if they were taking part in a triumphal procession. She opened the door with a flourish. It was only the second time Joanna had been in the room – the first had been when Uncle John had taken her in to show her the clock he'd mended and Aunt Ivy had hovered by the door the entire time, watching them anxiously.

As Joanna carried the oak box into the pretentious room, the air was still and heavy, tinged with beeswax and mothballs. Like stepping onto a theatre stage after the play had finished, and the actors had all gone home. What a sad place this was. It was reserved for entertaining company and showing off the family's wealth. But no one ever visited, so the room was silent and gloomy. Now, Aunt Ivy's sister-in-law and niece were her only company, and although they hadn't been forbidden to enter, both guests understood it would be frowned upon.

Joanna made a show of placing the box back on the crocheted mat to save scratching the surface of the sideboard and glanced surreptitiously around the room. It had occurred to her the previous week that not only did Aunt Ivy never mention her two grown-up children, but also, there was no evidence of them in the house. She'd assumed there'd be at least one family photograph that included her cousins, David and Amelia, and since she hadn't seen one elsewhere, it must surely be in the museum-like parlour.

But no. There were two framed photographs of Uncle John and Aunt Ivy on their wedding day. Two stern-faced people, rigid and uncomfortable in their wedding clothes. But no photographs of their two children.

Joanna had a terrible thought: perhaps both her cousins had died. No, that was nonsense. Uncle John would have told Ma, who'd surely have mentioned it. That's not the sort of thing to slip someone's memory. She'd ask Ma later what had happened to her two cousins. They were both several years older than her and had presumably left home and rarely returned. Perhaps there was a photograph of them in Aunt Ivy's bedroom.

Or maybe they'd left for good, and Aunt Ivy didn't want to be reminded.

While they tidied everything away in the kitchen, the sounds of children playing in next door's backyard drifted in through the open door. Aunt Ivy had been quiet during the meal; keeping herself aloof from the two unwelcome guests she held in contempt. However, at each shout and scream, she winced, and her loyalties shifted. Now, Aunt Ivy treated Joanna and Ma as confidantes, as once again, she expressed how much she detested living among people she considered inferior.

"This morning, I overheard Mrs Palmer in the corner shop say several of those dreadful Thomsett children next door were sick. You wouldn't think so from the din they're making. If only it wasn't so hot, I'd shut the door." She put the teapot down with a thud. "I wouldn't be surprised if they've all got scabies or some other ghastly disease. There are so many dirty children in that household, it shouldn't be allowed. And as for that fishwife three doors down, apparently, her daughter's in the family way again ..."

Joanna and Ma sipped their tea in silence. They both knew better than to disagree. Ma had tried several times to excuse the neighbours' behaviour, but Aunt Ivy wasn't interested. She wanted her own judgemental opinions confirmed.

Joanna realised she was holding her breath. Not because of what Aunt Ivy was saying about the Thomsetts next door or the other neighbours – she barely knew them – she was dreading what was almost certainly about to come. Once Aunt Ivy started listing the real and imagined slights and insults she endured from her neighbours, she seemed to feel her judgement and comment were required on other topics. Since Ma and Joanna were a captive audience, those topics often related to them.

"Consider yourself lucky you don't have to put up with such a trial, Rose. I've begged John to sell up and move. But no. Really! Men! It's all right for them. They're out all day. They don't have to deal with the riffraff in the neighbourhood."

"John loves this house, Ivy. It's where he and I were born."

"Well, you would stick up for your brother, wouldn't you? But I suppose it's too much for you to understand, with Tom having been under your feet all the time. If he'd got himself a job like he should have done after he came back from France, you and Joanna wouldn't be in such a dire position. Negligence. That's what I call it."

Ma's hand shook as she put the cup back on the saucer, although she kept her voice steady. "Tom came back with shell shock after doing his duty to king and country."

When Aunt Ivy sniffed and pursed her lips, she might as well have voiced the words both Joanna and Ma knew she was thinking, *Shell shock? Stuff and nonsense! You mean he was a malingerer!*

Ma abruptly changed the subject, her voice artificially bright. "Well, it's Friday tomorrow. Payday. I'll be sure to have your money ready for you on Saturday as usual, Ivy."

"Good. And are you any closer to finding a place to stay?"

"I'm still looking, but it shouldn't be long."

Aunt Ivy's sniff conveyed the words, *One day is too long for me.*

Once they'd finished their tea and tidied away, Ma excused herself, saying she was tired. Joanna followed her upstairs to their bedroom.

Aunt Ivy had inhaled sharply, and her eyebrows had risen in annoyance that her sister-in-law and niece preferred to go to their room rather than spend the evening with her.

Ma grunted with the effort of climbing the stairs. The hot day had obviously drained her. How could Aunt Ivy have taunted her like that? As Joanna followed Ma into their bedroom, she wondered why her aunt was annoyed at being left alone that evening. Was it possible she was lonely? If so, it was her own fault. If life was as unfair to her as she claimed, then she only had herself to blame for being so nasty.

Ma and Joanna knew all about unfairness. It was when your beloved husband or father came back from a war a broken man and died at an early age. It was when you had to leave your home and friends and live with an aunt who despised you.

But as Ma had told Joanna countless times since Pa

had returned, life wasn't fair. And it appeared she was correct. Those who deserved a chance were denied it, and those who had their share were given more than they needed. How Joanna longed for the courage to stomp downstairs and shout at her aunt. She'd tell her to stop being unpleasant to Ma and instead of resenting her husband staying in Brighton, she ought to be nicer to him. Then she'd have fairness. In fact, she'd have it all – a lovely husband, a comfortable home, an enjoyable life … She was about to add 'a family' to the list when she remembered her cousins.

"Where are David and Amelia, Ma?"

Ma sat on the bed and groaned as she eased her stockings over her swollen ankles. "Well, as far as I know, David joined the army and is now in India. Amelia's married and living somewhere in Sussex. She used to write to me from time to time, but obviously not while I've been living here."

"Why doesn't Aunt Ivy ever mention them?"

Ma shook her head sadly. "They both fell out with her and haven't contacted her since."

Joanna wasn't surprised her cousins didn't want to spend time with Aunt Ivy. Nevertheless, it was still shocking to hear they'd rejected their own mother. "What happened?"

"Oh, typical Ivy. She tried to run their lives. David fell in love with a girl who lived across the road, but Ivy wouldn't accept her. She said the girl was too common to become part of their family. In the end, David joined the army. And as for Amelia ... She was always such a clever girl. She wanted to study to be a doctor, but Ivy wanted her to marry well and stay at home. I expect you've guessed what happened."

"She ran away?"

"Exactly. She became a nurse. One day, I wouldn't mind betting she'll go back to her studies. But your aunt will probably never know."

Joanna nodded. "That's sad. But she doesn't deserve any family if she treated them like she's treating us."

"That's one way of looking at it." Ma lay back on her pillow with a sigh. "You're still young and have little experience of life, but one day, perhaps you'll see it doesn't help to come down to her level, Joey. You must rise above it. Now, we have no choice. We must take all her unkindness without comment because we dare not anger her. But even so, we need to be understanding—"

"*Understanding?* Ma! She's got everything and we've got nothing! Shouldn't she show us understanding?"

"Shhh! Of course, she should, but put yourself in her shoes, Joey. How hard must it be for her to see how well we get on together? Each time she sees us, it must remind her of her failed relationships with her children. That's no excuse, of course, but I find it helps me to be more sympathetic."

"I suppose ..." Joanna wasn't convinced.

Ma lowered her voice to a whisper. "Just think. She doesn't even know she's got grandchildren."

"Grandchildren?" Joanna stopped brushing her hair in surprise. She was finding out so much about the family to whom she'd given little thought.

"Amelia has a boy and a girl. I've lost touch with David, but he may have children, too. So, Ivy has at least two grandchildren, but she has no idea they exist. And if things stay the same, she never will."

Joanna still couldn't rid herself of the idea her aunt had brought it on herself. "That's sad," she murmured, "but I still think you're very kind. She's made some horrible claims about Pa, and you. How can you bear it?"

On several occasions, Aunt Ivy had hinted both Ma and Pa had been unfaithful during the years Pa had been in France. It had all been veiled as if a joke, but Joanna had been horrified. And she knew it had shocked Ma.

"I don't suppose for one minute your aunt believes Tom or I were unfaithful. She's just a strange, complicated, and bitter woman who fears her husband has another woman. And I suspect he has."

"I don't understand how Uncle John could have married her. Much less why he stays."

"Poor John. Even as a young boy, he always took the easy way out. But I think he genuinely loved Ivy once.

And as strange as it may seem, she loved him in her own way."

"What happened?" It was hard to believe they'd once loved each other.

"Ivy's family is wealthier than ours. Her parents warned her not to make such a poor match, but she carried on anyway. I think she expected her father to forgive her and to subsidise her and John. She even thought her father would give John a job in his store. But he refused. I suppose Ivy's bitterness grew from there."

"Well, thank goodness Uncle John stood up to Aunt Ivy and took us in. She'd have seen us on the streets."

"Ah, by the way." Ma's tired face lit up with enthusiasm. "I've been keeping this to myself until I was more certain, but I think you need some good news. John's been helping me find a new house and it shouldn't be long now, my Joey. Please tell me you can put up with your aunt's bad temper for a few more weeks until we've saved enough."

"Ma! That's wonderful! Where will we be going?"

"I'll tell you all about it when the time comes, but I can promise you it'll be miles from your aunt. We'll start a new life."

"Can we afford it?" Please let it be true! Was it possible that at last, life was showing them some favour?

"Well, it's been a stretch, but I put everything we

had after your pa died, all the money we've saved and …" She paused for a second. "I sold a few things, too." She slid one hand over the other and Joanna realised Ma's top hand was ringless.

"Oh, no, Ma! Not your rings!" And then another thought. "Not your wedding ring?"

Ma sighed and moved her hands apart. Not one ring remained.

"Oh, Ma!" A lump formed in Joanna's throat.

"Don't fret, Joey. I don't need rings. But we do need a home."

"But your wedding ring …"

"Pa would understand. I don't need a ring to remind me how much I love and miss him. Truly, it's better this way."

Joanna lay down beside her mother, her arms crossed beneath her head, staring up at the ceiling. Soon, they'd leave Aunt Ivy behind with her disagreeable ways and her miserable life. New home, new friends. Just a few more weeks …

Joanna turned over and clung to the edge of the sagging mattress, trying not to roll into the dip in the centre. The closer she got to Ma, the more they'd warm each up on this humid evening. Months before, when they moved into the house, the bedroom had been chilly, with drafts from the ill-fitting windows, and then they'd clung together in the bed, warming each other, and giving comfort. Each night, Joanna had held her mother while sobs racked her body at the loss of her beloved, Tom, until sleep had overtaken them both.

Joanna awoke at dawn. It was cooler than it had been all night, although still warm. She felt as though she'd only just fallen asleep.

Echoes of the waking day drifted into the room from the street outside, and Joanna knew she'd soon have to get up. The milkman's horse *clip-clopped* – metal against stone – accompanied by the rumble of cartwheels over cobbles and the frenzied clinking of glass bottles. The driver coughed – a hoarse, hacking bark, then several grumbling growls. He called a croaky greeting to someone, then turned the corner. The sounds faded. As Aylward Street woke up, front doors opened and closed, and footsteps rang out as neighbours set off down the road to begin their day at work. From the sound of heavy boots against the pavement, the passers-by were men heading towards the docks.

Joanna sighed and squeezed her hot, gritty eyes tightly shut. They ached as if she'd been reading all night. She'd have to pay attention at work because Miss Bartle had been irritable with the heat the previous day and it was likely to be as uncomfortable today. Now her new life was so close, she dared not risk losing her job and setting the date back even further. It had been such a joy to see Ma's face light up when she'd told Joanna about the new home.

Perhaps life could play fair after all. Aunt Ivy had pushed everyone away and now had no one. Joanna and Ma had worked hard, and they'd been given a second chance, even if it was without Pa.

Ma hadn't slept well either. After a cup of tea and a slice of bread and jam, they tidied the kitchen, ready for Aunt Ivy, and quietly left the house. As usual, Joanna accompanied Ma to the laundry. It added to her journey time, but it was pleasant to talk without fear of Aunt Ivy snooping. That morning, Ma had been quieter than usual. Joanna had encouraged her to eat a little more than the mouthful she'd managed, but she'd said she had no appetite. It was understandable. Joanna hadn't been hungry either.

As they drew closer to the river, a gentle breeze moved across the water and stirred the heavy air. That was promising. Perhaps the day would be slightly cooler after all, although Joanna knew Ma would swelter all day while she worked. She kissed her goodbye at the door of Reilly's Laundry and hurried back to the main road to catch the bus towards the City.

Joanna arrived at Tredegar, Murchison & Franklin ten minutes early, but Miss Bartle's greeting was frosty. "Good morning, Miss Marshall. I hope you'll pay more attention to your work today than you did yesterday."

"Yes, Miss Bartle." Joanna clenched her teeth. Any mistakes had been the supervisor's not Joanna's. But of course, she couldn't say that. Instead, she patted her hair, tucking stray curls back into place after her dash to work. Best not to give Miss Bartle anything else to criticise.

"The Dragon's on top form today," whispered Elsie, the girl who sat next to Joanna. She nodded towards Miss Bartle. "Don't worry, love, yer hair's fine. You'll be pleased to hear this. Jessie told me she'll be getting married soon. When they replace 'er, it'll probably be with someone younger than you. The Dragon'll have someone new to torment. She'll forget all about you then."

Joanna worked hard all day. She barely looked up and when she did, she ensured her eyes didn't stray to the clock – something that annoyed Miss Bartle. She ate her lunch in the shady churchyard across the street but hurried back to arrive at her typewriter five minutes early. By late afternoon, her fingers thrummed with the repeated *tap, tap, tap* of the keys. At half-past five, she finished the report she was typing, pressed the carriage return with a *ding* and eased the paper out of the machine. She rotated her shoulders and tipped her head backwards, trying to relax the muscles that had been working furiously all day.

What had Ma's day been like in the hot, steamy

laundry? As Joanna followed the other girls out, trying not to appear too eager to leave – something else that annoyed Miss Bartle – she wondered whether Pearl, the laundry's owner, had allowed Ma to sit down and rest her legs.

Not much longer and they could both give up their jobs. Joanna squeezed her handbag tightly. At least she'd been paid, and the unopened wage packet was safely inside. She couldn't wait to add it to Ma's money.

As she left the typing pool, Ted, one of the messenger boys, called out to her. The previous day, he'd invited her out to the cinema, but she'd gently refused. She didn't need more complications in her life. And anyway, Elsie had warned her off him. "Before you know it, he'll have 'is hands all over you. Best tell 'im to sling his hook."

"Hello, Miss Marshall. I didn't think you'd still be 'ere. False alarm, was it?"

Joanna frowned at him.

"Yer mum. She's all right then?" he added.

"Mum?"

"Yeah. I brought a note up for you earlier to say she'd been taken ill. I gave it to the Dragon."

Joanna stopped abruptly, causing several girls to glare at her as they moved around her and past, down the stairs.

"You brought a note for me?"

"Yeah. About half-past two, it were. Don't tell me Bartle didn't give it to you!"

"No." The word caught in Joanna's throat. She reached out to hold on to the banister. Perhaps he'd been mistaken, and the note had been for someone else.

As if reading her mind, Ted said, "The message were definitely for you so I brought it straight over. I put it right in the Dragon's hand."

Joanna shivered. It couldn't be true. Perhaps Ma's ankles had swollen further. But why would they call her? Joanna's chest tightened and her heart boomed like a warning bell.

"Thank you, Ted." Joanna turned on her heel and took the stairs two at a time, running back to the typing pool. Miss Bartle was still seated at her desk. As Joanna entered, she said sharply, "Miss Marshall, that is no way to enter the typing pool. This is a place of business, not a park."

But Joanna was beyond caring. "Do you have a note for me?"

Colour rose to Miss Bartle's cheeks. Anger because a junior staff member had spoken so rudely, or guilt because she'd failed to pass on a message?

"I ... I believe I may have a note for you." She slid sheets of paper over the surface of the desk until she found it.

Joanna's jaw dropped open, and she stared at the

woman, speechless. The colour in Miss Bartle's cheeks deepened. "I can't be expected to pass on every note as it arrives on my desk. While you are being paid by Tredegar, Murchison & Franklin, you work. You do not take part in personal correspondence."

Joanna snatched the paper from her, unfolded it, and read. Ted had been correct. With a strangled cry, Joanna turned and fled down the stairs, past the girls who were gossiping in the entrance hall, and out into the street.

The sun still beat down, its rays reflecting mercilessly off the tall stone buildings of the City. She dodged between pedestrians hurrying towards the bus stop. If there was no bus, she'd run from stop to stop. Even if it meant running all the way to Reilly's Laundry.

"Joanna! Where on earth have you been? I telephoned your company hours ago." Pearl Reilly held her hands, palms upward, an expression of horror on her face.

After her mad dash from the City to the laundry in such heat, Joanna's head was thumping and her throat burnt.

"I ..." But really, what was the point of explaining? "How's Ma?"

"I don't know. They took her to the London."

"*The London Hospital?*" Joanna's heart was pounding after the run.

"I wouldn't have called you at work unless it'd been really serious." Pearl's lips were set in a straight line.

"Serious?" Joanna could scarcely push the word past the lump in her throat.

"Yer mum fainted and hit her head. It didn't look good."

Ma. Fainted. Hospital.

Joanna spun around and stumbled towards the door and out into the street.

At the top of the steps of the London Hospital, Joanna doubled over, fighting for breath. She wiped her forehead with the back of her hand and bit her quivering bottom lip to stop herself crying. As she entered the building, sweat trickled down her back.

Where should she go?

Nurses in starched uniforms bustled past, helping patients, and pushing wheelchairs through corridors, pungent with the tang of antiseptic. White-coated doctors with stethoscopes swaying from side to side across their chests, strode purposefully by. Porters pushed trolleys with determination. Visitors carried bouquets. Everyone on their way somewhere and too busy to stop and ask the bewildered young woman if they could help.

"Joanna!" It was Uncle John, calling her from further down the corridor. He opened his arms, and she flew to him, clinging on and sobbing into his chest.

"I got home a few hours ago, and there was a message from Pearl Reilly. Where have you been, darling?" Uncle John stroked her hair gently.

"No one told me Ma was sick until I was about to leave this evening. I came as soon as I could. How is she? Where is she? Can I see her?"

Uncle John drew her to the side of the corridor, out of the stream of people. He swallowed, his eyes brimming with tears.

"Uncle John! Please!" Dread squeezed her heart in a vice-like grip.

A tear spilt over and trickled down his cheek. He raised his glasses and angrily wiped it away. "Joanna, darling. We must both be very brave." He swallowed. "Rose only regained consciousness briefly before she passed away. I was with her. I held her hand … She wasn't alone …" His voice trembled and he couldn't say more.

Joanna's heart pounded so hard, the drumming filled her ears, drowning the hum of the people in the corridor.

Thub, thub, thub.

The sounds of life mocking her loss.

She stared uncomprehendingly at the sea of faces around her. Smiling, preoccupied, harassed, hopeful. So many expressions, but none filled with grief like her and

Uncle John. How could they be untouched when a tragedy was being played out before them? How was it possible for life to carry on as normal when Joanna's world had shattered?

No. It was too cruel. It couldn't be true. Joanna had walked through the streets with Ma that morning. They'd talked about the new life they'd have together, away from Aunt Ivy. And now, a few hours later, Ma had gone.

Joanna squeezed her eyes tightly shut. If only Miss Bartle had told her when the note had been delivered, she might have been able to do something. She might have had the chance to say goodbye. A bitter taste rose in her throat. Why hadn't she seen how ill Ma was? She'd let down her father, now her mother.

Uncle John held her close and waited until her tears had subsided.

She was empty of tears. Empty of feeling. Hollow.

Life was unjust. Fairness? There was no such thing.

Joanna remembered little about the journey home. Her first recollection was of Uncle John sitting her down in the kitchen in front of the stove in his armchair and wrapping a blanket around her. Despite the heat, she shivered, her teeth chattering. He held a cup of hot, sweet tea with a large dash of rum to her lips.

"Can you give Joanna something to help her sleep,

please, Ivy? I'll let her office know she won't be in tomorrow, and then I'll sort out a few of the formalities."

Joanna remembered getting ready for bed, and the bitter taste of the herbal sleeping draught she forced past the lump in her throat. Then she lay alone in the middle of the sagging bed, listening to the sounds in the street and the intermittent muffled conversation from below. People carrying on with their business, in what for them, was simply another day. She fought the childish urge to hold on to the belief that the doctors had been mistaken and Ma would recover.

Happening so soon after Pa had gone, she'd barely had time to come to terms with his loss. And now ...

Alone. The word tiptoed after her as she drifted in and out of sleep, unable to distinguish dreams from reality. Shortly after midnight, she was sure Ma was in the room, putting her clothes in the wardrobe, getting ready for bed, but as Joanna called out, the figure froze and melted into the shadows. Joanna wiped the tears from her eyes and when her vision cleared, the room was empty. Then, the full force of her grief and loneliness crushed her.

Finally, she fell into a deep, troubled sleep. She didn't wake until late morning when the harsh rays of the sun crept across her swollen eyelids. The door opened slowly with a squeal as the rusty hinges protested, and Joanna opened her puffy eyes.

Ma?

It must be Ma. No one else entered the room without knocking.

No, of course, it wasn't. And it would never be again.

It was Aunt Ivy. Calculating eyes surveyed her – so different to Uncle John's gentle, tear-filled eyes. Had her aunt ever shed a tear for anyone other than herself? Now, her gaze darted about the room, as if taking an inventory.

"Well, you're awake at last. Up you get. You can't lie in bed all day. It's not good for you. When times are hard, it's best to keep busy." Her voice was brisk.

There was a knock at the door. Her aunt jumped.

"Ivy? Joanna? Can I come in?"

"Yes, Uncle," Joanna called, hoping his appearance would send Aunt Ivy away.

He ignored his wife and turned to Joanna. "Oh, my darling girl, I still can't believe we've lost her."

"I've just been telling our poor niece it might be a good idea to get up. Life goes on ..."

"Indeed." Uncle John frowned as he glanced at his wife over the top of his glasses. "Well, perhaps you'd be good enough to bring Joanna some tea and a slice of bread to give her the strength to get out of bed." He gave Joanna the glimmer of a smile and winked.

"Of course," said Aunt Ivy. Her eyes narrowed and

her lips clamped together as she left the room.

As soon as they heard her footsteps on the stairs, Uncle John took an envelope from the inside pocket of his jacket and smoothed it flat. He crouched by the bedside and handed it to Joanna.

Speaking urgently, he kept his voice low. "Rose asked me to deal with a few things for her. I don't know if she told you, but she was in the middle of buying a place in the country for you both. She gave me the money for the final instalment last week and asked me to pay it in for her, but I didn't get around to giving her the receipt ..." He paused and swallowed, unable to continue. A clatter from below made him jump, and he forced himself to carry on. "I need to be quick, darling, before Ivy comes back. Take this envelope, hide it, and keep it safe. As well as the receipt, there's a little money that was left in there and I've put a few pounds in. I can't afford more."

Joanna sat up. This was quite unexpected. "No, Uncle, I can't take your money."

"Hush." He looked over his shoulder at the door, then dropped his voice further. "Take it and hide it from Ivy, or she'll find some way of getting hold of it. She'll claim she's owed it in rent. Of course, I'd back you up, but it's easier if she doesn't know you've got it in the first place." He ran his hand through his sparse hair and shook his head with an expression of despair.

"She's so unpleasant to people. In the end, they all turn against her and leave. I think the only thing she understands is money. She thinks I'm unaware she goes through my pockets and takes whatever she finds. Everything goes into a box hidden at the bottom of her wardrobe. I suppose it comforts her to think that if she was ever completely alone, she'd be able to live independently. Anyway, I know Ivy hasn't been kind to you and Rose. Perhaps I should have stayed around more to look after you both, but the truth is, I can't bear to be in this house with her. So, I'm sorry, darling girl, I really am." His eyes flicked to the door. "I'll arrange the funeral and then I'm going away on business to Brighton. Once I go, she'll stop at nothing to force you out now your ma's gone. I've got a cousin in Brighton who'd be glad to take you in. I can ask her if you like, and I promise to keep an eye on you ..."

The rattle of cup on saucer announced Aunt Ivy was climbing the stairs.

"Think about it, Joanna. I'm sorry to hurry you. Probably the last thing you want to consider at the moment is the future, but once I go away, I won't be back for months ..." He placed his finger on his lips, his eyes begging for her forgiveness. She nodded, understanding his need to get away from his disagreeable wife.

Aunt Ivy opened the door and after placing the tray

on the bedside table, she stood with arms crossed, preventing further conversation.

Joanna felt the envelope beneath the blankets on her chest – the only link she now had with Ma.

Despite her aunt's advice to get up, she stayed in bed, sleeping fitfully with the envelope against her heart. What should she do? She knew nothing about making decisions. Until a few months ago, her parents had steered the course of her life. She'd done as she'd been told willingly and without question. Now, the burden of choice lay heavy. It was merely an envelope, but the significance of the contents seemed to crush her.

What makes you think you can start a new life in a place you've never heard of with no friends or job?

One thing was certain: she couldn't stay with Aunt Ivy. Life would be intolerable.

So, go to Brighton. Ask your uncle to manage everything. He'll look after you.

But would he? Who could tell where he'd be living? His home was in Stepney even if his heart wasn't. And would his cousin be any more welcoming than Aunt Ivy?

If Ma had provided a home for her, perhaps that was where she belonged.

Her thoughts spun. She wasn't ready to strike out on her own. Too young. Unprepared. Afraid. Alone.

But the contents of the envelope demanded action. She had neither experience nor anyone to advise her.

Well, she would choose before evening.

Whatever option she chose would stand as much chance of being successful as if she'd thrown dice.

While Joanna drifted in and out of sleep, she dreamt she and Ma were living in their new house in Dunton, Essex. It had been a curious mixture of the house in which they'd lived in Wimbledon with Pa, Aunt Ivy's house and a mist-shrouded castle.

Whatever Aunt Ivy had put in the sleeping draught had left her feeling heavy and listless. When she finally awoke that evening, her first thought was of Ma, followed by the stabbing pain of loss. Then came the fresh realisation she was alone.

She'd decided on a course of action. She was going to seize the chance of a new home. A new life in Dunton.

Dunton. She whispered it slowly, trying to become accustomed to the shape and sound of the word. One day, it would be second nature to give her address as Dunton. There was a friendly sound to it and if she didn't know anyone there, well, she'd eventually get to know people.

Anyway, who did she have in London?

Her father's brother and his family lived miles away in Devon. The only relatives she had in London were Uncle John, who'd soon be spending most of his time in Brighton – and Aunt Ivy. There were her cousins, but

David was probably still in India and Amelia lived in Sussex. She'd lost touch with her school friends from Wimbledon and hadn't been in her current job for long enough to make a close friend – it hadn't helped that Miss Bartle didn't allow talking at work.

No, Joanna had no ties to London.

The woolly feeling in her head faded like mist in the heat of the sun. It was time to be positive. She'd find a job in Dunton, make friends, and start a new life. Determination coursed through her. She'd envisage her new life and make it happen. But the more she tried to conjure up images in her mind's eye, the more obvious it was that her imagination was bare. The faces that drifted into her mind were people she already knew. The streets and houses were places she'd already visited. How could she visualise her new life when she knew nothing about it? That merely reminded her Ma wouldn't be there to encourage and support her. Determination turned to doubt. How large was Dunton? Was it a tiny village? Would there be people her age there? What about a job? Was it large enough to have a business that employed shorthand typists?

The money in the envelope wouldn't last long.

Joanna's eyes alighted on Ma's sewing box, and she could almost hear her saying, 'Everyone wears clothes, Joey. That means that people who wash, mend, or make clothes will rarely be out of work for long.'

Well, if she couldn't get a job typing, she'd heed those words and wash, mend or make clothes. She wasn't a gifted needlewoman like Ma, but she could make simple garments and she'd surely improve.

Trying to regain some of the earlier determination and momentum, she decided to pack her bags at once and make arrangements to leave as soon as the funeral had taken place. There was no point waiting any longer. Aunt Ivy would be glad to see her leave and anyway, this room held too many memories of Ma.

She got up and took down the battered suitcase from the top of the wardrobe. It was hard to say which items she couldn't find, but gradually, she noticed that certain of her mother's belongings were missing. The silver-framed photo of Joanna as a baby that usually stood on the dressing table had gone. The pearl brooch that had been Pa's first gift to Ma and the ornate scissors that Grandma had left her, which were always tucked into a pocket inside the sewing basket, were not there either. Joanna sat on the bed, shaking her head in disbelief. They were all items which Aunt Ivy had – at one time or another – admired.

Uncle John's comments came back to her. Was it possible her aunt had taken them? When she'd half-woken and thought Ma had been in the room the previous night, had it been Aunt Ivy looking through the wardrobe? The rum and the sleeping draught had muddled her thoughts and perceptions. No, it wasn't possible. Even a woman as bitter as Aunt Ivy wouldn't have taken the cherished belongings of a woman who'd only just passed away.

And yet, Aunt Ivy had a hardness that defied belief. Was it possible she'd deprive her niece of the few things that had meant so much to her mother?

Joanna hunted through everything again, searching under the bed, at the bottom of the wardrobe and in each of the drawers. The items definitely weren't in the room and yet, she knew the photograph had been on the dressing table the morning Ma had died. And who else had access to it?

There'd be no point confronting Aunt Ivy. She'd deny it and Joanna could scarcely insist on searching the house for it, much less demand access to the secret box Uncle John had told her about in her aunt's wardrobe. If she mentioned the box, Aunt Ivy would know Uncle John had told her and that would cause problems for him. Anyway, she could have hidden the items anywhere. After Joanna had left, it would be easy to remove the photograph and claim the silver frame was her own. Who, other than Uncle John, would recognise Ma's pearl brooch? It would be unfair to involve him, and if she waited until he'd gone, it would be her word against Aunt Ivy's.

Joanna sat on the bed and sobbed. The trinkets would

mean nothing to Aunt Ivy. If she pawned them, they wouldn't be worth much, but they were the last few links with Ma. And now they were gone.

Joey, they're just things. Don't cry, it's people who matter, not things. Make a new life, my love ...

Joanna dried her eyes. This would not beat her. She knew Ma would have urged her to pack up and live the new life she'd planned. So long as she had needles, thread, scissors, and fabric, she'd be able to make a little money until she got a proper job. Thankfully, the needles and a plain pair of scissors which her mother kept at the bottom of the sewing basket were still there as well as the black velvet, the box of jet beads and roll of silk cord Ma had put in the sewing basket ready to be sewn together. Joanna realised the bags Ma had completed, but hadn't yet sold, were nowhere to be found.

Had Aunt Ivy taken them too? Ma had promised one of them to Joanna for the Tredegar, Murchison & Franklin Christmas dinner and dance, to which all employees of the company were invited. Since there had been little money to spare, she'd also altered one of her own dresses for Joanna. An evening under the scrutiny of Miss Bartle hadn't been appealing and Joanna hadn't looked forward to it, but the other girls had said it was a lot of fun, especially after Miss Bartle had drunk a few sherries. But now, there'd be no Christmas Dance, and in fact, no more Tredegar, Murchison & Franklin after she handed in her notice.

Joanna hunted through Ma's rag bag in case she'd put the finished velvet bags in amongst the pieces of fabric. There was no sign of them. Ma had been meticulously tidy, folding pieces of fabric so they didn't crumple, but inside the rag bag, everything was in disarray. It looked as if a probing hand had been hastily inserted, searching for anything of interest. Joanna tipped everything out onto the bed and at the bottom, found a coarse canvas bag. If Aunt Ivy had come across that, she'd obviously decided it was too rough and ordinary to take. Joanna held it up and wondered if it would be possible to embellish it and sell it, but the best you could say for it was that it was large and strong. It would undoubtedly be ideal for carrying belongings to Dunton. She held the rough fabric against her cheek, breathing in the faint but distinctive perfume Ma used to wear. This might not be the velvet bag her mother had intended for her, but Joanna would cherish it as if it had been made of cloth of gold.

A week after Ma's funeral, Joanna slowly climbed the stairs of Tredegar, Murchison & Franklin. It was to be the last time she would enter this building as an employee. In one way, it was a relief. Since Ma had died, Miss Bartle had treated her extremely harshly. Elsie had suggested she might be embarrassed about having failed to pass the message on. She told Joanna Miss Bartle had been in trouble. She'd been called into Mr Tredegar's office to explain why she hadn't conveyed such an important message. But Joanna suspected Elsie had made up the story to make her feel better. There was no way Elsie would know what went on in Mr Tredegar's office on the top floor. And why should Mr Tredegar care about a message not being delivered to a nonentity in the typing pool? Nevertheless, she appreciated that Elsie cared enough to invent a story.

Of course, there was a possibility it was true, and that would explain Miss Bartle's bad mood. Joanna's presence would be a constant reminder. Perhaps it was a good thing. At least Joanna's last few days were so unpleasant she had no qualms about leaving. She couldn't wait to get away from the hateful woman.

Joanna worked hard all morning and was grateful the supervisor was occupied with two typewriters that were broken and needed attention. Shortly before midday, Ted came into the typing pool and told Mrs Bartle that Mr Franklin had asked to see Miss Marshall. Miss Bartle waved him brusquely away, telling him to pass the message on. With a wink at Joanna, Ted said Mr Franklin was waiting for her.

She'd never been called into any of the partners' offices, so she was rather alarmed.

"It'll just be yer references, love," Elsie whispered.

"And hopefully yer wages."

Mr Franklin smiled at her when she entered. "Please sit, Miss Marshall. I'd like to convey all the partners' condolences for your sad loss. I believe there was a regretful mix-up which resulted in you not receiving a message in time. Please accept our sincerest apologies. I've taken steps to ensure that sort of thing never happens again. Not that you'll gain much comfort from that, I'm sure." He shook his head and frowned. "However, on to happier things." He slid an envelope and her pay packet across the desk. "I'd like to thank you for all your hard work while you've been with us, Miss Marshall, and to wish you luck. Where are you moving to? I understand you'll be leaving London."

"Yes, sir. I found out after my mother passed away, she'd just bought a property in Essex. I haven't seen it yet, though."

"Whereabouts in Essex?"

"The Plotlands in Dunton, sir."

Mr Franklin's face lit up. "Dunton you say? I know the Plotlands well. We've worked for several clients who've bought plots of land down there. It's becoming quite the fashion."

He smiled, and after thanking him, she rose to leave.

"Oh, I just had a thought. An old friend of mine is one of the senior partners in a solicitors right near Dunton. It's on the High Road in Laindon. Richardson,

Bailey & Cole. Good solid company. If you're looking for a job, best go there and when they see my letter of recommendation and your references, I'm sure they'll find something for you."

"Thank you, Mr Franklin."

What a lovely man. So, the partners had been aware that Miss Bartle had failed to pass on the message. Perhaps Elsie knew more than Joanna had given her credit for. Under different circumstances, it would have been nice to get to know Elsie and the other girls, but it was too late now.

At the end of the day, the girls tidied up and then stayed on in the typing pool, much to Miss Bartle's indignation. "Haven't you girls got homes to go to? Normally, you can't wait to get out of the door."

"Won't be long, Miss Bartle. We're just saying goodbye to Joanna." Elsie handed Joanna a small gift.

"We clubbed together. They're for your new home," Elsie said.

They'd bought her an embroidered tablecloth and matching napkins. Joanna fought back tears. The enormity of what she was about to do suddenly struck home. Although she hadn't been there long enough to feel part of this group of women, they'd been kind enough to make a collection and buy her a thoughtful gift.

But from now on, she was no longer part of

anything. She was completely alone.

As she left the building, she wondered if this was how birds felt when they realised they had wings that would allow them to fly. Did they have an immense sense of freedom, followed by the realisation that the skies were so huge, they might easily get lost?

Ma's receipt showed she'd paid twelve pounds for a property on Second Avenue, Dunton.

The printed letterhead gave the address as Whitechapel Estates, Maynard Street, London E1

Beneath that, it said:

P. Dale & Co 'Solicitors Commissioners for Oaths'.

Handwritten in loopy script, below the letterhead, was:

18, Second Avenue, Dunton Essex.

Received of Mrs Rose Marshall, the sum of £12–0–0 (by cheque)

by J. Parker for P. Dale & Co.

The day after Ma's funeral, Joanna went to Whitechapel Estates in Maynard Street to see if she could find out more about her new home.

When she entered the office, a sandy-haired man glanced up from his desk, gold tooth glinting as he smiled. After looking her up and down, the smile dropped, and he frowned. "Yes?"

She obviously wasn't someone he thought was going

to bring him business. And, of course, he was right. Her eyes swept the office, taking in its shabby chaos. Sagging shelves laden with ledgers and books, a full ashtray on his desk, and the rubbish bin overflowing onto the grimy linoleum. She looked for signs of someone else, preferably a girl who might be more welcoming than the flabby man. It was obvious no one had worked on the other desk in the office for a while, so the man was her only option.

"I've come about some property my mother bought." Joanna was polite but firm. Something she'd learnt from Ma. She must now start behaving more like an adult if she was going to be taken seriously. And this man was not taking her seriously. With her head held high, she walked to his desk and held out the receipt. He stared at it.

"Property?" He spoke sharply and studied her with guarded eyes from under heavy brows.

His reaction puzzled her. Did he think she'd come to complain? If she was going to learn anything at all, she needed to convince him she wanted to know where the property was and a little about what to expect when she got there.

"I … I just wanted to know exactly where it is. I've looked on a map, but I can't find it …"

He narrowed his eyes further and regarded her with an unblinking gaze. "You're looking for directions?"

"Yes, please."

"To Dunton?"

She nodded.

He held out his hand for the receipt and after she'd passed it to him, he smiled, showing off the gold tooth. "So, you and your family are off to our little piece of heaven in Essex, are you? Well, this is one of the best spots." He tapped the receipt with satisfaction, then looked up at her speculatively. "I wonder if yer parents might be interested in further investments in land? It just so happens I have further plots available. Going like 'ot cakes, they are." He stood, and leaning across the desk, he held out a sausage-fingered hand. "Jonas Parker, proprietor of Whitechapel Estates. Sit, sit, Miss ..." He glanced at the receipt again. "Sit, Miss Marshall."

There was no point wasting his time and allowing him to believe he might make a further sale to her parents, so she explained her situation.

Mr Parker linked his hands behind his neck and leaned back in his chair. He surveyed her thoughtfully. "I see. Well, if you take my advice, Miss Marshall, you'll sell up. You're a might young to be starting out on yer own in the country, far from everyone you know. I'd be happy to take it off yer hands, although I couldn't give you what your mother paid for it. Times are hard. But I could run to eight pounds. You could walk out of here now with the cash and be in the West End in no time.

Think of all them frocks you could get with that much money. Now, what d'you say?"

"But didn't you say they were going like hotcakes?"

His eyes narrowed, and his smile slipped, but his reply came quickly. "For fresh land, yes. There's great demand. But with all the paperwork that'd have to be done to resell yours ..." The corners of his mouth turned down and he shook his head as if it was worthless.

His explanation didn't sound likely, but she knew nothing about the property market. She was still smarting at his comment about buying frocks. The cheek of the man. Joanna kept her voice level. She needed to know the best way to get there. To hint she suspected he was trying to swindle her probably wasn't the best way to go about it.

"Thank you for your kind offer, Mr Parker, but I've made up my mind, and this is the place I want to make my home. My mother sacrificed a lot to get it, and I intend to live there."

Mr Parker scratched his ear and peered at her with a frown. "Quite, quite. So, I take it your mother never had time to tell you much about it?"

Joanna shook her head. "That's why I came in. I intend to move there as soon as possible, but I'm not sure of the best way to get there."

"Ah, that's because it's such a recent development. New and innovative. You won't see it on old maps." He stood up and walked to a large map fixed to the wall and beckoned to her to follow. "This is Dunton Plotlands." With a sausage finger, he stabbed at an area of geometrically arranged roads. "It's near Laindon. See here?" He ran his finger along a dark line with bars across it like a long fishbone. "That's the railway line to Laindon Station, here." He stabbed the map again.

Joanna was no wiser. She'd never heard of Laindon and didn't know where it was relative to London.

Mr Parker stared at her expectantly. "I tell you what. I'm taking a group of potential buyers down to see the place next Saturday. Why not tag along with us? There're still plots to be had, but they're going fast and I'm expecting a large group. Anyone who's anyone is building a weekend cottage out in the country."

"That would be wonderful. Thank you, Mr Parker." She'd rather not have to rely on him. There was something about him she didn't trust. But perhaps it would be better to go with a group. She'd never travelled far on her own before and even seeing it on a map hadn't helped her. Yes, better to go with a man she distrusted than to risk getting lost on her own.

"And in the meantime, missy, think about my offer to buy your land. I might even be able to stretch to nine pounds. You say your uncle's been helping you? Perhaps ask him? I'm sure his instincts will be keener than yours." He shrugged as if it didn't matter to him, but a half-smile played across his lips.

"Thank you, Mr Parker. My mind's made up. But I appreciate you allowing me to join your group."

"Well, if yer uncle can't get you to see sense and you're still determined, I leave on the 9:55 train from Fenchurch Street next Saturday. We'll do a quick tour of Laindon before we go off to Dunton for a look around the Plotlands. There'll be plenty to celebrate, so I'll provide the bubbly. Don't be late or you'll be on yer own." He stressed the final word and shrugged.

Joanna left the office. What an unpleasant man. But at least now she had a plan. She'd leave for her new home on Saturday.

That night at supper, Joanna had nothing to say. Neither did her aunt, and the meal was more strained than usual. Joanna hadn't told Aunt Ivy she'd handed in her notice, nor that on Saturday morning she'd be leaving. She intended to get up early and creep out before her aunt was up. Of course, she'd leave the money she and Ma owed for their rent. Then she'd walk out of Aunt Ivy's house forever. Was there anything she'd miss? She looked around the room.

Nothing. Nothing at all.

The only pleasant memories of this house would be of Uncle John and Ma. It had been their childhood home, and they'd undoubtedly had happy memories of the house before Aunt Ivy had entered their lives, but Joanna could only recall their unhappiness within these walls.

On Saturday, she'd walk out without a backward glance.

Her heart raced as she considered how her new life would begin. Saturday. No more tasteless meals eaten in critical silence. No more of her aunt's disapproving sniffs. Freedom.

"Pass the salt, please, Joanna. By the way, what do you plan to do at the weekend?" Aunt Ivy held out her claw-like hand for the salt pot.

Joanna coloured slightly, and after passing the cruet set, she lowered her head. "Nothing, Aunt Ivy." Well, nothing she wanted her aunt to know about.

Early on Saturday morning, Joanna got up, washed, dressed, and quietly carried her suitcase and bags downstairs, leaving them by the front door. She had the rent money in her hand to leave on the kitchen table and after she'd eaten some breakfast, she'd tidy away and leave.

She gingerly opened the kitchen door to avoid the squeak and was about to enter when she saw her aunt sitting in her armchair by the fire. Wearing a dressing gown and with her long, grey hair loose around her shoulders, she'd obviously just arisen.

"So, it was as I thought. You were going to creep

away like a thief in the night. How typical! I take you and your mother in when you had nothing, and this is the way you repay me."

Joanna was so surprised to see her, she stepped back in alarm and nearly dropped the money. Her aunt rarely got up this early.

"H ... How? How did you know?"

"People rarely pack all their belongings in a suitcase if they intend to remain. I saw it last night when you went into Mrs Thomsett's next door."

"You went into my room?" It was worse than that. Joanna had put the case back on top of the wardrobe where it had always been. She'd only have discovered Joanna had packed up her belongings if she'd snooped inside the wardrobes and drawers. Then, she'd have seen they were empty.

"I went into *my* room," her aunt corrected her. "This is *my* house, and I deserve to know what's going on."

It was unbelievable. Aunt Ivy had practically admitted prying in Joanna's room.

"But you don't want me here anyway!" Joanna's voice grew shrill.

Aunt Ivy's face deepened in colour, her eyes bulged, and her mouth twisted in rage. She leapt to her feet. "You wicked, ungrateful girl! This is my house and I deserve to be warned when you intend to leave. And, of course, there's a question of the money you owe."

Joanna held out her hand to show she was going to leave the money. She placed the notes and coins on the table. Aunt Ivy strode towards them, and with one finger, pushed the coins apart, her lips moving as she silently counted.

She breathed in, the sound rasping in her throat. "That's not enough. You dishonest girl!"

Joanna had been brought up to be polite to her elders, especially family members. All her life, she'd shied away from confrontation, but this was too much. If she was going to live successfully on her own, she must learn to stand up for herself.

She swallowed, forced her shoulders back and said calmly, "That is everything I owe you. In fact, since Ma's been gone, you've only had one person to feed, so I believe this is more than I owe you. And if we're discussing dishonesty, I know you took some of Ma's things. I can't prove it, but I know you have them. So, you have more than you deserve from Ma and me, and I won't leave a penny more." She clasped her hands behind her back so her aunt wouldn't see them shaking.

The breath grated in Aunt Ivy's throat again. "Liar!" Her voice was low and menacing. She took a step towards Joanna and raised her hand to slap her, but she was too slow. Joanna quickly stepped away, turned on her heel, and left. She slammed the kitchen door behind her and ran down the passage on quivering legs to her case and bags. Aunt Ivy threw open the kitchen door and yelled, "Go then, you ungrateful wretch! Good riddance! Don't ever darken my doorstep again! You won't be welcome, whatever your uncle says!"

Joanna grabbed her bags and fell out of number 10 Aylward Street. She fumbled in her pocket for the key and threw it onto the hall floor, then slammed the door. Once she was safely on the other side of the road, she looked back at the house for the last time.

Chapter Two

Joanna had expected to feel light and free as she made her way to Fenchurch Street Station to begin her new life. Instead, the final unpleasant encounter with Aunt Ivy had cast a shadow over the day that had barely begun. In her right hand, she held the suitcase. Across one shoulder, the canvas bag hung; bulky and cumbersome. She'd put the other smaller bags in one larger one and held that in her left hand. Individually, each piece wasn't impossibly heavy, but the further she walked, the more her thoughts and bags weighed her down.

She'd given most of Ma's clothes, shoes and hats away to Mrs Thomsett next door. She hadn't told her aunt, but there was no doubt she knew and was angry. Many of the garments would have fit Aunt Ivy, but Joanna couldn't bear to think of her wearing Ma's clothes. It wasn't as if her aunt needed more of anything. Mrs Thomsett, however, was always trying to feed and dress a constantly growing family. At least she was grateful for Ma's cast-offs, and if they didn't fit anyone, they'd be lovingly altered until they did. Besides, Aunt Ivy would have sneered and criticised, although she'd have taken anything available and sold it if she hadn't wanted it herself.

When Ma had packed up their belongings after Pa died, she'd known there wouldn't be room to store boxes in Uncle John's house. Even if there had been, Aunt Ivy would have made a fuss, so Ma had sold most of their belongings and intended to buy new when she had a place of her own.

After Joanna had given Ma's clothes away, there was little left, and now she was carrying everything she possessed. It wasn't much to show for her brief life, but it was enough to slow her progress. She stopped repeatedly, swapping case and bag from one hand to the other to ease her muscles. As she walked, she held everything away from her legs, so she didn't trip, and the journey was taking longer than expected. She'd intended to arrive early and have a cup of tea while she waited, but by the time she reached the station – hot and flustered – there were only fifteen minutes until the train departed.

Her eyes darted back and forth over the crowds of people. Suppose she couldn't find Mr Parker? He'd made it clear he wouldn't wait. As she looked up at the clock to check how much longer before the train left, she spotted him and a group of about a dozen people standing beneath it.

Stop panicking, she told herself sternly. Calm down. Everything is going to plan. Her racing heart slowed, and as she walked towards Mr Parker, the bags didn't seem as heavy, nor her muscles as fatigued. At last, she felt optimistic.

Mr Parker stood out with his beige, checked suit, red bowtie, and boater, and she wondered how she hadn't seen him immediately. Several more people joined the group, and the excited chatter grew louder. As Joanna approached, Mr Parker looked up and recognition lit his eyes. He stepped forward, and with his gold tooth glinting, greeted her as if she was an old friend. "And here, ladies and gents, is our youngest buyer. A lady of wonderful discernment. You need look no further than to this example of a young modern woman starting out on her own in our little bit of heaven in Essex."

Joanna blushed. Judging by Mr Parker's behaviour when she'd first met him, she'd expected him to ignore her. He knew she didn't intend to buy anything from him, nor sell him her property. Yet, he was outrageously making use of her for his own ends. Even worse, several members of the group nodded with approval, as if she'd endorsed Mr Parker's business.

A new couple arrived, drawing Mr Parker's attention from Joanna, and she slipped into the crowd to hide, grateful not to be the focus of attention. She found herself next to a small, tired-looking woman, carrying a baby in one arm and holding onto the hand of a small girl.

"D'you work for Jonas Parker, dear?" the woman asked. Her voice sounded as weary as she looked.

"Oh, no."

"I wondered. Only you looked rather uncomfortable when he used you as an advertisement."

"I ... I was a bit surprised. I've only met him once. I went into his office the other day to find out how to get to Dunton, and he wasn't very helpful at first. In fact, he only seemed interested in persuading me to sell my property."

The woman wrinkled her nose. "Probably at a knockdown price. Typical Parker. Oh, 'e's a sharp one and no mistake. I'm Mary, by the way, Mary O'Flanahan and this is Jack." She raised her shoulder, lifting the sleeping baby. "And this is Gracie." The small girl lowered her head and shrank behind Mary, peering out shyly.

"I'm Joanna Marshall."

Mary looked down at Joanna's suitcase and bags. "So, you're going to Dunton on your own? If you don't mind me saying, you look very young."

Joanna told Mary about her parents and inheritance.

"I expect we'll be neighbours," Mary said and nodded at a large man who was talking intently to Mr Parker. "That's my 'usband, Frank. He's had a win on the horses and the money's burnin' a hole in his pocket. He's always wanted to own a bit of land and grow some nice fresh veg, so I don't think Parker will have to work too hard to sell him anything." She sighed and her shoulders sagged.

"Don't you want to go to Dunton?"

"I don't mind where I go, dear, but I just wish my Frank would settle to something. He can't seem to make up 'is mind. But perhaps moving to Essex will keep him on the straight and narrow ..."

Mr Parker pulled a pocket watch out of his waistcoat with a flourish. He checked it against the station clock and then consulted his list. Jabbing one sausage finger at each person, he conducted a headcount, and satisfied, he announced, "Everyone's here, so follow me, ladies, gents and kiddies."

The group, like a flowing teardrop with Mr Parker at its point, moved forward and joined the crowd at the ticket barrier.

"You'd best keep close, dear," Mary said. "It's going to be packed. You don't want to get separated from the group. Although don't worry if you can't see anyone you know on the train. You'll probably get pushed off at Laindon, whether you want to get out or not." The lines on her face softened and as she smiled, the years faded away. With surprise, Joanna guessed they only differed in age by a few years.

Once through the ticket barrier and onto the platform, Joanna understood Mary's warning. The carriages were filling quickly – men and women, young and old, carrying children in arms and on shoulders. Babies screamed, children wailed, and fathers shouted. Mothers seized hands to stop their offspring from straying. Older children helped adults carry or drag baggage across the platform and into the carriages. Boxes, baskets, tool kits, rolls of fabric, lengths of timber, buckets. One man cradled three slender saplings, jabbing his elbows with fierce determination to keep the crush of bodies away from his delicate plants. Everywhere, people pushed and shoved to get aboard the train.

Joanna, Mary, and the two children squeezed into the corner of the carriage and watched as people inserted themselves into spaces and placed small children on top of anything that would bear their weight.

The guard's whistle sliced through the air. Doors slammed and with a puff of steam and a lurch, the train pulled out of the station. Jammed in behind a large woman with a crate of squawking chickens, Joanna craned her neck to watch the rows of terraced brick houses gradually give way to cottages with gardens. The hard black, grey and brown lines of London softened until they became a blur of green.

"Blimey, it's 'ot today. I'm melting." The woman with the chickens wiped her face and neck with a handkerchief. "Mind you," she said to no one in particular, "it'll storm by the end of the day. You mark my words." She moved slightly to one side and Joanna had a better view out of the window.

How different this was from London, with its busy, teeming streets and grimy buildings that towered above, and blocked out the sunlight. Here, the landscape stretched as far as she could see, with gently rolling hills and fields edged with hedgerows. Joanna had the same floaty feeling she'd experienced when she'd left Tredegar, Murchison & Franklin for the last time. So much freedom it overwhelmed her. Was there such a thing as too much freedom? How would she ever get used to such openness?

Perhaps she wouldn't. Panic gripped her. She'd focused so much on the journey, fearing she'd get lost, she'd given little thought to a destination she couldn't imagine. The only image in her mind was the map on Mr Parker's wall with its grid of roads. Suppose she didn't like Dunton?

Don't be ridiculous. It's only a few miles from London. Not some far-flung foreign country.

Her eyes filled with tears when she remembered it didn't matter that Dunton was only a train ride away from London. After Aunt Ivy's last words, there was no going back.

But then again, there was nothing to go back to – nor for. She didn't belong anywhere.

I will belong in Dunton, I will.

She wiped the tears away angrily.

"The next station's Laindon," called Mr Parker from somewhere in the carriage. "Everyone with the Whitechapel Estates group who's visiting Dunton, please get off at the next stop. And if anyone in the carriage wants to buy a lovely plot of land there, you're welcome to join us."

Someone called out from further along the carriage, "Yer too late, mate, most of us are already Plotlanders." People laughed and others jovially added their comments.

Once the train had stopped, passengers grabbed bags, boxes, animals, and children, before they poured onto the platform. Joanna kept close to Mary and the children as the mass of people moved slowly as one towards the station exit. Ahead, Mr Parker's raised hand waved invitations to the viewing, which he handed out as he walked along.

Outside the station, the group gathered around Mr Parker, keeping out of the way of the other passengers, most of whom set off in either direction along the High Road laden with packages and other paraphernalia.

Once Mr Parker had done his sausage-fingered headcount and was satisfied he'd accounted for everyone on his list, he instructed the group to follow him. Waving his arm high in the air, he set off along the

High Road.

After the train journey through so much open countryside, Joanna was pleasantly surprised at the variety of shops and offices along Laindon High Road. She'd imagined a tiny village with only one or two shops. But here was everything one could wish for. Smaller shops than in London and possibly not as fashionable, but it would be a long time before she had enough to buy luxuries. By that time, she might have enough money to travel to London to go shopping.

An idle daydream.

But at least she was looking on the bright side and imagining herself doing well in the future. Of course, that relied on her getting a job. She suddenly remembered Mr Franklin's words when he'd given her his reference. A tingle of excitement ran through her. There, ahead on the right, was Richardson, Bailey & Cole Solicitors. That was surely a wonderful omen. As soon as she'd settled into her new home, she'd come back with Mr Franklin's reference and enquire about jobs. If not, they might recommend somewhere.

Mr Parker stopped outside the Laindon Picture Theatre and waved his hand grandly, as if it belonged to him. "All the latest films are shown at the Picture Theatre—"

"They're showing Moulin Rouge? That ain't new. I've already seen it," someone at the back said.

Mr Parker ignored him. "The theatre has a stage for live shows too. Now we'll be making our way over to Dunton shortly. There'll be a horse and cart for those who can't make it under their own steam. But first, I wanted to tell you that although we have quite a few plots, they're selling fast – and of course, the prices will rise very soon. So, if you want to take advantage of our special offer today, don't delay. See me and we'll come to an arrangement." His eyes raked the crowd and alighted on Joanna. "This young lady has invested in a plot and is looking to buy another." He slipped into the crowd and put his arm around Joanna's shoulders. "She has vision, ladies and gents. A thoroughly modern young woman. She's looking to the future."

Joanna blushed and froze, wanting to shake the man's hand off her shoulder but not wanting to appear rude. Again, people looked eagerly at Mr Parker. Joanna hoped they hadn't been swayed by such nonsense. She was grateful when someone asked him a question and she slipped out from under his hand. Once she'd found her cottage, she need never see the ghastly man again, even if he had been kind in letting her join the group and paying for her ticket.

Mr Parker announced that since the weather was fine, the champagne would be served picnic-style in Dunton. The bottles and glasses rattled alarmingly in the back of the cart as the horse pulled them to the top of one of the grassy, rutted avenues. George, the cart driver, set up the trestle table in the field and set about unpacking the glasses and bottles while people found flat areas to sit and enjoy the sun.

Such a vast expanse of grass. The only similar place Joanna had visited had been a park. But this was unlike any park she'd ever seen – not an open area in the middle of a town or city surrounded by smoke and traffic noise. Here, the air was crisp, and carried notes of late summer flowers and grass. Joanna closed her eyes and breathed in deeply. It was so refreshing after the grimy air of London.

From Mr Parker's description of Dunton as 'a little bit of heaven in Essex', Joanna had imagined a picturesque village like the painting on Ma's old biscuit tin. She soon discovered there were no quaint thatched cottages with beautiful pargetting and roses growing around the door in the Plotlands of Dunton. The grandly named 'avenues' were no more than grassy tracks where the wheels of vehicles or carts had churned up the ground, leaving deep furrows. As Mr Parker's wall map had shown, the roads were arranged in a grid, but as far as Joanna could see, that was the only nod to conformity. She was used to suburban roads filled with identical houses, such as her parents' home in Wimbledon and Uncle John's house on Aylward Street in London. The

Plotlands were a shock. Joanna couldn't believe the assortment of structures on each plot. From bell tents to wooden huts. From a disused railway carriage with patterned curtains at the windows to a brick-built bungalow with an ornately decorated veranda. Each home was distinct, and many were currently under construction.

Empty plots stood vacant and overgrown on either side of each avenue, like missing teeth in a smile. Some were marked with pegs and string and were presumably up for sale. Others had fences or some man-made barrier, such as planks of wood, showing the owner had marked its boundaries.

When George had finished setting out the glasses, Mr Parker called everyone to order. "My assistant, George, will make sure you all get something to help you celebrate. So, ladies and gents, help yourself." Mr Parker smiled benevolently as a young man poured champagne into the glasses and people surged forward.

While everyone was queuing, Joanna approached Mr Parker. "Excuse me, please. I wonder if it would be possible to direct me to my property."

"Certainly, missy." He smiled and handed her a glass. "Here, drink up! We'll be going past it on our way home. There's plenty of time. Enjoy yourself! It's not every day a girl gets taken out into the countryside and offered bubbly."

"But if you could just point it out—"

"My dear! Trust me when I say you'll find it much faster if I show you. I've never met a lady yet, who could follow directions. Just be patient. I've got some business matters to sort out first and then we'll drop you off. Never you fear." He raised his hand to catch someone's eye, cutting off Joanna's response.

She was sure she could follow directions, but then again ... It wasn't like navigating around London with its plain street signs and house numbers. Many of the cottages only had names, so it wasn't even like she could work out the numbers of the plots in between. She sighed and sipped the bubbly drink. It was the first time she'd tasted champagne, and she suddenly realised how thirsty she was – and hungry. If Aunt Ivy hadn't been waiting in the kitchen and taken her by surprise, she'd have had time for breakfast.

"Careful, love, it's easy to get carried away drinking that stuff." Mary pushed her way through the crowd to stand next to Joanna. "I've got an egg sandwich, if you like."

Joanna thanked Mary for her kindness but refused. She detested eggs but wouldn't have accepted one, anyway. Mary had probably only brought enough for her family. And it wasn't her fault Joanna had been so thoughtless.

"Well, guess what? My Frank's bought a plot and

signed the contract. Looks like we'll be neighbours – at the weekend, anyway. He plans to come down on the train each Friday night and go back on Sunday. I wish 'e'd waited till I'd seen it before he signed. But he said he'd take me there now."

She turned and, cupping her hands around her mouth, she called Gracie, who was at the far side of the field playing with two young boys. Jack woke up at the sound of his mother's shouts and grizzled. Mary glanced at Frank, who slowly walked away with Parker and several men. She bit her lip, as her eyes followed Frank.

"Gracie!" she yelled. Her voice, sharp and anxious.

Jack began to cry. The little girl hadn't acknowledged her mother's call, and Joanna could see the indecision on Mary's face as she looked back and forth between her daughter and husband.

"Mary, would you like me to keep an eye on Gracie while you go and see your new home?"

Relief flooded Mary's face. "Oh, would you, love? That would be so kind. I won't be long. Frank says it's just to the left up there. I need to make sure he doesn't get carried away."

Joanna finished her drink and accepted another one from George. At least it warmed her stomach and gave the impression it wasn't so empty. She sat on the grass and leaned on her suitcase, breathing in the smell of newly mown grass. Gracie and the two boys ran back and forth along the hedgerow, picking berries and eating them. How marvellous to have so much open space in which to play. At the thought of blackberries, her stomach grumbled, and she wondered if perhaps she might pick a few. She could save them for later.

Later!

The realisation she *had* no food for later hit her with a stomach-churning lurch. The shock of encountering Aunt Ivy in the kitchen earlier had driven all sensible thought from her mind. She'd missed breakfast, and it had taken her so long to get to the railway station there'd been no time for a cup of tea or a bite to eat when she'd arrived there. If she'd been thinking at all, she'd have assumed she could go to a corner shop and buy some provisions. But she hadn't been thinking, neither had she seen any corner shops in the Plotlands. And worse – tomorrow would be Sunday, and the shops in Laindon would be closed. She couldn't wait until Monday before she bought food. Her stomach squeezed in protest.

Foolish. Foolish. Foolish.

There must be something she could do.

Was there time to return to Laindon to buy something?

Where was Mary? She couldn't leave Gracie alone after having offered to look after her. As Joanna got to her feet, the world blurred and swam. She staggered and as she righted herself, she heard a young girl crying.

Oh, please don't let it be Gracie.

Joanna blinked and her vision cleared sufficiently to see a sobbing Gracie running back towards where she'd left her mother. When she failed to see her, she stopped abruptly, and her cries grew louder. Joanna shook her head to clear it and ran towards the girl. "Don't worry, Gracie! Mummy will be back in a moment. She's just gone somewhere with Daddy."

But Gracie wasn't to be comforted. "That boy pushed me over. I want my mummy." She pointed across the field at the boys, her bottom lip quivering.

"Are you hurt?" Joanna asked.

"No, but I feel sick. I want Mummy."

Joanna looked towards where she'd last seen Mary. There was still no sign of her or Frank. The girl's face and hands were stained with what looked like blackberry juice. But supposing she'd eaten poisonous berries?

Oh, where was Mary?

Then, a group of people turned the corner on their way back to the field and Joanna spotted Mary among them. She waved frantically.

"Don't worry, love, Gracie's just eaten too many blackberries," Mary said to Joanna when she reached them, and the little girl had shown her the berries she had in her pocket. "She's fine, aren't you, my brave girl?"

Gracie nodded, her eyelashes still wet with tears.

"Thank you for looking after Gracie, love. You must be really keen to see yer new home. When's Parker going to take you?"

"He said he'd show me when he's finished his business, but actually, that's probably a good thing because ..." She swallowed, the shame of her stupidity still raw, but she might as well confess. Mary might be able to help. "I realise I should have brought some food with me. I'm going to have to go back to the High Road to get something. If I wait too long, the shops'll be shut."

"There's a general store just down the hill," Mary said, her voice full of concern. "Hendersons, I think Parker called it. Why don't you leave your suitcase with me, and nip down there quick? You can be back in no time."

It was the strangest thing. Although Joanna knew she was upright, it was as though the world was tilting, first one way, then the other. She was tempted to sit down for a few minutes and allow her head to clear. But she dared not delay. Suppose Mr Parker should get back and find her gone? And worse ... suppose he should finish his business and take the group back to Laindon Station. Mary wouldn't know where to leave Joanna's belongings.

No, she wouldn't stop. She'd buy something for supper in the general store and hurry back. Strangely, the thought of food nauseated her. Had it been too long since she'd eaten? Or had she had too much sun?

The feelings of nausea grew, and once inside the shop, she knew she must choose something quickly and get out into the fresh air. It was hard to think clearly. Cheese? No, the smell made her stomach churn. Her eyes alighted on a can of soup on the shelf behind the counter. That would be bland. She bought two cans and some biscuits, and after paying, she hurried outside.

Right? Left? Which way? Why couldn't she hold on to her thoughts and follow them through? They were like the birds that fluttered in the hedgerow. When she approached, they rose as one and darted this way and that, only to settle further off.

Think!

Left, yes, she must turn left. She remembered noticing she was going downhill as she approached the shop. Now, she walked uphill, her head swimming, trying to note any landmarks. Other than unusual cottages and buildings on the plots, there were few distinguishing features. It was lucky she hadn't wandered off trying to find her own cottage.

Her own cottage.

What did it look like? She'd worry about that later. First, she must hurry back to the field where she'd find

Mr Parker and the others.

Hopefully.

She nibbled at a biscuit, but it was dry and almost sucked the moisture from her mouth.

Heavy, grey clouds gathered on the horizon, rumbling like a waking beast. If Mr Parker left for London, Mary would have to go too, and Joanna's belongings would be left in the field. She walked as fast as she could, eyes moving right and left, anxiously seeking the way back. If she got lost now …

Thankfully, Mr Parker and his group were still there, and since she'd gone, the atmosphere had grown more festive. There was a shared feeling of fulfilment. Many were drunk, both on champagne and the excitement of having purchased a patch of the countryside.

Champagne. Was that what had made her feel so strange? Mary had warned her. Well, it hardly mattered now. It was too late to do anything about it. It was yet another indication of how unfit she was to look after herself. She squeezed her eyes tightly shut, as if trying to banish that thought.

After nervously glancing at the oncoming bank of purple and grey cloud, Mr Parker checked his pocket watch. As he waited by his trestle table for a man to finish signing a form, his smug expression suggested he was satisfied with his day's business. George had stowed away the empty bottles and glasses and hovered, waiting to pack everything away and load it onto the cart.

Mary nudged Joanna. "I'd go and remind him if I were you, love. He's too interested in his bank balance to worry about anyone else. I bet 'e's forgotten all about you. He'll want to be leaving soon …" She nodded her head towards the dark grey skyline. "I wouldn't mind betting it'll storm later."

Joanna didn't like to make a nuisance of herself, but Mr Parker had promised he'd take her to her property on the way home and he was now fastening his briefcase. George carried the trestle table to the back of the cart and Mr Parker placed the briefcase, map, and papers on the seat at the front and climbed up.

"Mr Parker?"

He swung around and she could see from his expression he had indeed forgotten her. A look of annoyance crossed his face.

"Mr Parker, you said—"

"Yes, yes! What's the address? I'll check on the map."

It was 18, wasn't it? Or was it 16? Or … Why couldn't she think straight?

She took the envelope out of her pocket and handed it to Mr Parker. He removed the receipt, glanced at it, and consulted his map. "Right, you go down that avenue and take the first on the right. It's on the left, a little way down."

Was he sending her there on her own?

She stared at him, wondering if she'd misheard.

"Now, if you'll excuse us, I've got to get these folks back to Laindon for their train. You'd best hurry yerself. It looks like rain."

"B … but I thought you said you'd take me …"

His face hardened. "Yer surely not suggesting I put everyone out and give them a soaking just for your benefit? I'm sure you'll manage. Look, see that flag?"

Joanna turned and looked in the direction he was pointing. A green flag at the top of a tall pole flapped above the rooftops.

"Well, that's Green Haven. It's right next door to your place. If the flag's flying, it means the folks are at home." He handed her back the envelope. "Have you thought any more about selling to me? I've had an offer for five plots side by side, and I could do with yours. I'll give you a good price. If we shake hands on it now, I'll take you back to London and you'll walk away with, shall we say … ten pounds? You can't say fairer than that." He leaned towards her, his voice a whisper. "Sell up now, girl, otherwise I'm afraid you might regret yer stubbornness …"

Joanna staggered backwards in alarm. She kept her voice level. "Th … thank you, Mr Parker, but my mother bought it and I want to live there."

He flapped his hand at her in dismissal. "Fair

enough. But remember, I want your land. My offer won't be as good the next time I see you. And trust me, you *are* going to want to sell. You really ain't prepared ..."

As the cart pulled away, jolting over the uneven roads, Mary leaned out and waved. The passengers chattered in the back of the cart, groaning, and shrieking as it pitched and tossed over the furrowed ground. The sound of their voices gradually faded until the cart turned the corner and was gone. Standing alone in the middle of the avenue, Joanna felt isolated and lost, as if her body no longer had weight or substance, and might simply float up into the vast sky and keep going until she disappeared.

The sudden movement as she bent to pick up her suitcase and bags increased the thumping in her head. She was nauseous and felt dizzy; she feared she might faint. Well, at least she knew her home wasn't far away. If only Mr Parker had told her that earlier, she could have been there by now. If it wasn't hard to find, why had he made it sound so complicated?

Such a horrible man. A bully. His threat had unnerved her, and she was grateful she wouldn't need to see him again.

Now, what had he said? Take the first on the right and it's on the left, a little way down.

Joanna started walking along the avenue, and at the

crossroads, as she turned right, another avenue opened before her. It looked very similar to all the others, except there were fewer houses along this road. She carried on towards the tall flagpole that Mr Parker had pointed out, looking up at the green flag. It flapped vigorously, its ropes slapping against the tall pole. Yes, it most likely would storm, as several people had predicted. The birds that had filled the air with their song a short while ago were silent as if holding their breath, waiting for the onslaught. A few fat raindrops splashed down, drumming on the grassy road, and stinging her bare arms. She wondered whether to stop and get a jacket out of her suitcase, but if she was almost at Green Haven, then she was nearly home. To stop now would only risk getting soaked. She arrived at the flagpole, panting; her head hammering. This wasn't what she'd imagined. There was no house next to Green Haven – merely a large stretch of open land. The next building was some way along the avenue.

Well, of course. When he'd said it was next to Green Haven, that was a relative term. In London, 'next to' would mean within feet – perhaps inches. In the countryside, it might be measured in yards.

By the time she reached the next house, the rain was falling heavily, and thunder grumbled in the distance. Steely grey clouds now covered the sky, blotting out the sinking sun. The smell of damp earth filled her nostrils.

The bungalow was plain, with a window on either side of a central door. Simple but, oh, so welcome. As she pushed the gate, she wiped the rain out of her eyes and caught sight of the name. Hawthorne. There'd been no mention of a name. She stopped. Was this her plot? How would she know? She only had a number. Next to the house was a shed, and outside that was a wheelbarrow and spade. They certainly hadn't belonged to Ma. She opened the gate fully, and walking up the path, knocked at the door. Other than the thunder, the wind in the trees and the rhythmic thudding of the rain, she could hear nothing. No sounds came from inside the house. She peered through the window. The room was sparsely decorated, but the personal items showed this house already had an owner. On the table, a bright tea cosy on top of a teapot. Two mugs nearby. A newspaper and a book. No, this was definitely not Ma's.

Had she confused Mr Parker's directions? She'd been muddling things all afternoon. Had she turned left instead of right? Or perhaps he'd said the house was on the right? If only she could clear her head and think. Perhaps Mr Parker had been wrong. He'd been in a hurry to escape. More interested in buying her property than in giving accurate directions. But it couldn't be far, surely? She walked back down the path and looked across to the other side of the road. There were three houses, but each one had a name – and, it appeared, an owner. A china ornament displayed in the window of one. Wellington boots stood under the porch of another. Two umbrellas leaning against the wall of the third.

The wrong avenue? Perhaps she'd missed a turning. She retraced her steps to the crossroads, taking care on the uneven road that was slippery with the rain. Was there a road further along the avenue on the right? Yes? Then it must be down there.

Her shoe rubbed her heel as it slipped in the wet, and the driving rain had soaked right through her dress. She wished she'd stopped earlier to put her coat on, but it was too late now. At least after exploring several of the roads, she noticed that between the houses were areas of land marked with pegs. Presumably those plots were still for sale. And on each plot, the pegs were numbered. She hurried back to the green flag, intending to check the number on the plot next door. That might give her a clue. She bent to check the peg at the corner of the plot next to Green Haven. It was hard to read, and she leaned closer. It occurred to her that, unlike London with its streetlights, when darkness fell in Plotlands, it would be so black she wouldn't be able to see a hand in front of her face – let alone find a cottage. The tight ball of fear in her stomach grew until she could no longer ignore it. She allowed the terrible thought to form in her mind.

Suppose there is no cottage?

Well, of course, there is! I have a receipt to prove it.

But the receipt hadn't stated what Ma had bought, just how much she'd paid.

No, there must be a cottage. There had to be.

She crouched and cleared the grass from the peg at the corner of Green Haven and the land next door. It was hard to see in the gloom, and she rubbed at it with her finger to allow the rain to clean away the mud.

Number 18. She stared at it and wondered if it was upside down. But it had been driven into the earth. This was number 18. No doubt.

The breath she'd been holding burst out of her mouth in a gasp of horror. It was her land. But there was no cottage. There was nothing at all. Simply a rectangular piece of ground covered in dripping grass and brambles.

How could that possibly be? She thought back over the conversation she'd had with Ma, but try as she might, she couldn't remember any mention of a building. Ma had spoken of their future home. Is that why she'd said they'd have to wait a few more weeks before they moved – so she could save to have something built?

Joanna sank to her knees in the mud. She'd given up her job and walked out of Aunt Ivy's house for a patch of weedy ground in this tumbledown, half-built part of Essex. She wanted to throw her head back and howl at the thunderous clouds that raced above her, pelting her mercilessly with rain. Ma had been right. Life wasn't fair. And since Pa had died, life had singled her out to deal her blow after blow.

Lightning zigzagged across the sky, impaling the black clouds. Once, she'd have run to her parents for comfort in weather such as this. Now, she simply wanted to curl up in a ball and push the world away. But that was childish. And that part of her life must finish now.

But what should she do? She couldn't go back to Aunt Ivy's house. That was clear. Perhaps she ought to look for Uncle John in Brighton? Tomorrow, that would mean taking a train back to London and then travelling out to Brighton. Or maybe there was a bus. But how would she find out? Perhaps now she was in Laindon, she ought to find a room to rent.

Enough! You're still behaving like a child. Get up and find some shelter for the night.

Joanna struggled to her feet. Next door, the rope slapped wildly against the flagpole, and she remembered Mr Parker had said the flag showed the family was at home. She opened the gate to Green Haven and hurried up the path towards the front door. Climbing the steps to the covered veranda, she knocked. Despite the flag proclaiming the owners' presence, nobody replied, and she peeped through the windows. However, it was dark inside the small wooden cottage. Silent. Empty.

Joanna sank onto the doormat, across which in large

letters was emblazoned the word, 'Welcome'. Pressing herself against the front door, as far from the rain as she could, she took shelter. Her stomach growled and clenched, and she ate the packet of dry biscuits, wishing she had more. How foolish to have bought cans of soup earlier. She had no means of opening them. But she'd assumed a home would be waiting for her. How naïve was that?

In the morning, she'd go to Brighton. She'd proved beyond doubt she didn't know how to live independently. She might be eighteen, but she knew as much about life as a child.

Joanna woke with a start. A light glowed brightly in her face, and behind that were two indistinct faces, both topped with dripping sou'westers. A gentle hand shook her shoulder.

"Hello, lovey ... Lovey?" The woman's voice was kind and anxious.

Joanna tried to focus. Her head thumped and her neck was stiff after having fallen asleep sitting up.

Who were these people? It was so hard to think.

Where was she? Realisation came gradually, as gentle hands helped her to her feet.

"Come in, lovey. You don't look good at all. What's your name?"

"Joanna," she whispered, her mouth dry and rough.

"Then come on in, Joanna, and dry off. I'm Sheila

84

Guyler, and this is my husband, Bill. Come on, that's it. Are you hurt, lovey?"

Joanna shook her head and burst into tears.

Sheila wrapped a towel around Joanna while Bill put the kettle on.

"I always say the world's brighter with a cuppa," Sheila said, guiding Joanna to a chair at their table. "Now, why don't you sit down and tell us all about it while Bill brews the tea?"

Joanna explained how she'd joined the trip with Mr Parker, believing he'd show her to the cottage Ma had bought.

"That would be Jonas Parker of Whitechapel Estates, would it?" Bill asked as he placed a mug of tea in front of Joanna.

She nodded as she picked it up and cradled it gratefully.

"Only I've heard about him before," Bill said. "We ain't never had dealings with 'im but quite a few of the people who've moved down from the East End to these parts have complained about 'is lies. Parker tells everyone there's mains water. But there ain't. We've got standpipes every so often along the avenues. There'll be mains water one day, but not yet a while. That Parker ain't nothing but a liar."

"Well, that doesn't help the poor girl now," said

Sheila. "If you've been wandering outside for most of the day, when did you last eat, lovey?"

Joanna admitted she'd only had a few biscuits earlier.

"And you had a glass o' champers on an empty stomach?" Sheila shook her head, setting her grey curls bobbing.

"Two," Joanna admitted.

"No wonder you're feeling under the weather. Right, give me two ticks and I'll make you something to eat. If only I'd known, I'd 'ave bought you back some cake. Bill an' I've just been to a birthday party. That's why we weren't home earlier. Lucky we were here at all. We were supposed to be staying with our daughter, Dolly. She's just had a baby. Our first grandson. Bless him. What on earth would you have done then? You'd have had to sleep outside all night."

She placed a plate of bread and ham, and a bowl of stewed apple in front of Joanna, who ate hungrily.

"You tuck in, lovey, while I prepare the spare bedroom. You'll stay with us tonight, of course. There's plenty more where that came from if you're still hungry."

Joanna awoke to the smell of frying bacon the following morning. It took several seconds to recollect where she was. No milkman coughing, accompanied by the clip–

clop of hoofs and the rattle of milk bottles. No doors opening and closing and heavy boots on the pavement. Instead, birdsong and Bill whistling along with them in the garden. Sheila humming tunelessly, somewhere in the house.

With the new morning, Joanna's head was clearer. Sunshine glided in through the gap in the curtains. It was as if the previous night's storm had never happened. A feeling of optimism washed through her. When she'd thought things couldn't get any worse and she'd wanted to give up, Sheila and Bill had found her.

Perhaps she'd be able to manage this new life – if they helped her as they'd promised. She had sufficient money to rent a room in Laindon and once she found a job, she'd save until she had enough to build a home. A small cottage – nothing as large as Sheila's – just something big enough for her. Not that Green Haven was large, but Joanna didn't need two bedrooms. When she could afford it, she'd enlarge the building.

Over breakfast, her hopes soared. Bill said he'd already met a few other Plotlanders earlier that morning and had told them what had happened to her. "We look after our own here in Dunton, don't we, Sheel?" he said to Sheila, proudly nodding his head. He told her how people had offered to donate items they no longer needed and to help when she started to build a cottage.

Build a cottage.

She hardly dared to form the words in her mind. Was it possible? But Bill continued to discuss the problem as if it was. He'd broken down the nightmare that had been too huge for her to contemplate into manageable stages. With help, each step was achievable. And the kind couple had promised they and other Plotlanders would help.

As Bill listed items the neighbours had promised, Sheila wrote them down. "I know Tom's got some roofing felt left over," Bill said, wiggling his finger at Sheila, indicating she should make a note. "Of course, one day you'll have proper tiles, but roofing felt will do until you're on yer feet."

Tom and Florrie Cavendish were their best friends. Bill and Sheila had been at the Cavendish's house the previous evening, celebrating Florrie's birthday along with many of the neighbours. That explained why no one had been home in the cottages Joanna had passed. Florrie and Tom's son, Sam, worked at Davidson's, the building suppliers in town. Tom said he was sure his son would help where he could, too.

Later, Bill showed Joanna the plans he'd had drawn for Green Haven. At first, he and Sheila had bought the plot to build a weekend home. They'd started with one large room, which included a kitchen area and a bedroom. And a toilet at the end of the garden.

"Green Haven looked a bit like a shed." Sheila polished her spectacles, then perching them on her nose, she peered at the plans Bill had laid on the table. "But it was lovely to escape from the smoke for the weekend. Dolly used to come with us too, then she started courting and, of course, now she's got her own home."

"We loved it so much we found we were spending more and more time here until it weren't worth paying the rent for our flat in the East End. Bill does odd jobs, and we grow much of our food. Life's cheaper here. Much better, whichever way you look at it. Anyway, we added two bedrooms and built a shed for Bill's tools and moved out here permanent like. Never looked back," Sheila said. Her expression saddened. "Although now Dolly and Ray have had their first baby, I wish we weren't so far away. But they love it down here, so p'raps one day they'll come here to live too."

Bill patted her hand. "They're bound to, Sheel. Especially now they've got the nipper. It's much healthier raising children in the country."

Bill pointed out the original building on the plans. "You could get yerself something simple to start – just to get through the winter. Then next spring, you could add a bedroom. It'd look a bit like a shed, to begin with, but so what? Many of the cottages around here started like that. And when you've got a job and you've saved a bit, you can extend as much as you like."

Bill made it sound so logical. So easy.

Sheila insisted Joanna stayed with them in Green Haven until she had a firm plan. For the next few days, she helped Sheila in the house and garden, getting used to the quiet of the countryside. She inspected her plot with Bill, measured distances from the boundary and dreamt of her new home.

"It won't take long to clear those brambles. I'll get some neighbours over and we'll 'ave it clear in no time. Don't you worry. You'll be growing your own veggies next spring; you mark my words."

Joanna wondered if that was perhaps a step too far. She'd never thought of growing anything, let alone vegetables, but the change of pace of life in this Essex backwater was soothing and she could see why so many of the neighbours had expressed their delight at having exchanged the busy, dirty City for this place of eccentric cottages, open space and birdsong.

On Thursday, Joanna accompanied Sheila to Henderson's, the general store. Next to the wooden building was the post office, and Joanna waited for Sheila while she telephoned her daughter for their weekly chat. It soon became obvious from Sheila's replies that Dolly wanted to come with their grandson, Billy, to stay for a while. Sheila pinched the bridge of her nose and glanced at Joanna. Of course, she'd want her daughter and new grandson to stay, but such a motherly woman wouldn't like to ask Joanna to leave.

Nevertheless, Joanna would have to go. Sheila's cottage would be full, with five adults and a baby. The time had come to make provision for herself. She broached the subject on the way back to Green Haven, and Sheila told her there was no need to move out. They could put a spare bed up in the main room if Joanna didn't mind squeezing in. Dolly's husband, Ray, probably wouldn't come anyway, as he found it hard to get time off work.

It was a kind offer and so typical of Sheila. As pleasant as the last few days had been, Joanna recognised she must find a job – and quickly. The following day, she'd go into town and find the solicitors Mr Franklin had recommended. If they didn't need anyone, perhaps they might suggest someone who did. Tightness squeezed her chest. Sheila and Bill had given her the confidence to believe in herself, but she wasn't ready to leave them yet.

Too bad. She'd simply have to get on with it.

When they got home, Sheila told Bill about Dolly, wanting to visit.

"Don't worry, I'll move out and find a room," Joanna said, expecting to see relief on their faces.

"No need, love," Bill said. "If you don't mind roughing it a bit, you can sleep in the tent."

He suggested he could erect the bell tent in which he and Sheila had slept when they'd first arrived in Dunton on their empty piece of land.

Sheila brightened. "Oh, yes! You could sleep in the tent and come in here to eat and wash. Yes, that's the answer. You can always rely on my Bill." She beamed at him.

The weather was still warm for the time of year, and Joanna readily agreed. The idea of sleeping in a tent wasn't appealing, but she couldn't think of a better solution. And at least being close to Sheila and Bill made her feel safe. But ultimately, she had to manage on her own. It wasn't fair to rely too much on the Guylers.

The following day, Joanna dressed carefully in a smart navy-blue suit and white blouse. Sheila, who'd worked as a hairdresser for many years, pinned her hair up, completing the business-like look. She offered to accompany Joanna into town to offer moral support, and afterwards, she said, they could buy some bedding. Joanna would need it when she slept in the tent and then later, she'd want it in her own home.

Overnight it had rained, although the morning dawned bright and clear, promising another warm autumn day. The roads, however, had not dried out after the storm the previous weekend and were waterlogged. Joanna picked her way as best she could around puddles, but by the time they arrived in town, her shoes were caked with mud.

"Let's add rubber boots to your list of purchases."

Sheila looked down at her own muddy boots. "I don't care what I look like. I wear them everywhere, but when you get a job, you'll want to wear shoes. You can leave your boots with Mr and Mrs Dalton at Holmcroft, change into your shoes and pick yer boots up on the way home. That's what most people do, and the Daltons are happy to keep an eye on them."

Joanna looked down at her dirty shoes, wishing she'd had boots with her.

"Don't worry, lovey," Sheila said, seeing her frown. "Mud's a common feature around here. You'll soon get used to it. No one'll bat an eyelid. You'll see."

The closer they got to Richardson Bailey & Cole, the more Joanna's confidence drained away. Why would anyone want to employ her? Since she'd struck out on her own, she'd been a failure. Without the help of her kind neighbours, she didn't know where she'd be.

She'd come to Dunton, completely unprepared for life alone. Her shorthand and typing speed were excellent, but if she couldn't take herself seriously, how could anyone else?

"I'm not sure, Sheila. Perhaps I should come back another day?"

"Absolutely not! Come on, chin up! If you go into their office looking like that, they won't offer you the time of day. You've got to puff your chest out, hold your head high, and pretend you're the bees' knees. If you believe it, so will everyone else."

Despite her doubts, Joanna laughed at Sheila with her chest exaggeratedly puffed out, and her arms bent and flapping like a bee.

Perhaps she could do it.

Perhaps this was a point where she grew up, took control of her life, and made things change.

Maybe people created their own fairness in life. It had been easy for her to blame Fate and avoid taking responsibility herself. From now on, she'd seize control. She pushed her shoulders back, raised her chin, and repeating under her breath, "I can do this, I can do this, I can ..." She opened the door to Richardson Bailey & Cole. The bell tinkled merrily.

"Good morning. May I help you?" A severe-looking woman rose as Joanna entered the office. She was tall and slim, with grey hair pulled severely back in a bun, and she had such an air of Miss Bartle about her that Joanna stopped abruptly.

"Good morning, I ... I,"

For goodness' sake, say something sensible!

The woman dropped her chin and peered over her glasses.

Joanna swallowed and started again. "Good morning. I've just moved into the area and I'm looking for employment. I wondered if you had any vacancies?"

Under the woman's scrutiny, Joanna looked down in

embarrassment, catching sight of her muddy shoes. She couldn't imagine what she looked like to this smartly dressed woman. Some of Sheila's careful work had come unpinned in the wind, and now she wished she'd checked her appearance in a shop window to make sure she looked presentable. But she'd been so afraid she'd lose her nerve; she'd rushed headlong into the office and made a fool of herself. Who on earth would want to employ her?

"What employment are you seeking, Miss ...?"

Joanna's mouth had gone dry. But if she was going to stand a chance of making a life on her own, she must regain some of the confidence Sheila had urged her to find. She took a shaky breath. "Miss Marshall. I am a shorthand typist."

"I see. Well, I'm sorry, Miss Marshall, the partners only employ office staff from the Black & Snowden Employment Agency in London. We will require a cleaner shortly ..."

"I was hoping to find work as a typist."

"Yes, of course. Well, may I suggest you visit Black & Snowden? If they put you on their books, we'd be happy to consider your application."

Well, that was plain enough. There was no point trying to persuade the woman. She'd been perfectly clear.

"Thank you." Joanna half-turned, ready to admit

defeat when she saw Sheila through the window in the door. Her face alight with a huge smile, as if ready to congratulate Joanna. Sheila believed in her.

Joanna turned back and said, "I have good references and a letter of recommendation from Mr Franklin from Tredegar Murchison & Franklin in London, if that would be any use." Joanna fished in her pocket and held out the letter. During the storm, the rain had soaked her bag and everything in it. The envelope was wrinkled, although, luckily, the letter had remained dry.

The woman stared at the crumpled envelope but didn't take it. "I see. Well, I'm sure that is most impressive. It will stand you in good stead when you apply for employment elsewhere. However, as I said, Mr Richardson is most particular about his staff. I'm sorry Miss Marshall." She hesitated, then added, "If you leave your name and address, I shall put it on file in case I hear of anything suitable, and I'll let you know."

Joanna gave the woman Sheila's address. There was no point directing letters to an empty plot of land – where would a postman deliver them? Then she turned sadly away and went out to Sheila, whose smile dropped when she saw Joanna's expression.

"Never mind, lovey, that's the first place you've tried. It's their loss. You'll get a good job soon. Perhaps try in Wickford or Billericay. You can get there on the bus. And they might pay better wages."

Chapter Three

The bell above the door into the reception area of Richardson, Bailey & Cole tinkled merrily, and the young woman stepped out onto the street, closing the door behind her. From his office off the main reception area, Ben Richardson watched her go. The bell may have tinkled merrily, but she was anything but merry.

Neither was he.

When he'd first heard her come in, he'd taken little notice. A new client, he'd assumed. He'd glanced through the window of his office door into the reception area and wondered if it would mean more work for him. He was slightly hungover and finding it hard to apply himself that morning.

How long would it take Mrs Pike to deal with her? He'd wanted more black coffee. In that uncanny way Mrs Pike had of appearing to read his mind, she'd brought him a cup earlier – although, it wouldn't have taken a mind reader to see he'd required coffee. The greyish tinge to his skin and the red, puffy eyes had betrayed him. At breakfast, his mother's pursed lips and scornful expression had told him she knew he'd had too much to drink the previous evening.

Ben had tried to concentrate on the contract on his

desk, but something about the young woman kept drawing his attention. She was beautiful. Not in the conventional sense, like a Hollywood film star made up to appear flawless. No, this young woman had natural beauty.

The wind outside had tinted the colour in her cheeks but as she'd talked to Mrs Pike, the colour had heightened. She'd been embarrassed. He'd almost imagined her toes curling. And at that thought, he'd wanted to see more than just the top half of her. He'd casually walked to the filing cabinet near the door so he could take a better look. She'd been smartly dressed, although her shoes were very muddy. Her hair had presumably been tidy when she'd left home, although tendrils of hair had blown free and now framed her face.

Mud and wind. Two of the pleasure of living in Essex. Two of the pleasures he'd liked to have been able to enjoy, rather than working in a stifling office.

Standing by the door, while pretending to search for a file, he'd heard Mrs Pike turn the young woman away. He'd sighed when he'd seen her expression of defeat.

Someone else whose dreams had been dashed. Although he doubted that working for Richardson, Bailey & Cole had been the woman's dream. Nevertheless, her disappointment and resignation had been clear.

Resignation. Yes, he knew all about that. He

slammed the file drawer closed with the heel of his palm and sat down at his desk. There was so much to do today, but he simply couldn't get started. Pushing the document that lay in front of him out of the way, he reached for a blank sheet of paper. He folded it, running his finger along the crease, then continued to fold. Finally, he opened it out to form a paper aeroplane. Leaning back in his seat, he aimed it at the light fitting dangling from the ceiling. The plane sliced through the air, then for no apparent reason, changed trajectory, spiralled downwards, and crashed to the floor. Promise followed by disappointment. Yes, he understood all about that, too.

He was tempted to fold another plane, but it had been childish, and achieved nothing.

It might be childish, but then doesn't everyone treat you like a child?

Until recently, he'd gone along with it. He'd grown up believing adults knew best. He'd obeyed his parents, studied to become a solicitor, and followed his father into the firm he'd founded with two colleagues. Ben had expected to work in London in their main office and had been disappointed when he realised he'd been placed permanently in the provincial office in Laindon.

Of course, he'd seen the sense. So many people were moving into the area, the Laindon office was becoming increasingly busy. And since he lived with his parents in

Priory Hall on a large estate just outside Laindon, he didn't have far to travel to work each day.

When he'd been a boy, he hadn't given much thought to the future, blindly assuming it would hold something exciting. He'd worked from one exam to the next. With only vague ideas about his destination, he'd focused on the journey. And then, suddenly, he was fully qualified. He had a position in an established firm, and he'd arrived without realising it.

He looked around his office. It was small but well-equipped. It was also lonely. Mrs Pike, with her rigid ways, sat outside, dealing with new clients and queries. But as courteous and efficient as she was, she was hardly good company. Of course, he met many people during the day, but he was dealing with their wills, deeds, and other legal documents.

Why had no one ever asked him what he wanted to do? If he'd been allowed to decide, he wouldn't be cooped up in an office, he'd be outside with the sun on his face, the wind brushing his skin and mud on his boots. He closed his eyes and imagined the acres of land he would farm if he had his way. And the sad thing was that it had been possible.

Still was possible.

The Priory Hall estate comprised acres of farmland, but once, when he'd broached the subject, his father had looked at him with incredulity, and said he didn't consider farming a suitable way for his son to waste his education. He hired a farm manager to look after the land. Did Ben realise how much money he'd spent on sending him to Eton? How much had gone into maintaining a suitable lifestyle for him while he was studying at Oxford? What the cost of his travels around Europe had been? No, of course not. And now, Ben wanted to let his parents down and become a farmer?

Ben had introduced the subject on several occasions, but it had always ended in a row. Especially when his mother had learnt of his hopes.

"Farmer? No Benjamin. No. That won't do at all. How can you possibly throw all your father's dreams back in his face? Have you any idea how much effort he's put into the business he's building up for his only son? If you have any regard for him at all, you'll give up this silly nonsense and concentrate on your career."

Ben hadn't mentioned it since.

Perhaps one day he'd be able to leave his father's company, but by that time, would it be too late? Farming wasn't something you just picked up – it took years of experience.

The thought that he'd never be able to live his life as he wanted pressed down on him like a great weight. He'd seen enough of other people's lives when dealing with their wills and inheritances to recognise he was remarkably fortunate and wanted for nothing. Shame pushed back against the heavy burden that was bearing down on him. How many people would like to be in his privileged position? Guilt mingled with shame. His parents had carefully planned his life.

Why did he feel guilty?

After all, he'd done everything his parents had asked of him. Or so he'd thought. There appeared to be one more thing they wanted. Something he'd only discovered a few days before, at breakfast. And that was why he'd drunk to excess the previous night and was now paying for it.

The morning he'd learnt of his parents' new demands on his life, his father had left early for London. His mother had joined Ben for breakfast, getting up earlier than usual. Had she deliberately risen early to catch him and plant the idea? Probably. Although it would be hard to tell. It could have been spontaneous, but Mama was very single-minded. Planning – not spontaneity – was her style.

Breakfast had started normally.

"Did you have a good evening, Benjamin?" she'd asked.

He'd replied that he had and continued eating, but Mama had other things on her mind. The previous evening, he'd accompanied Emily Bailey to a theatre in London. Not that he'd invited her. Papa had intended to go with Hugh Bailey, Emily's father, but he'd discovered he had a prior engagement which had slipped his memory. He'd offered Ben his ticket. Strangely, Hugh Bailey hadn't been able to go either and had given his ticket to his daughter.

The ploy had been so blatant, it had been laughable, but really, what difference did it make? He'd known Emily since she was a child, so it wasn't like they were strangers. She was home from a tour of Europe after leaving finishing school, and she was good company. Lively, animated, amusing. Pretty in an artificial sort of way with immaculately styled hair, expensive clothes that hugged her figure and expertly applied makeup.

The play had been enjoyable and overall, he'd had an agreeable evening. But Mama didn't want to know about the performance.

"So, what do you think of Emily?" It hadn't been a simple query. Ben had recognised the tone – it was a question of great significance. Importance dripped from it, like the honey she was dribbling onto her toast.

He'd been deliberately noncommittal. "She's pleasant."

"Just pleasant?"

"Yes, why?"

"Oh, no reason."

But he'd known Mama wouldn't let it drop. He'd chewed faster and despite desperately wanting a second cup of coffee, decided against it so he could escape.

But his mother must have guessed. How did she know him so well? Not for the first time, he'd asked himself if she could read his mind.

"It's just that I was wondering ..." She stirred the sugar in her tea and tapped the spoon against the bone china cup. "About you settling down. And I thought Emily Bailey would be the perfect choice."

He'd spluttered on his coffee. Well, at least she'd been very clear.

He took a deep breath. "No." He would be equally specific.

His mother sat back in her chair. "Well, early days." Her eyebrows had shot upward in surprise at his vehemence, but he knew she wouldn't give up.

The idea of an alliance between the two families had come up before but Ben had never taken it seriously. He and Emily had been children and he'd assumed their parents had been voicing pleasantries. Not making plans. During the last few years while Emily had been at school abroad, the subject hadn't been mentioned. Now she was home, and they were both of marriageable age.

Of course, the match would have been perfect. Not for him, but for the Richardson and Bailey families. Hugh Bailey had been his father's closest friend since they were at school, and it had been natural for them to set up in business together. They'd formed the company with an older solicitor, Ronald Cole, who was now semi-retired. It was a successful business, but marriage between Emily and Ben would bind them even closer.

Over his dead body.

Ben couldn't get that conversation with his mother off his mind, although he'd temporarily blotted it out the previous evening after he'd had more whisky than had been sensible.

He stood up and retrieved the paper aeroplane, screwing it tightly into a ball in his fist and hurled it into the bin. No, he would not marry Emily Bailey. Not for his mother and not for his father. Not for all the riches in the world. He winced as the dull ache in his head grew to a thumping crescendo.

There would be trouble when they realised his refusal was final, although, at first, there would be incentives. The promise of a house if they were to marry. And, if he resisted, pressure would be applied. Yes, there would be many such breakfasts, lunches and dinners with his mother, persuading, pleading, or demanding – and his father backing her up.

Ben could give in and make life easy. He'd done so thus far and had a good job and a comfortable lifestyle, so why not? He imagined life in ten years' time with the immaculate Emily Bailey and perhaps a nursery full of children. It would mean he'd have to commit to Richardson, Bailey & Cole and give up any hope of ever achieving his dream.

His thoughts returned to the girl who'd come in earlier. For some reason, her image was imprinted in his mind. Curls framing a beautiful face, not painted and artificial, like Emily's, but natural and perfect in its own way. He wondered what job she was seeking.

He stood up and walked into the main office. "Mrs Pike, who was that young woman who was in here a few minutes ago?"

He'd only recently persuaded Mrs Pike to stop calling him Young Mr Richardson, and she tripped over it now and corrected herself. "That was a young lady looking for a job as a shorthand typist, Yo ... er ... Mr Richardson."

"Don't we need a typist?"

"Yes, but your father is always most particular that we acquire new members of staff from Black & Snowden. They've always sent us first-class people."

"But the last woman left after two months because she'd been offered a better job in Billericay."

"Yes, I know, but those are your father's orders. It's a shame because she's been working for Tredegar, Murchison & Franklin. And Mr Franklin thought enough of her to write a letter of recommendation. But there's nothing I can do. I suggested she approach Black & Snowden."

"But surely if we require someone now and she's available, we ought to at least give her an interview? I'll speak to my father and clear it with him. Yes, leave it to me. I'll take full responsibility. After all, what harm could it do to interview her?"

"Well, if you're sure ... At least she lives in one of the new Plotland houses, so we know she's local, unlike the last one who complained about her bus ride from Billericay every morning."

"Excellent. Well, no time like the present. If you could invite Miss ...? for an interview, please."

"Miss Joanna Marshall."

"Well, if you could type the letter up now, it could go with the evening post."

What was he doing interfering in such a way? His father might be angry.

Good. Perhaps that was the point. For Ben to make a decision that differed from his father's.

He was grateful to his parents, but he wanted to be his own man. And, as a bonus, he'd ensure a young woman was interviewed for a job.

How selfless!

All right. He had to concede that Joanna Marshall had piqued his interest. A beautiful, young woman working in the office might just give him a reason to look forward to coming to work in the morning. But suppose she was unsuitable?

Well, there was one way to find out.

"In fact, I have to go to the post office later," he lied.

"I'll take the post this evening."

"Oh, that would be most useful, thank you, Yo ... er ... Mr Richardson. My sister's coming to stay with me over the weekend and I wanted to leave on time."

"Then why not leave half an hour early? I'll clear it with my father that Miss Marshall is interviewed when he gets back from the London office later, and I'll lock up and post all the letters."

Ben's father didn't return to the Laindon office that day. He telephoned to explain he'd be dining at his club in London with Hugh Bailey that evening, and he'd called Ben's mother to let her know. However, since she'd be out all evening too – at a bridge party – he wondered if Ben would take Emily out. Hugh had mentioned she was at a loose end that evening.

"No, sorry, Papa. I'm afraid I'll be working late tonight. I'm sure Emily knows plenty of men who'd take her out. She often sees Ian Padgett-Lane. He might be free."

"Indeed ... Well, if you're certain you won't be finished in time ..." His father sounded irritated, but he could hardly display annoyance at his son's dedication.

"Yes," said Ben firmly. "Yes, I'm certain."

Mrs Pike left half an hour early, as suggested. Ben waited in the main office until five o'clock, when he locked up and walked to the post office. He posted all the letters, except one. Tomorrow, he intended to hand deliver the letter.

He couldn't get Joanna Marshall's face out of his mind, and if only to rid himself of the image, he needed to talk to her. He told himself she'd probably be quite unsuitable.

Unsuitable for what? For working in the firm? Or were you thinking of something more personal?

For working in the office, of course. But as hard as he tried to convince himself of that, he couldn't get her out of his mind. Her voice had been soft and ...

Stop it!

It was one thing rejecting his parents' choice of a future wife but quite another to fantasise about a woman he'd only glimpsed through a window.

Tomorrow, if he found her, he'd discover the reality didn't match up to the vision in his imagination.

But suppose it did?

The following day was Saturday, and Ben left the office at noon. With the letter for Joanna in his pocket, he set off toward the Plotlands. He'd ridden near the area on his horse many times but had never ventured down the avenues. However, he had a mental image of the area from the map that hung on the wall in the reception. Many new clients had moved into the region, and it was useful being able to locate them on the map. Ben had spent some time that morning making a study of it.

However, the neat geometric representation on the map had not hinted at the chaotic nature of Plotlands. Rectangles of tangled undergrowth, small areas of woodland, cottages, huts, tents. They were all to be found one after the other in this strange new community about which, he realised, he'd thought he knew much but actually knew very little.

He found Green Haven relatively easily. It was one of the more robust structures that he'd passed, although it was still very simple. Not even as grand as the cottages his father's predecessors had built for the farmworkers on the Priory Hall estate.

He'd known the previous day that Joanna Marshall was a working-class girl, and now, the humble cottage told him – if he'd needed reminding – she was beneath him socially.

Does it bother you?

No, he decided, it didn't. Again, her face appeared in his imagination, and he tried to push it away. He was being foolish. How could he be so taken with a woman he'd never met? As soon as he spoke to her, he'd realise she didn't live up to his foolish image. It would be best to slip the letter through the letterbox and walk away, or perhaps not post it at all. Forget this idealised woman that lived in his thoughts. It was simply a reaction to his mother's assumption he'd eventually come around to the idea of marrying Emily. He'd spotted a woman who was obviously from a lower class and had become fixated on her because she was as far from Emily Bailey as it was possible to be.

Yes, that was it. And so, now he had it all sorted in his mind, he might as well hand deliver the letter and see for himself that Joanna Marshall was not the girl of his dreams. His mother had always maintained that people of the lower classes were uncouth, untrustworthy, and undesirable to know. The sooner he met the girl and got her out of his system, the better.

Anyway, she may well have found a job after she left Mrs Pike and wouldn't be interested in an interview. In that case, it was unlikely he'd ever see her again. And even if she got the job, she'd probably have a sweetheart.

Aren't you getting ahead of yourself?

Well, there was only one way to find out. Ben opened the gate to Green Haven and walked up the path. He climbed the steps to the veranda, and ignoring the letterbox, he knocked on the door. A woman with a pleasant, ruddy face opened the door and peered at him over her spectacles. She held out a basket containing eggs, and then, realising he wasn't who she was expecting, pulled the basket back.

"Good afternoon." Ben raised his hat. "My name is Benjamin Richardson, and I'm looking for Miss Joanna Marshall. Is she home?"

The woman blinked several times. "Well, yes." Her

eyes narrowed with suspicion. "What do you want with our Joanna?"

He took the letter out of his pocket and then realising that if he passed it to this woman, she might shut the door, he added, "I was passing so I thought I'd deliver this letter on behalf of Richardson, Bailey & Cole, solicitors."

"Benjamin Richardson, of Richardson, Bailey & Cole?" The woman's voice became more respectful, and her eyes opened wide.

"Yes indeed, but I am not *that* Mr Richardson. He's my father—"

"Come in, come in!" The woman stepped back, allowing him to pass. "I'm Sheila, by the way, make yourself comfortable. I'll go and call Joanna." She ushered him into a cluttered living room and after moving a clothes horse covered in underwear away from the front of the stove, she indicated he should sit in an armchair.

As she hurried away to the back of the cottage, Ben looked about. Unlike Priory Hall, where curtains and cushions matched, and ornaments were artfully arranged, this room had a haphazard look. Although it was shabby and untidy, everything was clean – even the air was filled with the scent of polish. This was a room where the belongings didn't shout wealth or taste. No one had considered symmetry or style. It was a room crammed with well-loved items – many handmade – and useful objects, like pens, scissors, books, and torches. To Ben, it appeared to be a room that was lived in, and a place of happiness.

On the table, a large architectural plan was held down at each corner with the salt and pepper pots, a bunch of keys and a pot of jam. A knitting bag with needles poking out sat on the other chair with a half-finished piece of crochet on top.

Ben smiled as he imagined his mother's face on seeing this muddle, although she'd probably have taken one look at the outside of the cottage and refused to enter. But he was not his mother, and he was learning that people shouldn't simply be categorised according to their social class or their bank balance. He'd seen enough at work, of wills and the affairs of nasty, rich people and their greedy, grasping relatives to know that wealth didn't always accompany a reputable character. Well, that was obvious.

During his privileged education, he'd known plenty of rich people. But what he hadn't realised until he'd started working was that there were pleasant and not so pleasant people amongst all classes. When he'd thought about it, that had been obvious, but his parents had ensured he'd grown up only seeing one aspect of the world. He'd never been allowed to play with the farm hands' children – just rich cousins and children of rich friends. He'd finally realised how little of life he'd seen, and he was appalled. Even now, he had to check and recheck his attitude toward people and situations to ensure he wasn't simply echoing his parents' views.

This was the first time he'd been in such a home, and this cottage in Plotlands was quite a revelation.

Joanna stood in the middle of her plot of land. She pretended she was peering through the windows that would one day look out over her front garden. She wiped the sweat off her forehead with the back of her hand. There was a great deal to do before that day. She groaned as mud smeared, slick and slippery across her skin. There was no point fishing in the pocket of the overalls she'd borrowed from Bill for her handkerchief because, by the time she'd pulled that out, it would be covered in mud too.

She'd got up early that morning and had started digging the foundations of her new house.

My new house.

Three tiny words that made her fizz with excitement.

Bill had joined her after breakfast and was helping her to dig into the heavy, waterlogged soil. One neighbour had some hard-core. Bill said that once that was packed into the holes, they could build brick piers on top. Then, they'd place wooden planks over those and before long, she'd have a floor.

A floor! Soon, she'd have a floor. Had anyone ever been so thrilled at the thought of owning a floor?

But she wasn't there yet. Before the brick piers could be built, she needed to dig the holes in the ground. Taking a deep breath, she placed her foot on the spade and pushed down hard. The heavy ground, full of clay, fought back against the spade and she transferred more weight onto it.

"Coo-ee! Joanna!"

She looked up and saw Sheila impatiently waving and urgently beckoning her from the back door of Green Haven.

Bill started back to Sheila, but she gestured at him to stay and pointed at Joanna. "Looks like she only wants you, love. Not sure what's going on. But if she's made a cuppa give me a yell, will you? I'm parched."

Joanna left her spade half-buried in the soil and ran back to the cottage, her fringe falling on her face, tickling her forehead. It would have to stay there. Both hands were covered in mud, and she didn't want to smear more dirt across her face than was already there.

Sheila was almost quivering with excitement, her face alight with an enormous smile. She mouthed something that Joanna couldn't understand, but as she drew closer, Sheila whispered, "It's Mr Richardson come to see you. Quick, quick!"

Richardson? The name was familiar, but she didn't

know anyone by the name of Richardson. One of the neighbours? Was Sheila excited because he'd come with an offer of help? She took off her boots at the door, dirtying her hands further, and padded across the wooden floor in her thick socks.

As she entered, a young man rose from Bill's chair, his hat in his hands, and smiled. He was well-dressed in a smart dark grey suit, but she knew she'd never met him before. She'd definitely have remembered his face. Dark hair and dark eyes that drank her in. She was suddenly aware of how dirty and scruffy she looked in Bill's overalls, standing in her stockinged feet. No wonder he was staring.

Who was he? Whoever he was, he couldn't be there to see her. And yet, his face lit up as if they were old friends. She half-turned to Sheila, silently signalling she didn't know this man, but Sheila nodded enthusiastically, her eyes wide with anticipation.

"Miss Marshall, please excuse my intrusion. My name is Benjamin Richardson, and I was passing this morning, so I thought I'd hand deliver this letter."

He held out his hands to shake hers. She bit her lip, and, looking at him with dismay, she pulled her muddy hands out of her pockets. "I ... I'm so sorry. I'm afraid I've been working outside."

He lowered his hand and nodded with understanding. His expression was half-puzzled and half-amused, but he placed the letter near the plans on the table. "Of course, well, perhaps you could open it at your convenience. It contains an invitation for an interview."

And then she remembered where she'd heard the name Richardson. She gasped and almost lifted her hand to her mouth, remembering at the last second it was muddy. "You mean you're Mr Richardson of—"

He held up his hand to stop her. "Of Richardson Bailey & Cole, yes. But not *that* Mr Richardson," he said with a laugh. "That Mr Richardson is my father."

"But you want me to attend an interview?"

Mr Richardson nodded. "As a shorthand typist," he added with a mischievous smile. "We don't employ gardeners. If you still require a job, that is ..."

"Oh, yes, I do! As a shorthand typist." She hid her hands behind her back. "But I thought you only employed people from a particular employment agency?"

From behind him, Sheila was frowning at her and making frantic gestures with her hands to stop talking herself out of a chance of a job.

Mr Richardson seemed to be lost for words, then regained his composure. "Ah, well, it appears we need a typist rather more immediately than was previously thought, and so I ... er ... we ... er, that is Mrs Pike, our office manager, wondered if you'd be able to come for an interview on Monday."

The woman she'd spoken to the previous day had been adamant they only took people from Black & Snowden's books. Well, something had obviously changed, and it meant she had an opportunity at last. Sheila was almost hopping from foot to foot, fluttering her hands, urging Joanna to accept.

"Yes please, Mr Richardson."

"Well, that's excellent news." His face lit up with a smile, and Joanna could only stare. He was handsome when his face was at rest, but that smile made her quiver inside.

Sheila, too, was quivering – with excitement. "Well, that's sorted. How about I put the kettle on, and we celebrate?"

Mr Richardson had evidently not realised Sheila was behind him. He jumped and his smile slipped, but not before giving Joanna a searching look.

He hesitated for a second, and then after thanking Sheila, said he had to be going. He'd delivered the letter as he was passing and had to be … He paused as if he couldn't remember. "I have to go to a meeting," he finally said.

It was an excuse to leave. Although, as a solicitor, perhaps he was dealing with deeds or some other legalities to do with a land sale. That was possible.

But in her heart, Joanna knew he hadn't wanted to

stay. Of course, he wouldn't want to drink tea in a place like this, especially with someone who was covered in mud.

He'd had such a strange expression on his face. What had he been thinking? Joanna simply couldn't imagine. No one had ever looked at her like that. She wondered whether he'd been too much of a gentleman to say he'd made a mistake after seeing her in such a dirty state. He must surely have doubted she'd be a suitable candidate to work in his company.

Well, he had only invited her for an interview. There'd been no offer of a job and Joanna realised sadly, as she followed him to the front door to let him out, there wouldn't be. If only he'd posted the letter and she'd been able to turn up at the office looking presentable, she might have stood a chance. Sheila had shown her where to leave her new rubber boots at Holmcroft for her return journey, so she could have arrived at the office looking smart.

At the end of the path, Mr Richardson turned, nodded politely, replaced his hat, and let himself out of the gate. Once in the avenue, he turned once again, his face half-hidden by the shadow of the brim of his hat, although she thought she saw distaste in his expression. He raised his hand and hurried away.

Sheila came up behind her. "Well, that is good news, lovey. And fancy him delivering it himself!"

"But I think he regretted it after he'd given me the letter," Joanna said.

"Poppycock!"

"But look at me!" Joanna looked down at her overalls. "They won't offer me the job now. It's hardly worth going."

Sheila crossed her arms. "Oh no, my girl! You ain't going to turn down this golden opportunity."

"But they can't afford to have someone disreputable working in their office."

"What d'you mean disreputable?"

"Look at me."

"There ain't nothing disreputable about hard graft, my girl. And hard graft is often dirty. When you turn up on Monday, you'll look as perfect as a new pin. I'll make sure of that."

Joanna said nothing. It had been humiliating enough for the senior partner's son to have seen her in such a disgraceful state, but what was the point of attending an interview in which she didn't stand a chance of being successful?

As if reading her mind, Sheila said firmly, "You will go, Joanna. You owe it to yourself. Just think of all that lovely furniture you'll be able to buy to go on your floor once it's built."

Sheila often nagged Bill to buy new furniture, and Joanna knew it was her dream to get rid of the old, mismatched armchairs that Bill loved.

"I'll need walls first, and a roof."

"Exactly! And that takes money, so we'll have no more talk about not going for your interview on Monday. You're going to amaze them with your shorthand and typing."

Joanna nodded.

"That's my girl! Let's celebrate with a cuppa. I bet Bill could do with one."

That's my girl.

Joanna smiled. She hadn't known Sheila and Bill for long, yet the generous couple had taken her in and treated her as if she was family. Yes, she would go to the interview on Monday. She could hardly do otherwise. Sheila was sharing her home with her, and it wouldn't do to look as though she wasn't taking every opportunity to get her own place. But she certainly didn't share Sheila's confidence which was based on her kind-hearted optimism rather than knowledge of Joanna's typing and shorthand speeds. Luckily, her speeds were good, and she was accurate, but there was so much more to working in a solicitor's office than shorthand and typing. She'd have to be well-groomed and well-mannered. So far, Mr Richardson and his office manager had seen her at her worst, and she had a lot of ground to make up if she was going to persuade anyone to give her a job.

Joanna searched Mrs Pike's face for any hint of how she'd done on her tests. She knew she'd been fast, but had she been accurate? And even if she had, would that be enough to get her the job?

Mrs Pike's eyes seemed to drill into Joanna but gave little away.

"Well, Miss Marshall. Everything seems to be very satisfactory. Very satisfactory, indeed." She smiled, but still Joanna held her breath. Despite those words, Mrs Pike appeared doubtful. The next word she uttered would be 'however' or 'but' and then would come the reason Joanna was unsuitable for the job.

Mrs Pike frowned and added uncertainly, "However, you seem very young ..."

Surely, she wouldn't reject her because of her age?

"Your typing speed is outstanding, and you are impressively accurate. Your shorthand is excellent. In his letter, Mr Franklin was most complimentary about your work. He said you were punctual, hardworking, and polite. Young Mr Richardson has assured me we need an employee immediately, so I have no reservations about recommending that the partners employ you. Well, other than your youth, of course. But perhaps that will mean I can train you in how best to suit the partners, and you can avoid the, er ... problems that your predecessors have had in insisting on doing things their way."

Joanna slowly and silently let out her breath.

She had a job!

She'd soon have her first wage packet and be able to buy the timber for her new floor. Her cottage would soon be underway. Sheila had been right to nudge her towards going for the interview. Perhaps life wasn't fair or unfair – you simply had to make things happen. Take control.

The following day, a letter arrived at Green Haven, delivered by Bert, the postman. Joanna eagerly slit open the envelope and read the contents. It was confirmation that from the following Monday, Miss Joanna Marshall would be an employee of Richardson, Bailey & Cole Solicitors, Laindon Office.

During the week she prepared for the big day, cleaning her shoes until they shone, going into Laindon, and with her precious savings, buying a new blouse. Unfortunately, the shop in Laindon didn't stock the latest fashions, and it was rather plain, but at least it was new and would make her appear efficient.

She also carried on digging holes and by the end of the following week, not only would she have received her first pay packet from her new job, but the brick plinths would be built. Then she'd be able to purchase the materials ready for Bill's friend to lay the wooden floor.

Chapter Four

On the Monday that Joanna started work, Sheila got up at the same time to make breakfast and accompany her to Laindon. She claimed she had shopping to do, but Joanna knew she was there for moral support. Sheila skipped from one topic of conversation to another; encouraging, warning, and trying to amuse Joanna and take her mind off her nerves. It was as if Sheila was as nervous as she was – or even more so. Joanna began to fear she might deliver her to the office, as one might take a child to school on its first day.

But as soon as they reached the High Road and could see the office, Sheila stopped. She wished Joanna luck, then with a last piece of advice, "Remember, never—"

"Never borrow and never gossip!" Joanna finished.

Sheila gave a self-conscious laugh. "Yes, well, I may have mentioned that once or twice before, but it's good advice."

Joanna laughed. "Thank you." She placed a hand on Sheila's arm.

"For a bit of advice, my mother drummed into me?"

Joanna didn't reply. They both knew she was thanking Sheila for far more than that.

Sheila patted Joanna's hand, smiled her

encouragement, and turned in the opposite direction. "Well, I'm off to Barlow's for a new toasting fork. Bill broke the other one. You go in, lovey, and show them how it's done …"

Joanna watched Sheila go. She was now on her own.

But she could do this.

She'd impressed Mrs Pike at her interview.

Not that past successes were important now. What mattered was what she did in the future. She couldn't afford to make serious mistakes or to upset anyone – not Mrs Pike nor any of the partners.

She took her handkerchief out of her pocket and screwed it up in one fist, then passed it to the other, drying her palms. They'd been so damp, she feared she'd be unable to turn the doorknob. And as for shaking anyone's hand … But this time, she wouldn't be ashamed of her hands; she'd scrubbed them until they were red, removing every trace of mud from her skin and beneath her nails.

When she entered, Benjamin Richardson was in the reception area, chatting with Mrs Pike. They both looked up and smiled. Joanna tucked her handkerchief back in her pocket and stepped forwards feigning confidence she didn't feel.

"Ah, Miss Marshall, early I see," Mrs Pike said, glancing at the clock on the wall and nodding her head approvingly.

Mr Richardson held out his hand, and the hint of a smile lifted the corners of his lips. So, he hadn't forgotten how filthy she'd been the previous week. She quickly thrust her hand forward, eager to show it was clean. His eyes opened slightly in surprise at the determined way she'd pushed her hand forward. She groaned inside. It had been unladylike. Too forceful. *What must he think?*

He took it anyway. "Welcome to Richardson, Bailey & Cole, Miss Marshall. We're very pleased to have you join us. Mrs Pike will show you the ropes and please don't hesitate to see me if you have a problem. Well, I'll leave you ladies to start work."

Please don't let my hand be sweaty.

Joanna was so concerned her palm was too moist; for an instant, she didn't notice he was still holding her hand. She looked up in alarm and their eyes locked.

"Well, Miss Marshall, you've arrived on a busy day, so shall we get started?" Mrs Pike indicated a desk opposite hers. "If you'd like to sit there."

Mr Richardson abruptly let go of her hand. "Quite. It's going to be a busy day." He picked up a folder and disappeared into the office to her left. After taking her coat off, Joanna sat at her new desk and noticed if she glanced sideways without turning her head, she could just see him through the window in his door, sitting at his desk.

"First, I'd like you to type these up, please, Miss Marshall."

Joanna's first day in Richardson, Bailey & Cole had begun.

Throughout the next few weeks, Joanna learnt Mrs Pike's preferences, and she carefully noted her expectations. The supervisor was particular about office practice, requiring everything to be done methodically. She was strict like Miss Bartle, but scrupulously fair. After a few minor errors which Joanna had rescued, she was confident she was settling in well.

By the end of November, Mrs Pike trusted Joanna sufficiently to leave her in charge of the office. The supervisor in the London office had been taken ill and Mrs Pike had been asked to replace her until new arrangements could be made.

At first, Joanna had been nervous at being left alone. Ben Richardson had checked up on her and made sure she wasn't struggling. One day, when she'd taken tea into his office at eleven o'clock, he'd insisted she bring her tea in and share the cake a client had brought him.

All the partners had been in London with Mrs Pike, and Mr Richardson had encouraged Joanna to stay longer than she should. He was such good company. Always respectful and polite, but there was something about the way he looked at her that fired a warmth deep in her belly. It was like the looks she'd seen on the faces of other men. Ted, the messenger at Tredegar, Murchison & Franklin, had surveyed her similarly, but somehow, his glances had been uncomfortable. Or perhaps it hadn't been his glances, but more his coarse comments and constant pestering to go to the cinema or a dance with him. Joanna had always declined. Mr Richardson, however, had been completely respectful.

During the previous years, she'd spent much of her free time with her father, sharing the burden with Ma. There'd been no time for friends. She'd never stepped out with a young man, so she wasn't used to male company. Of course, Ma had warned her of men and their desires, and she wasn't naïve enough to consider that even if Mr Richardson had asked her out on a date that his intentions would be honourable.

A date? With Mr Richardson? What a preposterous suggestion!

Well, of course. She knew that. She knew enough about his family to recognise they were from a different world. No, if Ben Richardson showed interest in her, it would be for only one thing. But he hadn't. He'd been a perfect gentleman. Saying nothing that could be misconstrued. It was just his eyes ... The suggestion of something she couldn't define but which made her glow inside and yearn for something, although exactly what, she wasn't sure. It was like grabbing at clouds.

At the beginning of December, Mr Richardson Sr

came into the office looking for Mrs Pike, obviously having forgotten she'd returned to London for the day.

He looked at Joanna over the top of his spectacles and his eyebrows rose as if he doubted she was capable of finding a pencil. "Miss Mitchell, I'd like tea in my office now."

"Yes, sir." Well, 'Mitchell' was close to 'Marshall'. Closer than 'Findlay', which he'd called her the last time he'd spoken to her. And she could certainly manage to make a cup of tea.

"And please arrange the normal flowers for the Christmas Dance. You know the sort of thing." He waved his hand irritably and disappeared into his office.

She didn't know the sort of thing. And neither was she able to ask him when she delivered his tea because he was on the telephone. He gestured for her to leave the tea on his desk, then continued his conversation.

Joanna went back into the reception area. Why hadn't she spoken up when he'd first asked her? He had an abrupt manner that Joanna found disconcerting, but surely arranging the wrong thing was likely to upset him more than if she'd asked him to explain what he wanted?

She glanced at the telephone on Mrs Pike's desk and wondered if she dared use it to phone the London office to ask Mrs Pike what to do. Then, as she sat down at her desk, she glanced to the left and saw the younger Mr Richardson was staring at her through the window.

When their eyes met, he smiled and beckoned her into his office.

"Did my father ask you to order the Christmas decorations?"

"Yes. Well, I think so. He asked for the normal flowers for the Christmas Dance."

"Didn't Mrs Pike mention them?"

"No, she didn't say anything. I'm so sorry, Mr Richardson. I should have told Mr Richardson ... I mean the other Mr Richardson."

He laughed. "It must be tricky with so many Mr Richardsons. Might I suggest you call me Ben when we're together? Of course, you'll have to refer to me as 'Mr Richardson' to everyone else, or even the dreaded 'Mr Richardson Jr'. There's nothing like the word 'junior' added to your name to make you feel inferior."

Joanna smiled. How did this man always calm her worries and fears?

"And yes, I imagine you're thinking, well, at least Richardson is his name. I know surnames aren't my father's strong point, Miss Mitchell. Or is it Miss Findlay? To save confusion, perhaps when we're together, I could call you Joanna?"

"Yes, of course ..." She paused, wondering if she dared use his given name. Well, why not? He'd told her to. "Of course ... Ben."

He smiled at her, and her breath caught in her

throat. "Excellent … Joanna. Now, I understand you have a problem regarding Christmas flowers?"

Ben explained that each Christmas, most of the larger shops and businesses along the High Road organised a Christmas Dance for all their employees and families, which practically included everyone in Laindon. It was a huge affair and each year the hall was packed. Since its inception several years ago, Richardson, Bailey & Cole had organised and paid for the Christmas floral decorations.

"Mrs Pike usually arranges everything, and she orders everything from Rosie's Posies next door. You could pop in there and ask. They'll have records of what we've previously ordered. Mrs Russell will give you an estimate and I expect by that time, Mrs Pike will be back to take over."

Joanna had noticed the florist shop next door to the solicitors, but although she'd have loved to have enough money to buy Sheila a huge bouquet to thank her for all her help, Bill grew flowers in the garden so Green Haven always had plenty of full vases. Anyway, the best gift she could give Sheila would be to move out and into her own home. Not that either Sheila or Bill had expressed a desire for her to leave. Far from it.

"Would you like to go now? I'll deal with anything until you get back," Ben asked. "I'll leave my door open and keep an eye on the reception area."

"Yes, please. And thank you." At least she could report she'd carried out his wishes if Mr Richardson should enquire.

She smiled at Ben, and he returned the smile with that lopsided, boyish grin that made her stomach swoop and soar.

The bell over the door into Rosie's Posies jingled as Joanna entered. It was cold and damp, with the distinctive smell of wet flower stems and assorted floral scents. A young woman came into the shop, an apron over her clothes and a matching scarf over her shoulder-length blonde hair.

Her face lit up when she saw her customer. "Ah! Miss Joanna Marshall. And a very good morning, to you."

Joanna laughed. "How d'you know my name?"

The young woman smiled delightedly. "My mother knows everything – she's the busiest busybody in town and the worst gossip. She pointed you out shortly after you started work next door and told me ..." she counted the points off on her fingers. "First, you're new in town, secondly you live with Sheila and Bill Guyler and finally, you're the latest addition to the solicitors next door." She held up three fingers. "Am I right or am I right?"

Joanna smiled and nodded.

"I'm Louisa, by the way. Louisa Russell. I meant to come in and introduce myself, but things have been so hectic. Now let me see. I'm guessing you've come in about the floral decorations for the Christmas Dance?"

"Yes, but I'm afraid I don't know what to ask for." How lovely to discover she was working next door to such a friendly girl. Louisa was about her age, and it was hard not to be affected by her engaging smile.

"Say no more." Louisa held up a hand. "Since Mrs Pike is currently working in London, Mr Richardson Sr must have asked you to come in, and I expect he didn't explain what was required. Am I right?"

Joanne nodded and smiled. "Did your mother tell you that? And if so, how did she know?"

"No, I worked that out myself. There's been a succession of women working in your office who've had to organise floral displays for one event or another – either for the solicitors or for the Richardson family. Several complained about Mr Grumpy Richardson Sr. I knew he was in Laindon today because I saw him go into your office this morning. It's the beginning of December. And here you are looking flustered. It all added up."

"Well, can I leave it all in your very capable hands, please?"

"Certainly. Now we've dealt with the business. Tell me about the other Mr Richardson. The very handsome and desirable Young Mr Richardson."

Joanna blushed. "I know little about him. Since I

started, he's worked several days a week in London, covering while Mr Cole's been on holiday." While that was true, Joanna didn't say that when he was in Laindon, he'd always made time to talk to her. If Mrs Pike was there, he'd always started a conversation with her and drawn Joanna in. But when they were alone, he perched on the corner of her desk and told her amusing stories about the office in London. He sat so close to her, she'd wondered if he could hear her heart thudding in her chest. Those dark eyes had looked into hers with such ... With such what? She had no way of describing it, but somehow, it felt as if he wasn't looking at her as others did – just seeing her face, her clothes and judging her on her outside appearance. Ben Richardson seemed to look inside her.

"Ooh! You've got it bad." Louisa placed both hands over her heart and pulled what she assumed was a lovesick face.

"What? No! I was just remembering I forgot to do something," Joanna lied. Her cheeks flaming again.

Louisa smiled knowingly. "You wouldn't happen to know the dashing Young Mr Richardson's favourite colour, would you?"

"No. Goodness, why on earth would I know that? Or even want to know that?"

"Well, I want to know so I can order a dress in his favourite colour." Louisa's face broke into an enormous grin, and Joanna couldn't tell if she was serious.

From beneath the counter, Louisa brought out a pile of *Mabs Fashions* magazines.

Wiping away a puddle of water and some leaves, she placed them in front of Joanna. She took the top one, *Mabs Fashions for December,* and turned to a page she'd already marked.

"What do you think of those?" She tapped the evening dresses illustrated on two impossibly tall, thin women. "The pattern's included in this issue."

Both dresses were similar, but with different sleeves and collars.

"Of course, I can't afford silk, but Mrs Waverley has some beautiful Rayon in stock and once it's made up, no one'd ever know the difference. And with the money I save on fabric, I'll be able to buy a new hat and shoes. At the Christmas Dance, I want at least one dance with the dashing Young Mr Richardson. I danced with him last year and he's divine. But I absolutely don't want to partner the irritable Old Mr Richardson, although he does his best to dance with most of the local women. He even waltzed with my mother last year. You can tell he hates every minute but give him credit; he carries on until he's partnered everyone. Although he might just be doing it so he doesn't have to dance with his sour-faced wife. Anyway, what are you planning to wear?"

"Me? I ... I'm not sure I'll be invited ..."

"Of course, you will! All the employees of shops or businesses along the High Road are invited. You're welcome to borrow any of my patterns if you like."

How tempting it would be to make a beautiful gown. But she didn't have money to spare on a new dress and wasn't sure her dressmaking skills were up to it, anyway. She could have managed a day dress, but not anything as fancy as Louisa was about to attempt.

"Thank you, that's kind, but I think I have something that might be suitable." If Joanna was invited, she'd have to wear the dress Ma had altered for the Tredegar Murchison & Franklin Christmas party shortly before she'd died. It was cream, overlaid with black lace. Joanna had taken little notice of it, not caring what she'd look like. She'd only accepted the invitation because it had been expected. The entire evening hadn't sounded appealing, even if the other typists had giggled as they'd described how the previous year, a tipsy Miss Bartle had accidentally thrown her drink over Mr Tredegar's suit. There was nothing to say Miss Bartle hadn't learnt her lesson and would be sober and disapproving all evening.

"I'm sure you'll look splendid." Louisa smiled. If she'd guessed Joanna couldn't afford anything new, she gave no sign. "I mean to say, with your hair and face, you'd look splendid in an old sack and army boots!"

As Joanna hurried back to the office, she smiled to

herself. Not only had she carried out Mr Richardson Sr's wishes, but she might also have found a new friend. And, in a few weeks – if Louisa was correct – she'd attend a Christmas Dance. It was strange that although she'd scarcely given any thought to the Christmas party in her last job, the prospect of the Laindon Christmas Dance filled her with excitement. It would give her a chance to meet people in the area where she now belonged. But deep down, she knew it was more than that. If Ben had danced with Louisa last year, why not with her this year? Joanna breathed in sharply at the thought of dancing with him. Of course, that wouldn't happen. But the thought of his body touching hers. His hand on her back and the other in hers, holding her close. It was so thrilling; she shivered.

He won't dance with you.

Well, of course, he wouldn't.

Ben was in his office on the telephone when she returned. He caught her eye and smiled as if he hadn't been holding a conversation with someone on the other end of the line. As if he'd been talking to her.

The following day, Mrs Pike returned to the Laindon office and asked what had happened while she'd been away. She was pleased when Joanna told her she'd placed the order for flowers and decorations, and gave her a list of everyone who would be invited. Joanna bit her lip to keep from smiling when she saw her name beneath Mrs Pike's. Mrs Waverley from the draper's and haberdashery a few doors along the High Road was responsible for issuing invitations, although Mrs Pike warned Joanna there was still plenty to do.

"But at least you've now placed our order. I was going to do that today, so you've saved me a job."

Shortly after, Louisa came into the office and handed her mother's estimate for the floral decorations to Mrs Pike. As she turned away, she winked at Joanna, mouthing the word 'lunch'; her raised eyebrows silently added a question mark. With her finger concealed from Mrs Pike, she jabbed it towards Rosie's Posies. Joanna smiled and nodded, then carried on typing as if no exchange had occurred. She suspected Mrs Pike wouldn't approve of friendly chatter during work time, and obviously, so had Louisa.

At midday when Mrs Pike gave Joanna a nod, she tidied her desk and, taking her sandwiches and her coat, she went next door to Rosie's Posies. Louisa and her mother were waiting for her.

"This is my mum, Betty."

"I know all about you, Joanna, dear," Betty said.

Louisa winced. "Yes, thanks, Mum." Then, turning to Joanna, she beckoned for her to follow. "I'll bring you down a cuppa, Mum," she called over her shoulder.

After they'd eaten their lunch, Louisa showed Joanna

138

the pieces of the dress she'd cut out. The fabric was pink.

"There wasn't enough time to wait for you to find out delicious Young Mr Richardson's favourite colour, so I decided on pink. I didn't want to risk not having a dress for the evening. I've also ordered new shoes and a hat from my catalogue. Heavens, I hope the shoes fit."

The florist shop was doing very well, and Betty was generous with Louisa's wages. Of course, Louisa handed most of the money back to her mother, but she kept the rest for what she called 'necessities'.

"I simply can't resist buying new clothes. And going to the cinema. How about you?"

Joanna explained she was saving hard to build a cottage.

Louisa held her hands together, her eyes wide with surprise. "A cottage! Heavens! How marvellous!"

"Well, just a tiny cottage. Hardly more than a room at first—"

"But that's so exciting and so ... *modern*."

"But the downside is I don't have much to spare for anything else."

"Well, in that case, I shall treat you to an evening at the cinema to celebrate your wonderful building project."

"Oh, I couldn't—"

"But you simply must. Most of my school friends have married or moved away and I *need* someone to go to the cinema with me or I shan't be responsible for the outcome. Now, how about Saturday evening? *Desert Song* is showing. I'm desperate to see it. Please say you'll come."

"Well ..."

"The Red Shadow is so handsome and so romantic. You'll love it."

Joanna was happy to agree. Being with Louisa was like being caught up in a whirlwind.

"Oh, how wonderful to be swept into the arms of someone as dashing and daredevil as the Red Shadow." Louisa sighed. She stopped and looked back at the posters outside the Laindon Picture Theatre showing the Red Shadow dressed as a sheikh, holding the beautiful heroine as he declared his love.

"If only real life was as romantic." Louisa linked arms with Joanna, and they made their way back to Rosie's Posies, where Joanna was going to stay the night.

"Hey, Lulabelle!" The cry came from behind, and as they swung around, Louisa gasped. "Heavens, it's Harry Simpson. I used to go to school with him. I haven't seen him for ages."

A delivery van was slowly following them and a young man with thick brown hair leaned out of the window and smiled at Louisa. "Got a kiss for a stranger returned, Lulabelle?"

"Certainly not! And don't call me Lulabelle. You know I always hated it!"

But Louisa didn't walk away, and Joanna could tell she was delighted, despite her sharp words.

"Who's your friend?" he called.

The van stopped, and Joanna recognised the name *Davidson's Building Supplies* on the side. A large man leapt out of the van and ran up to Louisa, arms outstretched to give her a bear hug. She squealed and batted him away – but not too rigorously – and he soon caught her up in his arms and swung her around.

The engine stopped and out of the driver's side of the van climbed Sam Cavendish, the son of Bill's best friend, Tom. Joanna had seen him several times when he'd delivered items to Green Haven. She'd also seen him at many of the house parties that took place over the weekend in Plotlands. It was customary for a family to throw their house open to everyone for a singsong and general catch-up of the week's happenings. Sheila had told her that during the summer, they took advantage of the warm weather to gather around a bonfire in someone's garden, but now it was colder; they crammed into people's homes. Sam had been at several of the gatherings and although he'd said little to Joanna, Sheila had teased her later, saying he was sweet on her. It was nonsense, of course – just Sheila matchmaking.

Joanna guessed Sam was about her age; tall and

muscular, with a face that would have been handsome had his expression not been so serious and guarded.

"A good, steady catch!" Sheila had remarked, but Joanna had too much on her mind to think about catching Sam Cavendish.

As Sam and Harry accompanied the two young women, Joanna discovered they'd all been at school together. Sam contributed very little to the conversation, and Joanna felt sorry for him. She'd noticed his shyness before, but even if he'd wanted to speak, it was hard to get a word in with Louisa and Harry chattering excitedly. Joanna tried to put Sam at ease and to talk about the parties they'd both attended. His replies had been curt and awkward, and she was relieved to see Rosie's Posies ahead.

He abruptly turned to her. "I could give you a lift home, if you like."

She thanked him for his thoughtfulness and explained she was staying the night with Louisa. His expression dropped immediately when he realised his offer had been rejected. It was like a tortoise, pulling its head into its shell. Joanna had seen enough of him to recognise he felt rebuffed and embarrassed. To cheer him up, she asked if he was going to the dance the following Saturday.

Sam's face lit up and Harry chipped in, "We're both going on Saturday. How about you?" He turned to

Louisa. "We could pick you both up in Sam's van, then you could arrive in style."

Joanna wondered if that would mean she and Louisa would have to spend the evening with Harry and Sam.

Sam said he had to pass Sheila's door to get to Laindon, and it wouldn't be any trouble to stop for her. So, it sounded as if he was simply offering her a lift and not as though it was a date. She wasn't sure she wanted to spend the evening with Sam, but she certainly didn't want to snub him again and risk causing him embarrassment. Her heart sank. Would he consider it a date? In her imagination, the dance had gained magical status. Lights twinkling like stars and Ben Richardson dancing with her all evening. Now, the thought of arriving 'in style' in a van with Sam and Harry and possibly having to spend the night with them reduced the sparkle. It was just as well. What Sam and Harry were offering was reality. What she'd been imagining was a fairy tale.

Spending the evening with Ben Richardson? How foolish to consider it.

During the previous week, Mrs Pike had frequently mentioned Mr Bailey's daughter. At first, Joanna hadn't noticed the name 'Emily Bailey' amongst all the other names she'd seen on lists for the dance. But Mrs Pike had placed special emphasis on it, and that had caught her attention. 'Emily Bailey' was always mentioned in the same sentence as 'Young Mr Richardson'. If Joanna hadn't known better, she'd have thought Mrs Pike was gently warning her not to become too attached to Ben. But that was nonsense. Joanna had barely spoken to him during the last few weeks – well, not when Mrs Pike had been there, anyway. Perhaps she was warning Joanna in case she should take an interest in Ben. But whatever the reason, it had been done in a kindly way, as if the older woman was watching out for her to prevent heartache.

Now, with the Christmas event appearing less like a romantic dream and more like the ordinary dance it undoubtedly would be, Joanna acknowledged Mrs Pike was too late. When she saw Ben and Emily Bailey together at the Christmas Dance, it would tear her heart in two. Sad but inevitable. Well, it wasn't as if she'd been completely naïve. She'd known that despite his smouldering looks and the energy that seemed to crackle between them when they were together, he'd never be more than her boss.

So, why not spend the evening with a young man who regarded her with hooded eyes that expressed desire? He wasn't as handsome as Ben, but when he smiled, his face softened and lost its intensity.

If she'd wanted to refuse Sam and Harry's offer of picking them up and escorting them to the dance, it was too late. Louisa had accepted on behalf of them both.

It was settled then.

Betty was waiting up for Louisa and Joanna to find out all about *Desert Song*. More importantly, she wanted to know who'd been in the picture theatre. And specifically, who'd been there with whom.

Joanna had recognised no one, but Louisa was used to such interrogation, and her observational skills were sharp. Having spent most of her life in Laindon, Louisa knew everyone except a few of the newcomers.

Her father had died when she was a baby and her mother had left the East End to live closer to her sister in Laindon. Betty had worked in several shops until she'd saved enough to buy Rosie's Posies. With the influx of people into Plotlands, she'd recently seen an upturn in profits. Families such as the Richardsons, the Baileys and other wealthy families had started to throw extravagant parties, vying with each other to be considered the most lavish and avant-garde. So far, floral displays had featured highly in their party arrangements.

While the three women sipped cocoa in Betty's kitchen, Louisa gave her an account of the people who'd been in the cinema. Inexplicably, however, she failed to mention meeting Harry and Sam on their way home. Louisa's eyes sought Joanna's, opening wide as if asking her not to tell her mother.

"Thank you for not mentioning Harry and Sam," Louisa said when they were finally on their own in

Louisa's bedroom. "We'd never have got to bed if I'd mentioned them. Mum would have wanted to know all about them."

Joanna frowned but said nothing. After all, there'd been nothing to tell. They'd simply walked from the picture theatre to Rosie's Posies. Why would Betty be interested in that? It was obvious Louisa liked Harry. Perhaps she wanted to keep it secret. After all, she was nearly nineteen. It wouldn't be surprising if she wanted to keep part of her life away from Betty's prying eyes.

Tears pricked Joanna's eyes as she wondered if she'd have wanted to conceal anything from Ma. She admitted to herself she wouldn't have told her about Ben. But then, really, what was there to tell?

It was obvious Louisa was too excited to sleep. She chattered about their evening, and Joanna noted the boundary between the two parts of the evening – the film and the chance meeting of an old school friend – had blurred. Or perhaps the romance of Red Shadow winning his girl in such an exotic location was colouring Louisa's memories of the coincidental encounter with Harry. The moving picture and reality were merging.

Harry had told Louisa he'd gone to Hastings to stay with his uncle and work on his fishing boat after they'd left school. He intended to buy his own boat one day. Although he was now staying with his parents, he would return to Hastings after Christmas, so if Louisa became too fond of him, it could only end in heartache. But Joanna suspected Louisa would take as much notice of a warning, as she'd taken of Mrs Pike's gentle hints. Or perhaps for them both, it was too late.

No, she'd simply listen to Louisa talk about the accidental meeting as if Harry had whisked her away into the desert and declared undying love, rather than a simple walk home when he'd teased her mercilessly. But perhaps that was how love began? After all, hadn't Joanna woven Ben into a world of her own imaginings?

Finally, Louisa fell silent, and sleep overtook them both. Joanna's dreams were filled with Ben Richardson, taking her in his arms. During the night, when she awoke, she wondered whether Louisa had dreamt of Harry, dressed in sheikh's robes, lounging in a lavish tent.

During the following week, Joanna was busy at work. Not typing nor taking shorthand notes, but with arrangements for the Christmas Dance. On Saturday morning, she and Mrs Pike had gone to the hall to check the decorations were in place. Louisa and Betty were there, and the hall had been transformed. Holly, ivy, red roses, and plenty of colourful ribbon and lace – all provided by Mrs Waverley.

"And," Louisa whispered to Joanna, "most importantly ..." She glanced upwards and mouthed the word 'mistletoe'. She smiled mischievously as Joanna saw the bunch suspended from one rafter.

"I wanted more, but Mum said that was enough," Louisa whispered.

Shopkeepers came and went, bringing food, drinks, glasses, extra chairs, and tables. Several members of the band arrived and tuned up their instruments on the dais.

"Well, Miss Marshall, you'd best go home and change," Mrs Pike said. "I know you young women take ages to dress for events."

"You, too, love." Betty nodded at Louisa. "I've got everything under control."

Joanna left Louisa outside the florist and walked home. She'd helped Louisa finish her dress, sewing on tiny beads around the neckline the previous evening when Louisa had despaired it would ever be ready. The gown was beautiful. She didn't envy Louisa her dress, but she wished she had something more fashionable. Too late now. But when she had a floor for her cottage, she'd be glad she hadn't wasted money on a new dress.

Sheila met Joanna at the door of Green Haven, triumphantly waving a black stole embroidered in cream and red. It was beautiful.

"Ah, lovey! I knew I had this somewhere, and I finally found it. This'll go with your dress a treat."

The stole was very expensive and had been packed away carefully for years, judging by the creases and the smell of mothballs. Joanna thanked Sheila and pecked her cheek. It was so generous and thoughtful. So typical of Sheila. Joanna hadn't even thought about a stole. It would make her outfit dressier – and yet, she wasn't sure she wanted to go to the dance smelling of mothballs. But she wouldn't hurt Sheila's feelings for anything. And after all, she could always take it off when she was there.

Sam pulled up in his van slightly earlier than Joanna had expected. He knocked at the door, and his eyes lit up when he saw her.

"You're beautiful," he muttered and awkwardly thrust a red rose towards her.

It looked like the ones Betty had used in the displays. Joanna wondered if he'd taken one earlier when he'd been in the hall, tacking up swags of red and green fabric under the careful supervision of Mrs Waverley. Perhaps that was what Louisa had meant when she winked at her earlier and announced Joanna would be rather colourful later. It had made little sense at the time since Joanna's dress was cream and black – hardly colourful. But perhaps she was being uncharitable. After all, didn't one red rose look much like another? Perhaps he'd bought it from Betty and that's how Louisa had known.

"Thank you," she said, wondering how to attach it to her dress. Sheila bustled forward and, taking the rose from Joanna, she tucked it into the hair that she'd taken ages to plait and pin.

When Joanna had looked in the mirror earlier, she'd been amazed at her sophisticated hairstyle. She hadn't tilted the mirror so she could see her dress. That, she knew, was not sophisticated. Everything was second hand except her shoes – and they were now old and slightly shabby.

"There," Sheila said, stepping back to admire the rose. "Now, off you go, lovey. I won't wait up. You have a wonderful time."

As Sam took Joanna's arm and led her down the path, she wished Sheila and Bill were accompanying them. Bill was resting in bed with a hot water bottle. He'd slipped and hurt his back, and Sheila had said she wouldn't go to the dance as planned, without him. It was such a shame because Joanna knew they'd both been looking forward to the Christmas Dance.

The path was too narrow for them both. Even so, Sam clung on to her arm as if, having been given the opportunity, he wouldn't let her go simply for lack of room.

Once in the van, Joanna tried desperately to think of something interesting to say and wondered if Sam would remain silent until they reached Harry's parents' cottage. If Sheila had been with them, she'd have chattered and filled the awkward silences, but Joanna barely knew Sam. They crept along so slowly, Joanna wondered if the van was about to break down. Sam gripped the steering wheel and stared stonily ahead while she twisted her handkerchief and stumbled over her words, trying to say something interesting – or indeed anything. From time to time, he glanced at her, but before he caught her eye, he looked back at the road.

Questions. Yes, ask him something. He'll have to reply.

"How do you usually spend Christmas?" It was the first thing to pop into her head, but thankfully, Sam smiled and, for the first time, seemed to relax a little.

"Sheila and Bill are coming over to our house for the day, so we'll be together."

We'll be together? Who did he mean by 'we'?

Sheila hadn't mentioned their plans, but it wasn't surprising she and Bill had arranged to spend Christmas with their friends, Tom and Florrie. Sheila would have expected Joanna to be with them too because she'd taken to including her as if she were a daughter.

Joanna had focused on the Christmas Dance and hadn't considered Christmas Day. If she'd thought about it, she'd have assumed Sheila and Bill would spend it with Dolly and her family.

Tears sprang to her eyes, and she swallowed to keep down the lump in her throat at the thought she wouldn't have Ma and Pa this year. She looked down, pretending to check her watch, hoping the tears wouldn't spill down her cheeks. She noticed the time. It had taken so long to creep along the road towards Harry's parents' house. In fact, Sam, seemed to go slower and slower. Every so often, he glanced towards her and smiled.

When they arrived, Harry was waiting at the gate.

"I thought you'd never get here." He threw open the door and piled in next to Joanna.

Sam glared at him. "Give Joanna some room, you oaf! You're too used to mixing with a bunch of fishermen. Keep away from her, you'll crush her dress."

But good-natured Harry took no notice of his carping tone. "You'll be complaining. I smell of fish next." Harry laughed delightedly. "I wouldn't mind, but your van stinks!" However, he pulled away from Joanna, giving her space.

It did, indeed, reek in the van. The smell of timber, tar and engine oil merged in an oppressive stench that hung heavily, and with the jolting of the van, Joanna began to feel queasy.

Sam sped up; the van juddering over the grassy road and they were soon in the High Road outside Rosie's Posies. Louisa had been watching for them from a window and as soon as they pulled up, she rushed towards the van. Harry leapt out and took her hand, then opened the door for her.

"You were so long, I thought you'd broken down," she said breathlessly. "I'm so pleased to see you. I didn't want to go on my own."

Sam said nothing, but Joanna noticed he was gripping the steering wheel even more tightly.

"I'll get in and you can sit on my lap," Harry said.

There was much laughter, as the huge, bear-like Harry got back in and eased a squealing Louisa onto his lap.

Sam seemed more concerned that Harry, with Louisa on top, kept away from Joanna. It was strange he was so concerned they shouldn't crush her. But perhaps it was sweet?

It wasn't far to the hall, and finally, Sam parked and rushed to the passenger door, allowing Harry and Louisa to spill out. He reached in to take Joanna's hand and help her out. Joanna told herself he was merely being a gentleman and she should be flattered, but somehow, the intensity of his gaze and the proprietorial way he held her arm alarmed her.

Don't be so childish. He's looking after you.

Yes, it was true. She simply wasn't used to anyone treating her so well, that was all.

With Joanna on his arm, Sam followed Louisa and Harry into the hall's vestibule.

She slipped free of Sam, ostensibly to take her coat off, but as soon as she'd hung it up, she stepped into a group of people and walked into the main hall with them, away from Sam. It felt mean to avoid him like that, but he couldn't surely intend to hang on to her arm all night?

She'd intended to arrive much earlier and now admitted to herself, it wasn't because she wanted to ensure everything was organised. Everything had been ready when she'd left a few hours before, so why should anything be different now? It hadn't been her responsibility, anyway.

No, she simply wanted to see if Ben Richardson was there. And Emily Bailey. One would bring her much pleasure. The other; much pain.

Joanna had seen the hall by day but, in the semi-darkness with coloured lights twinkling, it was transformed into a magical place. Winter spices and the sharp smell of pine trees filled the air, reminding her of the Christmas tree she used to dress with her parents on Christmas Eve. Dusty, tired areas of the hall were concealed by the subdued lighting and the decorations, and the few people who'd already gathered added to the excitement with their fancy clothes, high spirits and lively conversation. A setting for a fairy tale, she thought as her eyes roamed across the crowd for Ben.

The hall began to fill up, and Joanna hid amongst the crowd. Louisa and Harry wouldn't miss her, but she'd spotted Sam, who looked as though he was trying to get away from his boss. He was across the hall, but his eyes were roaming over the crowd as if he was looking for someone. Perhaps he was. He knew many people in the area; she reminded herself. It was conceit to imagine he only had eyes for her.

Mr Richardson Sr stood near the dais next to a tall, elegant woman – probably his wife, talking to the bandleader. The woman's long evening dress shimmered as the twinkling lights reflected off the beads, giving her a cut-glass effect. In fact, everything about Mrs Richardson – if that was indeed her – was angular and sharp. Mr Richardson tapped the microphone to test it and as the sound echoed around the hall, he checked his pocket watch. Presumably, he was waiting for seven-thirty to make his welcome speech and to start the event.

At the side of the dais, Mr Bailey, with a stylish woman on his arm – probably Mrs Bailey – stood chatting to elderly Mr Cole and Mrs Pike. Next to them, listening to Mr Cole, was Ben. At the same instant that Joanna's eyes fixed on him, he saw her and his expression, which had been one of polite interest in the conversation, transformed. Even from across the hall, she saw his eyes light up. He leaned towards Mr Cole, who was slightly hard of hearing, and gestured towards Joanna. Mr Cole nodded politely, and Ben shouldered his way through the crowds who were gathering to listen to his father, towards her.

Her heart soared like a bird in flight as she took in the pleasure on his face. For an instant, she allowed herself to believe it was because he was happy to see her and wanted to spend time with her. But she knew it wasn't true. It was more likely her presence meant that now everyone who worked in the Laindon office had arrived. Simply Richardson hospitality.

"Miss Marshall! Perhaps you'd care to join us over there?" He offered her his arm and as he led her towards the group, he placed his hand over hers protectively and whispered in her ear, "You look ravishing, Joanna."

That was more than hospitality, wasn't it?

But perhaps that was how people behaved in the circles in which he mixed. Their arms might have been touching, but a gulf had suddenly opened between them. She'd never been involved socially with anyone from a higher class before and didn't know what might be involved. The pleasure she'd felt under his admiration was crushed by the realisation there'd never be anything more than ... Than what? Attraction on her part and flirtation on his?

While he introduced Joanna to Mrs Bailey, the austere woman who'd been with Mr Richardson Sr appeared at Ben's elbow.

"And who is this young woman, Benjamin?" she asked, holding out a limp, gloved hand around which hung a diamond bracelet.

Ben introduced Joanna to the woman who – as she'd guessed – was his mother.

"Pleased to make your acquaintance, Miss Marshall. So, you are a typist in my husband's company?"

It had been subtle, but Joanna had noticed she'd added emphasis to the word 'typist' and simultaneously, her nose had imperceptibly wrinkled. Ben still had his hand over hers, and she felt him stiffen. Had he recognised his mother's disparaging reaction and was sympathising? Or was Joanna misreading everything?

Mrs Richardson flapped a hand towards her son and, with her gaze boring into the arm that was linked with Joanna, she said, "Benjamin, where are your manners? Miss Marshall doesn't have a drink and neither do I."

Ben squeezed Joanna's hand, and let her go, then walked away to get them drinks.

"So, Miss Marshall. How long have you been in my husband's employ?"

"Just a few weeks, Mrs Richardson."

"I thought I didn't know your face. I never forget a face. Although it's become remarkably hard to keep up with all the typists who pass through the office. They all seem to leave as soon as they arrive. That's the trouble with employing young women. No sooner have they settled in than they're off getting married. I expect a pretty girl like you will have a sweetheart?"

Joanna shook her head, but before she could reply,

Mr Richardson's voice boomed out and echoed around the hall. "Testing, testing, one, two, three ..."

Ben arrived back with glasses of champagne for his mother and Joanna, and Mr Richardson beckoned his wife urgently onto the dais to be by his side as he made his speech.

"Welcome everyone to the annual Laindon Christmas Dance," he began.

People cheered, and he waited for the uproar to subside, then read from a list, thanking everyone who'd been involved in the dance's organisation. He finished by wishing everyone a joyful Christmas and a healthy, happy, and prosperous New Year. He and Mrs Richardson raised their glasses in a toast and everyone in the hall responded, then loudly applauded, and cheered again.

As Mr Richardson and his wife walked off the dais, the conductor raised his baton and launched the band into a lively melody. Mr Richardson led his wife onto the dance floor, and everyone followed.

Ben turned to Joanna. "Would you care to dance?"

Would she care to dance? Joanna had dreamt of nothing else for days. Her heart was soaring so high now it might raise her off the floor.

She took his hand; grateful she hadn't needed to reply because the excitement had risen to her throat, and she knew she couldn't speak.

Ben glanced over his shoulder at his mother and father who'd waltzed across to the other side of the hall, and he quickly took Joanna's hand. He led her onto the dance floor, and steering a course away from his parents, they were soon hidden amongst the dancers.

"I apologise for my mother. She's somewhat overbearing," Ben said ruefully. "She's deeply old-fashioned in her outlook. People should know their place, that sort of thing. All very out of date now, thank goodness. People are people, as far as I'm concerned, but she's finding it hard to adapt."

The crush pushed them closer, and he leaned forward to speak into her ear. "But I was determined to dance with you – if you'd wanted to, of course."

"Oh, yes." She looked down shyly. It must be obvious how much she liked him.

"You realise I may have to ask Mrs Pike to dance just to throw Mother off the scent?" He laughed, and it appeared that against all odds, he was nervous, too. Was she imagining it? Perhaps it was an act. But if it was, then for the duration of the dance, she'd buy into the fantasy.

Dancing with Ben differed from the way she'd imagined. When she'd conjured up this moment in her mind's eye, she and Ben had been alone. There had been no dancers pressing close, no disapproving Mrs Richardson somewhere on the dance floor. And no Sam, who she suddenly realised was watching her from near the hall door. His eyes; hooded and impossible to read. She felt a stab of guilt for having slipped away from him. But this was just one dance with her boss. Nothing more.

And yet, despite all the distractions, when she closed her eyes, she was only aware of Ben. The warmth of his palm and the press of each fingertip on her waist as if he wanted to close his hand around her and hold on. His other hand cradling hers, gently but firmly. Two halves of a whole. The closeness of his body and his cheek against the side of her head, slightly rough against her temple. Her fairy tale dream had been magical, but the reality of dancing with Ben far surpassed anything her imagination could have conceived.

His breath caressed her cheek. "You're so beautiful, Joanna." As he whispered, his lip accidentally touched her ear, sending shivers of pleasure through her.

Or perhaps it hadn't been accidental? She realised she'd been holding her breath and, as she breathed out and then in, her nostrils filled with his cologne. Spicy. Woody. Masculine ... Divine.

"I wonder if I could talk to you later. On your own ..." He drew back slightly to seek an answer.

"Yes." She could barely speak. On her own? What could he possibly need to discuss with her on her own?

He smiled and pulling her close again, with his cheek against hers, he inhaled as if he were breathing her in.

He paused for a beat as if startled, and their rhythm was broken.

She froze, and forgetting her footing, almost stumbled. Of course! They were so close. If his scent filled her nostrils, then when he'd breathed in, he'd only have detected cheap soap and worse, so much worse – the distinctive smell of mothballs. Perhaps she still smelt of Sam's van? She almost groaned aloud. He was probably expecting the fragrance of expensive French perfume. Instead, he'd been treated to the pungent stink of mothballs. She stared at him; eyes wide in embarrassment.

He was looking over her shoulder. His nostrils flared momentarily. Annoyance?

And then she wondered if he hadn't been looking over her shoulder at all. The rose in her hair had been in his line of sight. The rose that was so like the ones in the floral displays. Did he think she'd taken one for herself? If she had taken one, would that be considered theft? No, of course not. But it certainly would be seen as the height of bad manners to remove a flower from the displays for personal use. She wanted to rip it from her hair, but that would only draw attention to it and further her embarrassment.

Their moment had gone. As the music changed tempo and the musicians launched into another tune, she drew away. It was best to get as far from Ben as she could, and save him from making his distaste clear. He'd turned away from her anyway, although she saw it was because Mrs Pike had tapped him on the arm to attract his attention. Ben frowned, his mouth set in an angry line as Mrs Pike spoke into his ear. Joanna pushed her way through the dancers, eager to escape. What must Ben think of her? His expression had said it all. How humiliating. And how much worse would it be on Monday when she'd have to go to work?

Joanna pulled the rose from her hair – unheeding that several of the carefully pinned tresses were pulled free and tumbled over her face. She dropped the flower on the floor. Let it be trampled underfoot – like her dreams. Everything had been perfect – even surpassing her imaginings, but it had all been an illusion. Ben had said she looked beautiful but compared to many of the dresses in the hall, hers was plain and old-fashioned. There was no hiding it. She was wearing a hand-me-down. Ben had been humouring her. And if he'd looked as though he'd meant it, perhaps he could turn that look on and off when he needed it. If her dress hadn't been enough to mark her out as a girl who could never associate with a man of Ben's class, she smelt as if her clothes had come from a second-hand shop. And then the rose ... Mrs Richardson had been quite right to remind her where she belonged.

With her head down, she hurried towards the hall

door, not having considered where she was going. But it didn't matter, so long as she was far from Ben. Someone stepped in front of her. She stopped and looked up into Sam's face.

"Joanna, has someone upset you?" He glanced towards the dais where she could see the top of Ben's head.

"No, no. I just needed some air," she lied. She certainly didn't want to explain her humiliation to Sam.

"Would you dance with me?" His voice was hesitant, and before she'd thought about it, she'd agreed. It would be better to behave as normally as possible. Yes, if she didn't draw attention to what had happened, then no one except her and Ben would know. She'd deal with the embarrassment on Monday. And perhaps he'd be working in London next week. Shortly after that, it would be Christmas and by the time everyone returned to work, Ben would have forgotten he'd ever danced with her.

Ben stared ahead, past the chauffeur's head, through the windscreen of his father's car. Stebbings had drawn up in the car outside the hall at midnight, as Mr Richardson had instructed. Ben had joined his parents. The dance had ended but people were lingering, in no rush to go home. However, for Ben, there'd been no point staying.

Now, sitting in the rear seat of the car between his

parents, childhood memories of long- ago journeys to and from school flooded back. Except this time, his father was snoring. His mother, however, was sitting ramrod straight in the seat and Ben knew it wouldn't be long before she commented on the evening, and specifically, his behaviour.

It was taking all his self-restraint not to yell at Stebbings to stop and then to climb past his father, get out of the car and walk home on his own.

But he might as well get it over with. He'd always shied away from confrontation, especially with his formidable mother, but tonight, he was prepared to clash. And for the first time, he was determined to do as he pleased. Not that it would help him now – his mother had made sure of that. She'd seen him dancing with Joanna and had decided to stop it. His evening had ended there.

Mother laced her gloved fingers, rings clashing. That heralded an important announcement.

Here it comes …

"Well …" She paused and glanced at her son to ensure she had his attention. "Such a shame Emily couldn't be at the dance tonight. The Baileys were so disappointed. But as Letitia said, her daughter has such a kind heart. Imagine volunteering to spend the evening with a sick friend. It must have been so dull. Still, it's most commendable. It shows an emotional maturity not usually seen in one so young."

Ben's eyebrows shot up in disbelief. Emily had told him she had tickets for the theatre in London. She'd mentioned it several times, stressing Ian Padgett-Lane had invited her out for the evening. Yet another attempt to make him jealous. She was wasting her time. He didn't care where she went nor with whom. Ian Padgett-Lane was rich, decadent, and selfish. Everything Ben scorned.

"Emily is such a fine girl, don't you think, Benjamin?" The gloved hands unclasped and one of them grabbed Ben's and squeezed.

He fought the urge to shake it off.

She acknowledged his silence with a martyred sigh and re-clasped her hands, rings clinking. "Emily is a wonderful example of good breeding. The Christmas Dance was delightful, as usual, but really, there was precious little breeding in evidence."

Ben squeezed his eyes closed and pushed his nails into the palms of his hands. He knew exactly what his mother meant, or more precisely, exactly to whom his mother was referring.

"So many common, little people pretending to be grand. No wonder you seemed to be out of sorts all evening. One might even say *moody*." She sighed again. "But I suppose we shouldn't think badly of those people. They're doing the best with what they have. And at least we helped to lay on a lavish spread for them. I'm sure it's the highlight of the year for most of them. And everyone seemed to have a good time."

Everyone except me.

Once again, his mind was in turmoil, trying to pinpoint exactly what had gone wrong. Over Joanna's shoulder, he'd seen his mother's scowl as her eyes followed him across the dance floor. Then, as the band played the end of one tune and he was about to suggest to Joanna, they slip away so he could talk to her. He'd seen his mother whispering to Mrs Pike. Mother's thunderous expression, the line of her gaze and above all, the pointing finger alerted him to what might happen next. And he'd been correct. Mrs Pike had nodded, adjusted her glasses, and glanced his way. Her expression had betrayed her discomfort. Then she'd begun to weave her way through the dancers, resignation written on her features. He'd turned away, but the tap on his arm had been insistent.

"Mr Richardson, your mother's feeling faint and has asked if you'll take her a glass of water, please." Mrs Pike hadn't been able to look him in the eyes. They'd both been aware of the silly subterfuge. Anyone could have fetched his mother a glass of water – if she had indeed felt faint.

Ben knew she hadn't.

Indeed, he didn't think his mother had ever felt faint

in her life. She wasn't the fainting kind. No, she simply wanted him back by her side, or more specifically, she wanted him away from Joanna.

None of that would have mattered, because he was going to talk to Joanna and declare his feelings to her. Of course, Mother would have been outraged, but he wouldn't let that stop him. Never before had anything in his life been worth standing up for. But now he'd found Joanna. The time had come.

Then, something strange happened. At the point when he'd spotted Mrs Pike reluctantly approaching, ready to deliver his mother's message, something had upset Joanna. She'd pulled sharply away from him. Had she seen Mrs Pike too? But so what if she had? Joanna couldn't have known she was on a mission ordered by his mother.

Then, while Mrs Pike was passing on the message, Joanna had fled, dropping the rose that had looked so beautiful in her hair. He'd followed her, but she'd run straight into the arms of a man. Ben thought he recognised his face but couldn't place him. A tall, well-built chap who'd given him a warning glare over Joanna's shoulder. After putting his thick arm around her, he'd led her onto the dance floor. Ben hadn't been able to catch her eye since then.

He'd returned to his mother, forgetting to take a glass of water and she hadn't remarked on it – having made a miraculous recovery. Throughout the evening, Joanna danced with the large, brooding man. Ben had been tempted to take part in the Gentlemen's Excuse Me Dance, cut in and replace the large man, but he suspected Joanna would be angry. In an instant, he'd lost her – if he'd ever had her at all.

What had gone wrong?

He'd wondered if Joanna had arrived with that man and, in asking her to dance the second she'd entered the hall, he'd inadvertently come between them. But surely Joanna would have said? The man had taken such a proprietorial interest in her, his large frame dominating her slender body as if was showing the world he'd claimed her for himself. An arm around her shoulders gently directing her in whichever direction he wanted. His body, carefully positioned between Joanna and Ben, preventing him from attracting her attention. And wherever Ben had been, the man's eyes seemed to be on him – wary, warning, menacing. Yes, *menacing* was a good word for the large man. There was something threatening about him.

Mother's rings clinked as she flexed her fingers. "Oh, by the way, I invited Hugh, Letitia and Emily to dinner tomorrow." She paused. "Did you hear, dear?"

Father grunted and sank back into sleep.

"And you Benjamin? You will be there, won't you?"

A bitter taste rose in his throat. He'd been prepared

for a fight. But what was there to fight about? If he'd had the conversation he'd planned with Joanna and she'd wanted to be with him as much as he wanted her, this journey home would have been different. He'd have stated his intention to live his life the way he wanted. He had a profession and even if he was no longer welcome in his father's firm, he'd find employment elsewhere. Of course, his lifestyle would be far simpler, but he'd be his own man and, with Joanna by his side, nothing else mattered. But now, what was the point of fighting with his mother? Joanna had made it clear she didn't want to know him. There was nothing to fight for.

"Yes," he said wearily.

"Well, I hope you'll be in a better humour tomorrow evening. No one likes a crosspatch. And I'm sure Emily will need a bit of cheering up after spending an evening by someone's sickbed. I expect you'll ensure she has a marvellous evening, won't you dear?"

The car pulled into the drive of Priory Hall, crunched over the gravel, and pulled up at the front door. Ben gently woke his father and followed him out of the car. He couldn't bear to spend another minute in his mother's presence. After rushing upstairs, he waited until he was sure his parents were in bed and, after checking the strip of light beneath the door, had disappeared, he crept down the stairs. He put his coat on and quietly let himself out of the back door, his breath hanging in clouds around his head as he walked to the summerhouse at the end of the garden. Turning his collar up, and thrusting his hands into his pockets, he sat on the cold, unyielding bench. There, he turned the evening's events over and over in his mind, undisturbed by anything except the night sounds from the countryside around.

Nothing made sense. How could it have gone so wrong? He surely hadn't been mistaken that Joanna was interested in him. Yet later, she'd spent the evening with the large man. His name had come to Ben. Cavendish. Yes, he worked for Davidson's Building Supplies. Ben had seen him driving the delivery van.

What had Joanna seen in him? One minute she'd stared into his eyes with such passion it had taken his breath away, and the next, she was in Cavendish's arms.

Had she been stringing them both along?

No. Not Joanna. She wasn't a flirt.

Then what?

He mentally retraced everything, but each time he arrived at that point on the dance floor where Joanna had stepped away in alarm and Mrs Pike had distracted him. Even the music replayed in his mind up to that point and died instantly, leaving silence.

What had happened? What? *What?*

The first dilute rays of the sun crept apologetically into the summerhouse, and he knew he had to return to his room, or he'd be missed. He walked stiffly back to the house. He was freezing. A frozen heart within a frozen body.

Joanna was still awake at dawn. She lay in bed, going over and over everything that had happened during the evening. The dance. Ben. The embarrassment. Sam. The kiss.

Sam had been so sweet and protective. His powerful arms around her had felt comforting at first, and she'd been grateful he'd asked no questions. He'd simply brought her drinks and danced with her. Every time she'd seen Ben, he'd been searching the crowd; concentration on his face as his eyes darted across the faces in the darkness. She guessed he'd been looking for her, but she couldn't imagine why.

He'd said he wanted to talk to her, and his eyes had been full of excitement and promise. But then had come his grimace of disgust and an instant later, Mrs Pike had appeared at his side, giving her a chance to slip away. Ben's look of distaste was imprinted on her memory – the eyes flicking into the ceiling in irritation, a flare of the nostrils and the angry set of his mouth.

But it was likely she'd never know the cause. By the time she saw him again, they'd be at work and that wasn't the sort of place to discuss anything personal. She certainly wouldn't remind him. It was all best forgotten.

Her thoughts then turned to Sam. Exactly when the safety of his muscular arms had become confining, it was hard to say. At first, it had amazed her how attentive he'd been. Louisa and Harry had danced together all night, but whenever they'd stopped to talk to her and Sam, his expression had changed and he'd made some excuse, whisking her away. Louisa had winked at her, evidently thrilled at being with Harry, and assuming she was similarly smitten with Sam.

But that had been far from the truth. Sam's face; open and honest, turned dark and brooding in the blink of an eye. Or was she just imagining it?

Then, after dropping Harry off at his parents' house, Sam had driven her home. When he'd pulled up, she'd waited for a second, expecting him to get out of the van and open her door, but he'd taken hold of her wrist. It had alarmed her until she realised his grip wasn't tight and she could have pulled away if she'd wanted. In that instant, she'd known he wanted to kiss her.

Her skin had prickled.

"Did you have a good time?" he'd asked.

She'd nodded.

"I really enjoyed taking you there and looking after you."

He had done all those things. Surely, she owed him one little kiss. She'd swallowed as he'd leaned closer and placed his hand against the back of her head. "It's a shame that rose fell out of your hair. I bought it for you, especially from Betty Russell. She charged me a fortune because she said she needed all the roses for the Christmas decorations. But it was worth every penny. It suited you so much."

Joanna had involuntarily drawn back. Or she would have done had his hand not been behind her head. His face had been so close, she'd smelt the beer on his breath. She'd closed her eyes. This was her first kiss. Of course, she'd be anxious ...

Joanna sat up in bed and held her hands over her eyes. Her first kiss. She'd expected nervousness and excitement, but the anxious fluttering inside had given way to emptiness. An aching, echoing hollow. The kiss had been as intimate as a handshake, although after, she felt as though Sam had stolen something from her. It had been so unlike her dreams. So disappointing.

At least, that was what it had been like for her.

Sam had broken away. She'd seen a light sheen over his brow, and he'd run a hand through his blonde fringe. Breathlessly, he'd said, "It's best we stop there in case we get carried away. You know I'm mad about you, don't you, Joanna? But we've got time."

And then thankfully he'd climbed out of the van, and she'd gratefully run up the path to Green Haven.

So, Sheila had been correct. Sam was keen on her.

Joanna lay back down in bed and looked at the clock.

She sighed. It was too late now to think about sleeping. Sam had offered to help her build her new cottage.

No, that wasn't true. He hadn't offered. He'd told her he'd be there early and would start work. Timber had been delivered the previous day, and she'd explained to him Bill had engaged a carpenter, but Sam had told her he'd work for nothing.

She should be grateful for his kind offer. What was wrong with her? She'd be able to save more and buy materials faster. The cottage would be finished sooner. That was what she wanted, wasn't it? She visualised the new floor. Previously, it had given her so much pleasure to imagine it. She knew it would just be a few planks nailed together, but it had represented the start of her new life.

Now, it didn't seem quite as exciting.

When Sam arrived at Green Haven the following morning, Sheila was still quizzing Joanna about the dresses, the food, the music, and whether the vicar had got tipsy. Sam was early, as he'd promised. Bill greeted him and together, they started work.

Joanna glanced at Sam out of the window. She'd tried to be upbeat and humorous in describing the previous evening to Sheila, but she hadn't been completely convincing.

"You seem a bit down, lovey."

Joanna assured her she was just tired because it had taken her a long time to get to sleep after such an exciting evening.

The explanation seemed to satisfy Sheila. "I suppose you could've slept in longer if Sam hadn't come. It's early to be up on a Sunday. Especially a Sunday after such an exciting Saturday night." She smiled conspiratorially, and Joanna looked away and stared into her mug.

The rhythmic rasp of a saw biting through wood penetrated Green Haven and sliced into Joanna's brain.

"I wonder if he's going to keep that up all day," Sheila asked, echoing Joanna's thoughts. But far from being annoyed, Sheila was delighted.

"I'm walking down to the post office later. I want to ask if I can use the telephone to call Dolly because I promised to let her know how her dad's back is."

Joanna felt ashamed she hadn't enquired about Bill's back that morning. What was wrong with her? Suddenly, within one day, life had become so complicated. Problems she couldn't pin down or define. Or perhaps there weren't problems at all.

"Would you like to walk down with me, lovey? You look like you need to clear your head. Oh, I say, you're not hungover, are you?"

"No, I just haven't quite woken up yet."

"I expect you didn't have time to get sozzled with

young Sam keeping you busy on the dance floor." She winked. "Now, if you'd rather stay home and watch lover boy, I don't mind."

"No, I'd like to go for a walk. Thanks, Sheila." Joanna couldn't wait to get out of the house to put some space between her and Sam.

"Well, if you're sure, lovey." She frowned as she regarded Joanna.

When Sheila got through to Dolly on the telephone, she told her about the improvement to Bill's back, but increasingly, there were long pauses while she listened, periodically expressing dismay. "Oh, dear." "Poor mite." "Oh no ... yes, of course."

The news wasn't good from the East End.

Sheila took a deep breath as she explained to Joanna what had happed to Dolly. "Poor little Billybub is unwell. The doctor thinks it's measles. But unfortunately, Ray's in hospital. He was rushed in a few days ago. Appendicitis, apparently. They've operated, and he's comfortable but won't be out for a day or two. Poor Dolly! She doesn't know which way to turn. The baby's crying all night and she's hardly had any sleep. She wants to come down here to stay so I can help her look after the baby."

Joanna realised why Sheila had looked so dismayed. Dolly would need the spare bedroom. Where could she go at such short notice?

"Now, I don't want you to fret, lovey. I know the last time Dolly came, you slept the night in the tent, but it's much too cold now. We'll put up the spare bed in the sitting room. I'm sure we can all cram in somehow."

But Joanna knew it would be a problem with so many people and a sick baby in the house.

When they got back to Green Haven, they inspected the work Sam and Bill had done. Sheila told Bill about Dolly and the baby coming to stay.

"Perhaps Joanna could sleep at my house? I'm sure my mother would be happy to put her up." Sam's eyes were bright with eagerness.

Sheila frowned as she looked at Joanna and saw her expression. "We'll be fine, thanks, Sam."

"No, I'm sure my mother will be really pleased. I'll take her things around now." Sam got up and turned towards Sheila's cottage.

"No," said Sheila firmly.

Sam stopped. "It's no bother. I'm sure Joanna would prefer our spare bedroom." Tendons stood out on his neck as he clenched his jaw. "You'd prefer that, wouldn't you, Joanna?"

"Joanna is so excited to see the baby," Sheila lied. "She'd be so disappointed if she missed him."

"But she could come back and see him—"

"Come on, lad, that floor won't get laid on its own," Bill said, picking up the rule and taking the pencil from behind his ear. "Joanna's relying on us."

Sam's face relaxed slightly, and he followed Bill.

Sheila jerked her head towards Green Haven, and Joanna quickly followed.

"Thank you, Sheila," she whispered when they were in the kitchen.

Sheila tipped her head to one side and peered at Joanna with appraising eyes. "You didn't seem too keen on the idea."

"No. It was kind but—"

"No need to explain, lovey. He's fallen hard for you, but there's a fine line between makin' plans *with* someone and making 'em *for* them. Don't let him make plans for you unless that's what you want. Right, let's make them a cuppa and a sandwich. The men'll be off to pick up Dolly at five."

While Sam and Bill drove in Sam's van to the railway station, Joanna inspected the building site. The men had finished the floor and had started on the walls. It was so kind of them, and Joanna was grateful to Sheila that she'd refused Sam's offer on her behalf. She was certain she'd now be at Florrie's if Sheila hadn't been there. It was disappointing. She'd thought she'd started to stand up for herself at last, but with Sam, it was especially hard to go against his wishes when she felt she owed him. Sheila had shown her how. In future, she must be firmer.

When everyone arrived back at Green Haven, Billy was asleep. Dolly was a younger version of Sheila, but now she had a look of desperation. Her eyes were sunken with dark smudges beneath, and her hair, which Sheila had once told Joanna was her pride, appeared to be uncombed.

"He's cried himself to sleep," she whispered and gratefully handed him over to Sheila. "It was a dreadful train journey. Everyone kept looking at me like I was killing him. One man asked me to shut him up."

Sheila gently bobbed up and down, rocking the baby in her arms. "You get a bit of shuteye while you can, lovey. You leave Billybub to me."

Joanna made up a bed in the living room, but before she climbed into it, she looked through the window towards her plot. The first stages of the structure were silhouetted in the moonlight. It wouldn't be long before she had her own home.

Chapter Five

On Monday, Ben rose early, eager to get to work to see Joanna. He'd rather have eaten breakfast alone, but his parents were already in the morning room. His father greeted him and after clearing his throat, adjusting his collar, and glancing at his wife, he delivered the news that Ben was expected at a meeting in London that morning. Furthermore, he'd be working there for the rest of the week.

Ben's mother neither reacted nor commented – as if she'd been too preoccupied buttering her toast to be bothered with business matters. There was no doubt: if she hadn't engineered this change in his diary, then she thoroughly approved, knowing it would prevent him seeing Joanna.

Mother had done her best the previous day to throw Ben and Emily together, and after the dance on Saturday, Ben had been so dejected he'd complied. Not, he acknowledged, that he'd acted with any great enthusiasm, but he'd been polite to Emily and had listened to her excited chatter during dinner and then afterwards while they played whist.

He'd half-expected Emily to slip up and accidentally reveal where she'd really been the previous evening. But she'd been thoroughly convincing, and it was only when she'd nudged his leg with her stockinged foot under the table and given him a glimmer of a smile that he'd appreciated how easily the lies dripped from her tongue. Their mothers had certainly been persuaded by her charitable and selfless actions.

His father cleared his throat, bringing Ben back to the present. "We have a potential new client I want you to meet in London, Ben." He flicked the newspaper and held it in front of his face to prevent further discussion. Perhaps it really had been an oversight on his father's part in not advising him he was expected in London that week. The run-up to the weekend had been hectic.

As his mind turned once again to Saturday evening, he felt icy fingers squeeze his heart. He'd been longing to see Joanna at work on Monday morning, even though he knew there'd be little opportunity to ask her what had happened.

He simply wanted to see her face.

Ben quickly finished his coffee and pushed his plate away. If he hurried, he'd have time to drop into the Laindon office on his way to the station.

Rather than wait for Stebbings to drive him and his father to town, Ben drove his own car and parked outside the office. It would be perfectly understandable if he had to pick up a few papers. Even if he didn't need them.

As he got out of the car, he saw Sheila walking

towards him, pushing a pram. She smiled as she recognised him, and then she abruptly stopped and held up her hand as if to keep him away from the pram.

She called out, "Mr Richardson, have you had measles?"

He was disarmed by the unexpected question. "I ... I don't know. Well, yes, I think so ..."

Sheila took a step backwards, pulling the pram towards her. "Only if you haven't, I'd keep well away if I were you. My poor little grandson's gone down with it. Smothered in a rash, he is. And very fretful with it. I wouldn't have brought him out, but we've run out of calamine lotion. He's been crying all night. Poor little mite." She leaned forward and peered at the baby. "You kept mummy up all night, didn't you?" Taking another step away from him, she said, "I'd hate you to go down with measles if you haven't had it, Mr Richardson. So, we'll keep out of your way."

Ben watched as she went into the pharmacy. Grandchild? He didn't know Joanna had any brothers or sisters. But then again, he reminded himself; he didn't know her well at all.

He must hurry if he was going to have any time at all in the office and still catch his train. As he walked up to the door into the office, he peered through the window. He couldn't believe his luck. Mrs Pike wasn't in the office, although her coat was on the hook.

Presumably, she was in the tiny kitchen at the back. Would she stay there long enough to allow him a few moments alone with Joanna? And if so, what would he say? He paused as he saw Joanna fold her arms on her desk and lay her head on them as if she was asleep.

Was she ill? Still, he hesitated, hand poised over the doorknob. However, an instant later, she sat up straight as Mrs Pike came out of the kitchen into the office carrying two cups of tea and placed one on Joanna's desk. That was unusual. It was normally Joanna who made the tea. She pushed the hair from her forehead and inserted paper into her typewriter, but every movement looked as though it were an effort. Her head was lowered; her shoulders sagged. He hesitated for a second and then carried on walking to the station. Instinct told him his presence would only make her feel worse.

Later that day, the bell of the door to the office tinkled gaily, rousing Joanna from her reverie.

"Miss Emily Bailey to see Mr Ben Richardson." The young woman's brows drew together as she surveyed Joanna.

Mrs Pike moved quickly from behind her desk, making it clear she was in charge of the office. "Is Young Mr Richardson expecting you, Miss Bailey?"

"Not as such, but I can assure you he'll make time for me." She craned her neck around Mrs Pike to peer into Ben's office.

"I'm sure that's the case, Miss Bailey, but as I expect you can see, Young Mr Richardson is not here today. He's working in the London office this week." Mrs Pike stood to one side so she could see into the empty office.

"Oh ... Well ... I see. How tedious. In that case, I shall telephone him when I get home. I wish to confirm our arrangements for Friday." She glanced at Joanna, holding her gaze for a few seconds and then with her nose in the air, she said, "Good day." And swept out of the office.

Mrs Pike blinked several times after the doorbell tinkled, signalling Emily Bailey's departure. She heaved an enormous sigh. "Well, that was the height of rudeness. And all for your benefit, Miss Marshall."

"My benefit?"

"Of course. I shouldn't speak ill of Mr Bailey's daughter, but really ... How ill-mannered. On the other hand ..." She paused with her head tilted slightly to one side, as if considering how to proceed. Finally, she said, "It was rather effective, if you consider her intention was to find out what you are like and how much of a threat you pose."

Mrs Pike held up her hand as Joanna opened her mouth to speak. "Before you say 'Me?'. Yes. You. I'm not one for tittle-tattle, Miss Marshall, but sometimes when you see a disaster about to happen, it's best to speak clearly. You and Young Mr Richardson have been

184

studiously pretending not to notice each other since the day you arrived."

Joanna flushed. So, Mrs Pike had noticed how much she liked Ben?

"I see you haven't denied it," Mrs Pike continued. "Good. That would have been an insult to my powers of observation, which are second to none. However, I happen to know Mr Richardson and Mr Bailey are both hoping their offspring will marry and unite the families. Which means our lovely Young Mr Richardson will be tied to that spoiled brat."

She nodded towards the door through which Emily Bailey had just disappeared. "Hopefully, he'll see sense and will choose his own bride. But either way, Miss Marshall – and it pains me to say this – it is most unlikely to be you. Mrs Richardson would never allow it. I don't wish to be the bearer of bad tidings, but whatever is going on, if indeed anything is going on, must stop. For your benefit. I fear it's your heart that will be broken." She softened her words with a sympathetic smile. "And of course, I hardly need to say that as far as anyone else is concerned, this piece of friendly advice was never voiced by me. Now, if you please, Miss Marshall, I think we both need a cup of strong tea."

The demand for tea was a way of giving Joanna a chance to be on her own to absorb the message and recover her composure. She went to the kitchen.

Had anyone else noticed how smitten she was with Ben? It seemed unlikely. No one else was there when she and Ben were together. No one else would have noticed how she repeatedly glanced into his office. Mrs Pike's message had been given with compassion. Joanna had seen a different side of the austere, stern woman who spotted the slightest error in her work and demanded it be repeated. Beneath the pristine grey suit jacket and opal brooch, beat a warm heart.

After two nights with little sleep, Joanna's eyes ached, and she couldn't think straight. Billy had cried on and off all night and no sooner had she fallen asleep than he'd begun again.

And now Mrs Pike's warning. It had piled more embarrassment on top of what she'd already experienced. But somehow, hearing from someone else's mouth what she'd always known with her head, finally convinced her heart.

It had been a dull week in the Laindon office. There wasn't much typing to do, so Mrs Pike decided they'd tidy up and check all filing. Mr Cole had dropped into the office twice, but only because he'd forgotten the partners would be in London during that week. Other than Emily Bailey on Monday, few other people had entered the office. Christmas Day would be the following week and it appeared no one wanted to deal with legal matters until the new year. By midweek, Billy was now settling at night, and Joanna had caught up with her sleep. However, she was pleased when Friday came. She'd missed Ben, although she was dreading seeing him, too. How could she be so torn?

Sheila made Joanna a cup of tea when she got home, but they'd hardly raised the mugs to their mouths when there was a knock at the door. On the veranda was a small girl. Her shoulders shook and between sobs, she managed, "I've wet myself. And I've dropped most of it …"

Sheila put an arm around the tiny child. "Gracie? It's Gracie O'Flanahan, isn't it?"

The little girl nodded.

"Come in, lovey. Does Mummy know you're here?" Sheila looked over her head into the darkness.

Gracie shook her head. "I came out to get w … water at the standpipe, but I dropped it. It went all over me." She looked down at her wet coat, socks, and shoes. "And Mummy's not well."

Sheila peeled the coat off her and placed it on the clothes horse in front of the fire. "Now you sit there, lovey, while I make you a nice hot mug of cocoa. When my Bill comes back from town, I'll get him to go and tell Mummy where you are."

"I'll go," Joanna said, putting her coat on. "Mary will be worried if Gracie's not home soon."

Joanna found the upturned pail outside Green Haven and filled it at the standpipe on the corner of the avenue. It had been no wonder Gracie had struggled with it – when full; it was heavy and awkward. At the O'Flanahan's house, she discovered Mary wrapped in a blanket, shivering. Her face was red, blotchy and beaded with sweat.

Joanna explained how Gracie had knocked at their door and was safe, drinking cocoa and drying off in Green Haven. "Don't worry," Joanna said. "I've brought your water, and Sheila will bring Gracie when she's finished her cocoa."

It was clear Mary was too sick to look after two young children. Her husband, Frank, had been away several days, working in London and wasn't due back until the next day.

Mary raised her eyebrows in a silent question at Joanna, who guessed what she was asking.

"Would you like me to stay tonight to keep an eye on the children while you go to bed, Mary?"

"Oh, would you?" Her shoulders sagged with relief.

Shortly after, Sheila arrived with Gracie. After helping Joanna put Mary to bed, she fetched an armful of blankets and pillows from Green Haven and placed them on the sofa.

"At least it's not as crowded here, lovey, and you'll be doing a good turn, too."

By Saturday morning, Mary was no better. Indeed, she seemed weaker. Joanna decided to call Dr Nichols and ask if he'd come to see her. She gave the children breakfast and then, after putting Jack in his pram, she suggested to Gracie they walk to the post office to use the telephone. Gracie, however, wanted to stay with her mother, so Joanna set off pushing the pram over the grass. It was such hard going; she wondered if it might have been faster if she'd carried Jack in her arms.

Ben urged his horse on, trying to catch Emily as her mare broke into a canter. Not that he wanted to draw level with her – he didn't want to be with her at all. A slight mist swirled over the Essex countryside and dew-hung spider webs sparkled on the hedgerows. But the beauty was lost on Ben.

His head pounded and the motion of his horse wasn't helping. Serve him right. He'd drunk too much the previous evening at a soirée given by his parents. The evening was another Richardson family Christmas tradition. Unlike the Laindon dance, only the wealthiest members of Essex society were invited to this event.

A string quartet provided the music – "None of that modern nonsense," Ben's mother had proclaimed. Although each year, she invited a group of local people into the house to ring out festive songs on handbells. Once their candlelit performance had finished, they were herded into the kitchen for mince pies and spicy punch. Then, presumably, they were dismissed. They'd certainly never been invited to stay.

The tinkling chimes of the bells in the candlelight had been the highlight of the evening for Ben. As the bellringers were escorted to the kitchen, Mother had signalled to the string quartet to play, and conversation had resumed. After that, Ben had done his best to avoid Emily, but she'd pursued him persistently. Eventually, he'd drunk too much port to care.

This morning, Emily had arrived at Priory Hall early. She claimed he'd invited her to go riding. He had no recollection of such an invitation. Well, let them ride. As soon as she'd had enough, he could go home. The fresh air might even clear his head. Hopefully, Mother wouldn't invite her for lunch. His stomach sank as he realised that Mother probably would invite her. Indeed, probably already had. Her matchmaking was relentless. But he would not give in. Not this time.

"Come on, Ben, let's go this way." Emily turned toward the road into one of the avenues of Plotlands.

He drew alongside her. "We need to go back. You've gone the wrong way."

"Wrong way? Whatever do you mean?"

"I thought you wanted to go over the fields."

"No, I didn't say that. I wanted to see where so many of Daddy's clients live. He often talks about Plotlands, and I wanted to see what it looked like."

The last place Ben wanted to go was anywhere near Green Haven. "No, let's go back and carry on across the fields—"

"Oh, Benny, don't be such a spoilsport. I want to see the disused railway carriage. Your mother said someone lives in it as if it was a house. Imagine that!"

He might have known his mother had aroused Emily's interest. He wouldn't put it past her to have told her about Joanna and her parents' house. Would Mother know? He sighed. When she put her mind to it, she could find out anything.

He'd head Emily off at the end of the road and guide her through the woods or to the High Road, and then this silly game would be over. He was determined to keep her away from Green Haven.

"Look at that! It's not a house, is it? It's more like a potting shed. Yes, look, there's smoke coming out of that chimney. Is it a chimney? Perhaps the shed's on fire." Emily shrieked with laughter and urged her horse on faster.

Ben stared at her back for several seconds. He narrowed his eyes and vowed to himself he'd never marry this girl who ridiculed people and their way of life.

"Goodness! Look at that house. It's so tiny. I had a doll's house bigger than that when I was a child. I wonder if they'd like some of my doll's house furniture."

She laughed, and Ben looked about to see if anyone had heard her words. He was ashamed to be with her. Ashamed of his life.

They reached a crossroads, and Ben turned towards the High Road.

"Ben? Where are you going? I wanted to go up there." Emily pointed in the opposite direction.

"I'm going home. These are people's homes you're ridiculing."

"Oh, Benny, where's your sense of humour, daahling? You were such good fun last night."

She caught up with him and drew level.

He couldn't bear to look at her. "Many of these people are the company's clients." How dare she sneer at people who hadn't been born into a family with a fortune deposited in the bank? And what had he been thinking in providing her with fun last night? At least now, the cool air was clearing his head. He almost wished it hadn't. He deserved a headache.

"Oh, honestly, daahling. I was only joking. I say, isn't that the girl who works in your office?" Emily pointed ahead. "I thought she was *Miss* Marshall. She's pushing a pram. But then these people seem to breed like rabbits. Or perhaps she's going to buy some coal … Oh, no, that's most decidedly a baby."

It was indeed. Joanna had scooped up a baby into her arms and was comforting it.

Thankfully, she'd taken the child into the post office and Ben carried on past, hoping Emily would follow.

"That *was* that girl who works in your office, wasn't it?" Emily said when she'd caught him up.

"What if it was?"

"If she's married, she ought not to be working in the firm's office. And if she's not married—"

"It's none of my business. Nor yours."

"Your mother thinks it is."

Ah, his mother.

So, Emily and his mother had been discussing Joanna. Typical.

But that wasn't what filled his mind. It was the image of Joanna with a child in her arms. When he'd last seen Sheila, she'd been pushing her grandchild in a pram. He'd assumed the child had belonged to Joanna's brother or sister. And perhaps it did. But suppose he belonged to Joanna? She'd never mentioned brothers or sisters. And on the day he'd met Sheila, she'd said the baby had kept his mummy up that night. Shortly after, he'd seen Joanna lay her head wearily on her arms as if she was exhausted. Had she lied about being married to get the job? Or lied by omission about having a baby? Still, it might not be hers …

Of course, it was. And what was more, his mother must have found out and told Emily. That was the real reason for her wanting to come here.

Don't be foolish. How would Emily know Joanna would be out with the baby?

But he was beyond reason. Everything inside twisted. If Joanna had a baby – there was – or had been a man. He wanted to give rein to his horse; to gallop until they were both spent at the thought of Joanna with someone else. Jealousy? No, he wasn't the jealous type. And yet now, it appeared the thought of Joanna with anyone other than him awoke such an intense reaction his body seemed to have locked into position; jaws clenched, muscles rigid. He needed to release the tension, or he'd break into a thousand pieces. Spurring the horse on, he galloped back to the field.

Behind him, he heard Emily's startled cry, then her shout. "A race, is it?" And far behind him, thundering hoofs.

How he longed to be alone with his thoughts, but even now he'd rudely ridden away from Emily, she was pursuing him. He slowed his horse. There was no point running; eventually, everything would catch up with him. The realisation he'd never have what he wanted rushed through him. He'd have stood against his parents, and he'd have refused to marry Emily if Joanna had wanted him. But she'd made it clear she didn't want him. Now his unwelcome glimpse into a private life he hadn't known existed had put her even more out of reach – if that were possible.

He stopped and waited for Emily to catch up. His tense muscles relaxed. He was exhausted, like a shipwrecked man who'd been swimming against a powerful tide and had finally washed up on shore. He was alive but had lost everything he held dear. The obvious solution was to go away, far from his mother's schemes and Emily's constant presence. But where would he go?

If you don't remove yourself, eventually, your mother will wear you down.

But another voice whispered that maybe his mother knew best. Perhaps she knew from experience that marriage to Joanna would ultimately make them both unhappy. And who would that benefit? Better that he should choose someone from his own class.

Joanna had been a last attempt at youthful wilfulness. But it had been doomed from the beginning. Now, perhaps he needed to think about the family and do what was best for everyone.

It would not, however, include Emily Bailey.

The walk from Mary's to the post office had taken twice as long as Joanna had expected with the pram. She'd had to steer a course from one side of the road to the other to find the flattest route and avoid shaking Jack too much. However, Dr Nichols had promised to visit Mary on his rounds later that morning.

He said she'd be up in a few days – nothing life-threatening – so long as she rested in bed to get over the worst of it. He wrote out a prescription and said he'd be dropping some tablets off to a neighbour later and would be happy to ask the pharmacist to make up Mary's medicine and deliver it on his way. By the evening, Frank hadn't returned, and once again, Joanna stayed the night.

He didn't return on Sunday either and although Mary felt slightly better; it was clear she wasn't well enough to get up or to look after two children.

But what about Monday? Joanna would have asked to take the day off, but she knew all the partners would be in the Laindon office in the morning for a meeting about the new year's plans. The firm had gained two very important clients, and the London office staff would need help. Everything would be announced at the meeting.

Joanna had called in at Sheila's on her way back from the post office to ask if she'd be able to mind Jack, only to discover that she and Bill were on their way out with Dolly and Billy. They were seeing them home to Poplar, staying overnight while Dolly visited Ray in hospital and then coming home on an early train.

"Bring Jack to Laindon Station on your way to work and as soon as we get there, I'll take him from you, lovey. We'll arrive before you start work, so you won't be late. I'll take him back to Mary and stay awhile to look after her and Gracie. So, you've no need to worry on anyone's account."

Joanna clung to the hope the train would be punctual. She couldn't take Jack to work with her.

Early on Monday morning, Ben drove his car to Laindon Station to pick up his father and Hugh Bailey. They'd both stayed overnight in the company's apartment in London. It wasn't far from the station to their office, but Ben wanted to judge their mood and, if it was suitably buoyant, to suggest he worked permanently in London. He'd find rooms somewhere and although he'd be summoned home periodically, most of the time he'd be in London – away from everyone. The previous day, after his ride with Emily, she'd stayed at Priory Hall for the rest of the day. He'd been correct. Mother had invited her.

Thankfully, his father had telephoned in the evening and asked Ben to look in his study for a file he'd mislaid. By the time his father realised he'd had it after all, he discovered he needed some figures from another document he'd left in his study. Ben had read them out over the telephone and by that time, most of the evening had gone. He'd remained in his father's study long after the call had finished, staring out of the window, and wondering what he was going to do. He didn't put it past his mother to be showing Emily wedding dresses in one of the many fashion magazines that arrived at Priory Hall each week.

He'd been wrong earlier. It was possible for him to run away. And although London wasn't that far, if he moved there, he'd put a large barrier between him and Emily. He'd immerse himself in his work and if that wasn't enough for him, he'd make the break completely and find a new post further north – somewhere like Edinburgh. Not that he wanted to go so far. He loved Priory Hall and the Essex countryside.

But did he love them enough to put up with Emily for the rest of his life? During dinner, he'd played a game, imagining what it would be like being married to her. During the main course, Emily described some of the 'hovels' they'd seen in Plotlands that morning. She and Mother discussed the local people and their shortcomings. Common. Uncouth. Ignorant. Their homes – tumbledown slums – laughable.

It had been too much. In the past, Ben would have privately considered such words unacceptable, but he'd never have voiced his opinions. Not only would he have been in a minority in such company, but it would have meant criticising his mother's opinions. Something that, as a young boy, he'd never dared to do. But he was a man. Not that his mother recognised that. As long as he lived under his father's roof, he'd remain a small boy in her eyes.

"Benjamin? Are you ill? You're rather pale?" His mother had dabbed her mouth daintily with a napkin. "Is the beef not to your liking? I'm finding it slightly tough myself."

Ben had assured her he was fine – as was the beef. At least the conversation had moved on, although he'd half-wished one of them would start again so he could defend the Plotlands and its people. He'd always avoided conflict. At the dance, he'd have welcomed it and now, he'd lost the perfect opportunity. *Coward. Say something! You say you're a man – well, act like one.*

He took a deep breath. "I must admit to finding your comments about the people of Dunton rather unacceptable." There. He'd told them. Not exactly forceful but he'd made a start. Either his mother or Emily would disagree and then he'd really get started.

His mother had made a little sound of disappointment. "Oh, Benjamin. Really. This is hardly the time nor the place. Now, Emily, do tell us about the Masterson's ball. I hear it was quite an event. Such a bore that we were unable to attend."

Ben had stared at his mother. How did she do it? She hadn't even given him the satisfaction of disagreeing with him. Well, this time, he wasn't going to be fobbed off.

"This morning, in Dunton—"

"Enough, Benjamin." His mother hadn't even looked at him. Her voice had been calm and self-assured. His opinion was irrelevant.

The telephone had shrilled, and the maid had hurried into the dining room looking flustered. "Mr Richardson Sr would like a word urgently, please, sir."

"Tell him we're dining." Mother had waved her hand dismissively.

Ben had leapt up. "It'll be important." He'd followed the maid into the hall, and the conversation he'd wanted to have with his mother and Emily had remained unfinished.

Ben parked the car and switched off the engine. He watched the passers-by on their way to work. The very people he'd let down the previous evening when he'd wanted to take a stand. He shook his head and groaned. There was no excuse. He could have finished what he'd been about to say, but he'd chosen the easy way out. On the other hand, it wouldn't have made any difference. His mother wouldn't have listened, and he'd have achieved nothing. She still considered him a child and the only way he'd demonstrate he was a man was if he moved out of Priory Hall.

He checked his watch. The train he hoped his father and Hugh Bailey had caught was due to arrive at Laindon Station in two minutes. A surge of determination lifted his spirits. He was going to be courteous, but firm. And if his father wouldn't allow him to move to London, then in the new year, he'd find another job. At the thought of Christmas with his family and the Baileys, his mood lowered slightly. But soon he'd be gone and would only return when he wanted. This was the start of his life.

Then he saw Joanna. She was pushing a pram.

At the sight of her, his heart beat so hard and fast he could hear pounding in his ears. Where was she going with the child? She crossed the road and entered the station. Was she leaving Laindon? He checked his watch again. She was due in the office in ten minutes. Surely, he'd have heard if she'd handed in her notice? Although she had a bag, it was too small to contain all her possessions.

It's none of your business where Joanna is going.

Ben got out of the car and, with head down and coat collar up, he walked to the station entrance. He stopped and peered in. Joanna wasn't in the queue at the ticket office. She was standing at one side of the ticket hall, her attention on the platforms.

She was waiting for someone. As the *chuff-chuff* of the approaching train slowed, she moved closer to the ticket barrier. With a hiss of steam and squeal of brakes, the train stopped. Doors opened and slammed before people passed through the ticket barrier into the hall and then out into the road.

Joanna stood on tiptoe and waved, having spotted

someone on the platform. Ben caught sight of the feather in Sheila's hat and her ruddy, round face smile with delight as she spotted Joanna. Sheila and Bill showed their tickets and after a brief conversation, Joanna glanced up at the station clock and handed the pram over to Sheila who swiftly pushed it out of the station and into the street. Ben stepped back and hid.

So, that was it. Sheila looked after her grandson while Joanna was at work. No mystery there then. Just a straightforward family arrangement. So why was his heart breaking?

He suddenly realised that although Sheila, Bill and their grandson had come out of the station, Joanna was still in the ticket hall. Ben looked back and just as his father and Hugh Bailey approached, he saw Joanna talking to a man. No one Ben recognised. He appeared to be several years older than Joanna. Surely not the child's father? No. There was no evidence of closeness. The man's hands were outstretched towards her, palm up, and his expression was one of disbelief. Outrage even. He said something and although Ben didn't hear the words; it must have been unkind because Joanna stepped backwards, her face aghast. She pointed outside to the road, and the man turned and hurried out after saying something else that appeared to be threatening or unpleasant. And then, unexpectedly, Joanna ran after him.

Ben watched as the man, pursued by Joanna, ran up to Sheila and harangued her. He roughly shouldered her to one side and after pushing Bill, who'd come to his wife's defence, he marched off down the road with the pram. Joanna, Sheila, and Bill looked at each other in disbelief and after a brief conversation, Joanna left them and ran along the road towards the office.

"Ben?" It was his father.

"Oh ... I ... err ... I came to pick you up from the station."

"That's very thoughtful of you, son."

"Yes, indeed, Ben. Most appreciated," Hugh Bailey said.

Ben suddenly realised that if he drove fast, they'd arrive at the office before Joanna, thus making it appear she was late.

"Did those figures finally make sense last night?" he asked his father, stalling for time.

"Yes, I'd inverted one of the amounts. But once you'd read them out, Hugh and I had it sorted in no time ... Well, shall we?" He gestured to the road. "We can't have Mrs Pike thinking we've forgotten about her, can we?"

"Yes, yes, of course. I'll just get a newspaper first. I shan't keep you a moment ..."

Ben drove slowly along the High Road until he saw Joanna run across further ahead and go into the office.

Well, at least she'd made it before his father and Hugh Bailey. If she hurried, she'd be in her seat, working when they entered. It had been a tiny thing, but he was glad he'd looked out for her – even if she'd never know what he'd done. Her life was already complicated enough without getting into trouble for being late to work.

He followed his father and Hugh Bailey into the office and, keeping his expression neutral, wished, first, Mrs Pike a good morning and then Joanna. Her face, too, was expressionless, although her cheeks were flushed, and he wondered if that had resulted from rushing to work or perhaps anger at whatever had happened outside the station. Presumably, a family argument. He took off his coat and hat and sat down at his desk.

It's none of your business.

So why was he so desperate to help her? Other than a brief, angry exchange, no one had stopped the man from taking the child. That must surely mean they recognised his rights to him. He must be the baby's father. But he was so much older than Joanna. A brute of a man. Perhaps that was why no one had challenged him. So, he and Joanna … He shook his head, still staring at his ink blotter. Was she married to him? It was hard to believe she'd have anything to do with someone who treated people with such a lack of respect.

Respect?

Wasn't that how his mother treated him?

Disregarding his right to live as he desired? And wasn't he allowing her to do so? There was nothing he could do about Joanna. With a man and a child, her life was already mapped out, and at least she had her parents to support her.

The sooner he got away, the better. Not only to claim his own life back, but to avoid the pain of seeing Joanna suffer.

Mrs Pike knocked at his door and entered. "Mr Richardson Sr is ready to start the meeting, sir ..."

He nodded and stood up. This was his chance. He'd hoped to sound out Father before the meeting, but that had been the last thing on his mind once he'd seen the man take the baby. This was his chance now. He'd volunteer to go to London and stay. He would make it happen.

Joanna knew Ben had entered the office. Despite hearing the voices of Mr Richardson and Mr Bailey, the chilly gust that had blasted in as the men opened the door carried the spicy, citrus smell of Ben's cologne. She lowered her head further, pretending to check her shorthand pad to hide her flushed cheeks. They were still hot after her earlier encounter with Frank when he'd behaved so outrageously. She'd tried to explain she'd been looking after Jack while Mary had been ill, but Frank had been beyond reason.

He'd been working in London for much of the time since she'd first met him, and he didn't know Sheila or Bill, so she could see how he'd assumed she'd handed Jack over to strangers to return to Mary. There hadn't been time for a thorough explanation if she was going to get to work on time – even if his anger had allowed her to get a word in. She'd run after him, afraid of what he'd do to Sheila, but Bill had seen him off. After snatching the pram, Frank had walked away.

After that, had been the dash to work and her cheeks had reddened further.

Mrs Pike had glanced at her disapprovingly over the top of her spectacles after pointedly looking at the clock. It had been a minute past the hour.

"I'm sorry, Mrs Pike."

At two minutes past the hour, Joanna had fed paper into her typewriter and as she placed her fingers over the keys, the office door had opened. Ben's cologne had announced his presence, and she'd closed her eyes, remembering that smell and the warmth of his body as they'd danced. The door slammed, bringing her back to the present, and she cringed as she recalled his grimace at the smell that enveloped her.

They gathered in Mr Richardson's office and Joanna kept her head over her notepad, taking the minutes. It was much as she'd expected from the snippets Mrs Pike had told her. The new year would bring more work.

Good. That was what she was there for and if the company was successful, she'd be more likely to keep her job. Assuming there were no more complications, such as being left in charge of baby Jack when she should have been at work. But once she had her own home, she'd be more independent. Yes, 1931 was going to be her year. She would make it so.

Then, two things surprised her. First, Mr Richardson announced she and Mrs Pike would get a Christmas bonus in their pay packets on Christmas Eve – only two days away. While Joanna was calculating how much faster she could build her cottage, the second surprise came. Ben asked if he could move permanently to the London office. It was a shock to his father – but not an unpleasant one, judging by his expression. In fact, it seemed to solve the company's increase in workload. The two senior bosses agreed Ben would start work in London after Christmas and would live in the company's apartment in Mayfair.

Disappointment, like a heavy weight, pressed on Joanna's chest. She wouldn't see him again – well, not until he came back to Laindon – but there was something about the way he spoke that made it sound final – as if this move to London was permanent. But surely, it would be better not to have the constant reminder of the embarrassment of the Christmas Dance?

'Yes,' her head told her.

'No,' her heart replied.

When the meeting was concluded, Ben went into his office to gather up his belongings. While Joanna and Mrs Pike tidied away their chairs, Mr Richardson and Mr Bailey continued to discuss Ben's move.

"I don't suppose Emily will be happy about Ben moving to London," Mr Richardson said.

"On the contrary, old man. She'll probably be delighted. She loves London life. Given half a chance, she'd move there tomorrow. This may just be what she's looking for."

Mrs Pike cleared her throat and signalled with her eyes that Joanna should hurry.

When Joanna got back to her desk, she began work immediately, trying to block out everything that had happened that morning. Frank's unpleasant accusation that she'd handed his son over to a stranger. Ben's request to work in London and then the knowledge that Emily Bailey would be pleased to spend more time with him.

You have no right to feel so hurt.

Ben deserves someone kinder than Emily Bailey.

Still, it's none of your business.

At midday, Joanna usually went next door to Rosie's Posies with her lunch. After such a trying morning, she'd rather have gone for a walk on her own, but knew that if she didn't go, Louisa would come looking for her. Since the Laindon Christmas Dance, Louisa had seen Harry on several occasions. Now, her conversations revolved around him, and her eyes lit up whenever his name was mentioned. Joanna was pleased to see her happy, but today, of all days, she didn't want company.

"You poor dear," Louisa said when she entered.

Was her face so miserable?

"Mum told me about Frank O'Flanahan this morning. Heavens! How horrid! She's heard he's mixed up with the wrong people in the East End. It's a shame for his wife, though. She seems nice. But it wasn't fair of him to take it out on you, particularly after you'd been helping his family."

Despite herself, Joanna smiled. So, Betty already knew all about the O'Flanahans, as well as the scene outside the station.

It was so easy to be with Louisa, and before long, Joanna told her Ben intended to leave Laindon and work in London.

Louisa tilted her head to one side and nibbled her lower lip. "I'm beginning to believe you care more for handsome Young Mr Richardson than you've ever admitted."

"No, no! That would be very foolish. He'd never be interested in someone like me."

"It doesn't stop a girl dreaming though, does it? I'm

probably being foolish spending so much time with Harry. He's going back to Hastings soon. But I just can't help myself."

"Well, I assure you, I'm not dreaming about Ben." Joanna realised her mistake as soon as his name left her mouth.

"Ooh! Ben, is it?" Louisa raised her eyebrows in mock disapproval. "Surely you don't address your boss by his Christian name?"

"No, of course not. I just wanted to make it clear I wasn't referring to the senior Mr Richardson. And 'Young Mr Richardson' is such a mouthful." Joanna made light of it, trying to deflect Louisa's interest, although she knew the heightened colour in her cheeks would be enough to provoke her curiosity.

If Louisa noticed, she made no mention and indeed appeared to be distracted.

"So, if you're not dreaming about Mr Ben Debonair Richardson, who are you dreaming about? Your handsome, brooding carpenter?"

"Sam? Goodness, no."

Louisa was an incurable romantic. "But you're going to the New Year's Eve Dance with him, aren't you?"

"No. He hasn't asked me." Joanna had seen the posters for the event in town, but after the last dance she'd attended, she had no desire to go – with or without Sam.

"Well, that's strange because Sam told Harry he'd invited you and you'd accepted."

"No, definitely not. It's not likely to have slipped my mind."

"Well, perhaps he plans to ask you and was being slightly over-optimistic? You'll see him at Christmas, won't you?"

Joanna nodded. Guilt twisted her insides. She'd avoided him as much as she could since the dance, although that hadn't been hard. He'd worked on her cottage over the weekend while she'd been helping Mary and the children, and at other times, he'd been there during the day when she'd been in the office. The walls were finished, and the roof was next. The cottage was ahead of schedule.

So why wasn't her heart soaring? Perhaps it was because Sam had dismissed Bill's carpenter, explaining to Joanna, he'd do it for nothing. While that was very kind, it meant she'd be beholden to him for all the work. He'd refused payment, but he must want something ...

She hadn't seen the cottage for several days because she'd been busy looking after Mary. When she'd been out, she'd taken an alternate route to avoid her plot – and Sam. There was nothing wrong with him. But his face lit up whenever he saw her, as if there was an understanding between them. At least, it was something he understood. He clearly liked her more than she liked him and although she didn't want to take advantage of his good nature, somehow, it always seemed she was at a disadvantage.

"Harry must have misunderstood about the New Year's Eve Dance. Perhaps he's going to ask you to go with him the next time he sees you. But I know he's got tickets." Louisa shrugged. "When he asks you, you will go, won't you? It'll be so lovely to see the New Year in together."

"I don't know ..." Another night with Sam's arms enclosing her?

Again, the memory of Ben filled her mind.

This must stop! Ben has gone. Do you want to be alone for the rest of your life?

Well, no. But then again, did she see a future with Sam? Perhaps if she got Ben out of her mind, things might be different.

"Are you worried about what to wear? I know you weren't happy with the dress you wore the other week," Louisa asked. "Not that there was anything wrong with it, of course."

Dear Louisa. But how could she tell her friend what was really on her mind?

At Joanna's hesitation, Louisa assumed she'd been correct. "Heavens, you don't need to worry about a dress. Borrow one of mine. I have lots. And I'm making a new gown for New Year's Eve. Let me show you ..."

Louisa opened a *Mabs* Magazine. "What do you think?"

Louisa was certainly skilful at dressmaking and very kind to offer Joanna one of her dresses. But … But what? If only she didn't feel so tired, she might be able to think clearly. Tonight, Dolly and Billy were home in East London. Frank was back with Mary. As soon as Joanna could, she'd go to Green Haven and sleep. Everything would look different in the morning. In two days, it would be Christmas Eve. It seemed everything was going her way. A generous man was building her cottage, and he wanted to take her out to celebrate the New Year. Her best friend had offered her an elegant dress to wear so she could see in the New Year in style. True, Ben would be gone, but then he'd never been part of her world, anyway. It was time to get over him.

After a good night's sleep, she'd wake refreshed and that hard, heavy weight in her stomach would be gone. Then it would be Christmas, shortly followed by New Year's Eve. The dance would herald the new. The year of 1931 would be hers.

The following day, Joanna felt slightly rested and although she wasn't looking forward to her first Christmas without both parents, she was determined to salvage something from the year and finish with good memories.

"This is a place of business," Mrs Pike had declared when Joanna asked whether they usually had decorations in the office. But she'd relented and allowed two paper chains crisscrossing in the windows.

"Mornin', ladies." Bert, the postman, placed a large pile of letters on Mrs Pike's desk. "It's chilly out there today." He rubbed his hands together and blew on them. "Oh, by the way. I keep forgetting …" He pulled a letter out of his bag and turned to Joanna. "Are you Miss Marshall from plot number …" He paused and scrutinised the envelope. "Plot number 18?"

"Yes."

"Well, I'd get that young man of yours to get a door on your home as soon as he can. Preferably with a letter box in it. It's not easy delivering a letter to four walls." He chuckled. "But I can see it won't be long. Your young man's working real hard. I expect it'll be wedding bells next, will it?"

"No! He's not my young man. He's just … a friend."

"Are you sure he knows he's just a friend? Only the last time I was over that way, he were talking about the place like it were his."

"No, he's just a friend who's helping me with the build."

"Shame it won't be done this side of Christmas." Bert winked. "But before you know it, you'll both be in there, cuddling up—"

"Thank you, Bert. We mustn't keep you." Mrs Pike moved towards him, as if to shoo him out.

"Well, I'll be back shortly, ladies. Still got more rounds before Christmas."

Joanna slit open the envelope. It was dog-eared and smudged as if it had been in the post for some time. She unfolded the letter and checked the date; it had taken nearly a fortnight to reach her. Quickly, she scanned the message and then gasped.

"Miss Marshall? Is there a problem?"

Joanna had the letter between her finger and thumb and stared at Mrs Pike with a shocked expression. "This says I have to vacate my land. It disputes my ownership."

"But didn't you say your mother gave you a receipt?"

"Yes."

"Then there's nothing to worry about. Who is the letter from?"

"Jonas Parker, the man who sold my mother the plot. He says she didn't pay the full amount, so it rightfully belongs to him."

"Well, we'll see about that." Mrs Pike held out her hand for the letter. "Mr Richardson Sr is here he'll make sense of this, I'm sure."

She carried the letter into Mr Richardson's office and beckoned Joanna to follow.

"Ah, Jonas Parker. An unpleasant petty crook. You say your mother gave you a receipt? Good. Well, I'm sure we can conclude this nonsense swiftly. Have you had many dealings with this man?"

Joanna explained she'd bumped into him during his last visit to Plotlands with a group of prospective buyers. He'd offered to buy the land from her once again. She'd told him she'd never sell. He hadn't been happy and as he'd left, he'd once again threatened she'd regret it.

"He probably thought he could send this letter, and you'd give in with no effort on his part. Nasty bully of a man. Bring in the receipt after Christmas and I'll write a letter. Parker will soon see you're not alone and he'll back down. So don't worry your pretty little head, Miss Mitchell, just leave it all to us."

Chapter Six

Florrie Cavendish and Sheila had pooled the money they'd withdrawn from the Christmas Club, and on Christmas Eve had bought a turkey and a few presents. Both women had been preparing for months. Florrie had made a Christmas cake in her log burner oven in November. During the same week, Sheila had filled Green Haven with steam when she'd cooked Christmas puddings on her paraffin stove. On Christmas Eve, Sheila had made dozens of mince pies and taken them to Florrie's to cook, filling the Cavendish's house, Speedwell, with the spicy, fruity aroma.

The two families had decided to share their Christmas Day and Boxing Day, as well as the expense. Tom Cavendish and Bill had worked together in the docks in East London years before. Tom had moved to Laindon and after marrying Florrie, he'd built a cottage and had turned his hand to building or any other available work. When Bill had moved to Laindon, they'd picked up their friendship again. Their wives had become friends. Both men considered themselves comfortable, but news of the Great Depression in the United States of America had caused everyone to worry. Who knew what might happen next? Everyone wanted to enjoy Christmas, but it was prudent to be careful with their finances.

They gathered in Speedwell for Christmas Day since it was larger than Green Haven, and they could all be seated comfortably around their table. The following day, they would spend in Green Haven, when the leftovers would be served.

The living room in Speedwell was festooned with colourful paper chains suspended between the corners of the room, and a huge red, fold-out, honeycomb bell dangling from the middle of the ceiling. The Christmas Club money had also stretched to paper hats and crackers, but Florrie had suggested a 'no gift' policy. "It's enough we'll be spending the day together. We don't need presents."

After the enormous meal, Sheila and Florrie carried dishes into the kitchen to wash up. Bill and Tom were deep in conversation about the problems caused by the Great Depression in America and the knock-on effects in England. Joanna stacked a pile of plates ready to carry out the kitchen, but Sam caught her wrist. With a shy smile, he slipped a small ribbon-tied box into her hand. "My Christmas present to you."

"But … but it was agreed no presents." Joanna looked down at the small box, her heart beating wildly. Throughout the entire meal, she'd been aware of his gaze resting on her and his leg brushing hers. Things were moving too fast, and she wasn't sure how to deal with Sam without hurting his feelings. And now, he'd given her a present. It was obvious he thought more of her than she did of him. If only he'd give her a chance to think about her feelings, but when she was with him, everything spun out of control.

"I know but under the circumstances ..." He smiled at her, and she had to keep reminding herself that despite his proprietorial behaviour towards her, they were not close. Had he assumed one kiss meant they were sweethearts? And what did he mean by 'circumstances'?

"Joanna, where are those plates?" Florrie called from the kitchen.

"Sorry. I'm just coming ..." Joanna slipped the box into her pocket.

"Thank you," she said, trying to keep her voice as neutral as was polite. He had, after all, given her a present. But she didn't want to add to the intimate atmosphere he was trying to create.

She carried the plates into the kitchen and had a sudden thought. Could the box contain a ring?

Oh, please, no!

The box had been too big, hadn't it? The shock of him holding her wrist and then giving her a present hadn't allowed her to take in the size. As soon as she'd put down the plates, she felt the box in her pocket. No, not a ring box, she was certain. But even so, she now felt more indebted to him than ever.

When the kitchen was tidy, Florrie, Sheila and Joanna brought tea and cake into the living room for the men.

"How about a game of charades?" Florrie asked.

"Before that, perhaps Joanna would like to open her present." Sam smiled at her.

Joanna flushed with embarrassment. Why had he drawn attention to it?

"Present? But I thought we'd agreed no presents?" Sheila said.

Florrie looked adoringly at her son. "Oh, you know my Sam. He's so generous and he always likes to do things his way."

Joanna, still with crimson cheeks, took the box out of pocket and untied the ribbon. Inside was a small, silver heart-shaped locket on a delicate chain. Both Sheila and Florrie gave a sharp intake of breath.

"That's a beauty." Florrie sighed, regarding her son with soft, loving eyes.

It was beautiful, but it was too much. Joanna knew she ought to refuse it but how could she do that in front of everyone without appearing ungracious? It was merely a Christmas present. Or was it? Did her acceptance of it mean she was accepting more than a necklace?

"Aren't you going to put it on?" Sam's eyes held a hint of pain, as if he knew she was considering refusing it.

Joanna lifted it from the box. She couldn't bear to see his hurt expression, so she fastened it around her neck. As she did so, she noticed the small furrows in Sheila's brow that always formed when she was worried. But Sam's face, on the other hand, had lit up. Was it such a bad thing to make someone happy?

"Drink up everyone," Florrie said. "I've got a marvellous idea for when it's my turn at charades."

Despite his shyness and obvious awkwardness, Sam took part in charades and Joanna could see how hard he was trying to please her – ensuring her glass was topped up with sherry and her plate full. He was most attentive, and when he made her laugh, his delight was apparent. Joanna caught sight of Florrie and Tom sending each other knowing glances as if they knew their son was keen on her and they approved. Sheila and Bill also exchanged glances, but those were less easy to read. Bill's eyes were half-closed as the warmth of the fire and the beer drained him of energy but Sheila, despite several glasses of sherry, appeared alert and wary. After a while, Joanna wondered if she was imagining Sheila's expression. Perhaps she was merely silently warning Bill not to drink too much.

Before the Cavendish family arrived at Green Haven on Boxing Day, Sheila tentatively broached the subject of Sam.

"Well, that was a surprise. Sam giving you a necklace after Florrie made such a to-do about not giving presents, lovey."

"Yes. I must admit, I was rather embarrassed."

"He's head over heels ..." Sheila studiously polished a spoon with a tea towel. "I'm just wondering what you feel about him. Not that it's any of my business," she added hastily. "Only you don't seem completely comfortable with him. He's not pushing you into anything you're not ready for, is he?"

"Oh, no. Nothing like that. It's just ... I don't know what I think about him. He's so good to me and I feel I ought to be more grateful. It's like something inside me is lacking. Or perhaps I just need more time." She'd been about to say she knew little about falling in love, but that wasn't strictly true.

Ben.

But did she love Ben? Or had she merely been strongly attracted to him because he was out of reach? Sam was there. She ought to concentrate on him.

"Mm. Perhaps." Sheila didn't sound convinced.

Bill came in from feeding the chickens, and Sheila abandoned the topic.

The easy camaraderie and laughter of Christmas Day

continued on Boxing Day when the Cavendishes arrived at Green Haven. Sam smiled when he saw Joanna was wearing his necklace. She hadn't wanted to but she'd guessed he'd be upset if she didn't.

The Cavendishes brought many of the leftovers from the previous day and Sheila had onions and vegetables chopped up, ready to boil with the turkey carcass to make soup.

After lunch, while the women cleared the table, Florrie looked at Sam, her eyes gleaming with excitement. "So, what do you young people plan to do tomorrow?"

"Well, I've arranged to borrow the van from work and I'm going to take Joanna to Southend for the day." Sam smiled at her triumphantly.

Joanna dropped the spoon she'd picked up. "What? No, I'm sorry, Sam, I'm afraid I can't. I'm going to Louisa's tomorrow. I'll be staying with her until the New Year's Dance."

Florrie's face fell and Sam frowned.

The ensuing silence was relieved only by the stertorous breathing of Tom and Bill, who'd both nodded off, and the ticking of the clock.

"But I've arranged everything I've booked a table in a restaurant on the seafront." Sam's puzzled frown had now been replaced by a darker expression. His eyes had narrowed.

"I ... I'm really sorry, Sam. I didn't know you had anything planned."

"Well, under the circumstances, surely you could tell Louisa—"

"Joanna can hardly let down her best friend, can she?" Sheila cut in, her voice carrying just the right amount of light-heartedness to thaw the chilly atmosphere.

"I think it might rain tomorrow anyway," Florrie said in an artificially cheery voice. "Perhaps you could take Joanna on another day?"

But Sam's earlier little-boy look of eagerness had become brooding and dark. His hands were bunched and a vein in his temple throbbed.

Joanna glanced at Sheila, whose eyes were as wide as hers.

Everyone looked at the floorboards, avoiding each other's gaze, until Bill woke with a snort. "Any chance of a cuppa?"

Sheila leapt to her feet. "I'll put the kettle on."

"I'll help," said Joanna, grateful to escape the awkward atmosphere.

Florrie remained with her son.

Once they were out of sight of everyone, Sheila shot Joanna a questioning glance, as if to ask what had just happened. Joanna shrugged and shook her head, her eyebrows raised. Sam's reaction had been completely out of proportion. He hadn't checked with her before he'd booked anything, so he had no right to behave as if she'd deliberately upset his day.

Sheila nodded her head reassuringly, as if to say, 'Don't change your plans, Joanna.' Bill joined them in the kitchen area and mouthed, "What happened?"

Sheila could only shrug, her bottom lip jutting out and her eyes wide.

"I'm going to get out the sloe gin," Bill whispered.

By the time they'd taken the tea into the living room, Tom had woken up. Either he was used to such an undercurrent, or he hadn't been awake long enough to detect it, but he cheerily suggested a game of Monopoly. It turned out to be an excellent suggestion. Everyone joined in, and after Bill had been liberal with his precious sloe gin, things livened up. Sam was still withdrawn; his earlier boyish excitement had disappeared, and even winning at Monopoly hadn't lifted his mood, but if it was affecting everyone else, they were careful not to show it. Nevertheless, Joanna felt guilty she'd almost ruined the day. How much easier would it have been if she'd simply changed her plans to fit in with Sam's?

After the Cavendishes had gone home, Bill tidied up the empty bottles. "Florrie's given in to that lad of theirs too often. I've heard some of his workmates talk about 'im. He likes his own way. Got a bit of a reputation. Trouble is, he's so big and 'andy with his fists, no one'll tackle him."

"Well, it weren't the end of the world. He should have asked Joanna first before booking a restaurant. It weren't anyone's fault. Just one of them things. But it would be a shame to let Louisa down." Sheila turned back to the washing up. "You be careful, lovey."

On Monday morning, Sheila walked into Laindon. She knew Joanna would be at work, but as well as buying fresh bread, she wanted to know how she'd been. Looking back on it, Joanna had been subdued the entire Christmas. Of course, she would have missed her mum and dad. But Sam hadn't helped. She'd felt awkward about his gift, and guilty because he'd made a fuss when she hadn't gone out with him.

Betty and Louisa were both in Rosie's Posies when Sheila entered. "Ah, good. Just the ladies I need. I haven't come to see Joanna. I want to ask you about her."

She explained about Sam's possessive behaviour and how he'd spent the two days of Christmas watching Joanna. "It sounds quite romantic, but for some reason, it alarmed me." To her surprise, both Betty and Louisa nodded with understanding.

"I couldn't bear it if he upset Joanna," Sheila said. "She's been down most of the holiday."

"Are you sure she wasn't upset because of that letter?" Louisa passed her mother a reel of ribbon.

"Letter? What letter?" Sheila asked.

"The one threatening her and telling her to get off her land."

Sheila gasped. "I didn't know nothing about that! When did that come?"

Louisa's hand flew to her mouth. "I … I thought you knew. But she told Old Mr Richardson, and he said not to worry. He'd sort it out after Christmas. I expect he's working on it now."

"No, I had a chat with Mrs Pike this morning and she said he won't be in till late morning," Betty said.

"So, I might have been worrying about Sam and it wasn't him upsetting Joanna at all. I wish she'd told me about the letter." Sheila nibbled her lower lip and shook her head sadly.

"She probably didn't want to bother you, especially with all that trouble with your Dolly and young Billy just before Christmas."

"Well, I'm certainly worried about her now. Poor girl. She's had more than enough heartache for someone of her age. She don't deserve it. I think I might pop next door and chivvy Mr Richardson up a bit. Over Christmas, he might have forgotten. He might need a little nudge."

"Do you think Joanna will be happy about that?" Louisa asked.

"She won't know, lovey. I'm going to wait till she comes in here and then I'll pop in."

"Well, she'll start lunch in about ..." Louisa checked the clock. "Half an hour."

"Rightio. I'll go to the baker's first, then I'll drop in next door all casual-like as if I was looking for her and while I'm there, I'll try to find out more. That'll sort out one problem, but as for that lad, Sam ..."

"He always was a dark horse," Betty said, "Beggin' yer pardon, Sheila, because I know she's your friend, but Florrie Cavendish spoiled him rotten. Didn't he cause problems at school, Lou?"

"Yes, he always wanted his own way. I haven't had much to do with him since we left school, but I thought he'd changed. He seems more polite now."

"Mm, I know what you mean," Sheila said. "He seems all right. Full of smiles, but then something'll upset him, and he looks like thunder. He keeps reminding Joanna of all the things he's done for her. I think that's the problem. She knows she owes him a lot. He's been working hard on her cottage, and he's given her some partly damaged building supplies. It saved her a lot of money. He's so good to her. And yet ..." Sheila wasn't sure how to continue. "And yet, somehow, it doesn't seem to be all selfless. Perhaps that's a nasty suspicious thing to say, but it's like he's fishing and he's winding her in slowly and surely, luring her in with his good deeds."

Ben's heart lurched when he saw Joanna at her typewriter. He hadn't allowed himself to think about her over Christmas. There had been a constant stream of relatives arriving and leaving Priory Hall. Thankfully, he hadn't seen Emily, although he knew he was expected to join her at a ball in the Savoy Hotel in London on New Year's Eve. Well, he'd worry about that on the day. He'd get out of it somehow.

Not that he hadn't thought about Joanna over Christmas. He'd thought of her often, but he hadn't allowed his mind to dwell on her. It was senseless to wish for the impossible. He'd even fooled himself into believing he had his emotions under control, but one look at her and his resolve drained away.

He'd politely enquired whether Mrs Pike had enjoyed her Christmas and then asked Joanna. After that, he'd hurried into his office to find the files he'd need in London. The sooner he found them, the sooner he could leave. And yet, he found himself at the filing cabinet near the door, not searching in the 'A' to 'D' section, but glancing sideways, through the window, watching Joanna type. She was biting her lower lip as if she was troubled and he longed to ask her what was wrong.

She's probably made a typing error, he told himself. It wouldn't be anything more serious than that. But what if it was?

It's none of your business.

Mrs Pike suggested Joanna go to lunch, and she slipped on her coat and left. Now, at last, he could concentrate. He had two more files to find, and he was tempted to ask Mrs Pike, but she appeared to be busy.

The bell tinkled over the door. It was so soon after Joanna had gone out, he expected it to be her returning because she'd forgotten something. Instead, it was her mother, Sheila.

Mrs Pike greeted her and instead of asking for Joanna, to his surprise, Sheila asked if his father was there. Ben nudged his door slightly open and listened.

Sheila enquired about a letter Joanna had received, laying claim to her land. Ben knew nothing about such a letter and was surprised to discover Mrs Pike did. She informed Sheila that Mr Richardson Sr was running slightly late but would be in soon, and Sheila wasn't to worry because Joanna had told her she had a receipt. It was a mistake and would easily be resolved.

Sheila thanked her and left.

Ben went into the main office. "Was that Miss Marshall's mother?" he asked nonchalantly, as if he'd been so busy, he hadn't listened closely to the conversation.

Mrs Pike's brows were knitted. "Indeed not, Mr Richardson. Miss Marshall's mother passed away a few months ago."

Ben stared at her. "Then who was that?"

"Sheila Guyler. Miss Marshall's next-door neighbour."

"But I thought Sheila lived in Green Haven ...?"

"She does. Miss Marshall gave Green Haven as her address until such time as her cottage is built. She's staying with Sheila."

"Until her cottage is built? Wait! Is this the land she's been warned to leave?"

"Yes. Do you know about the letter?"

"No. Well, yes ..." Now Mrs Pike would realise he'd been eavesdropping. But too bad. He needed to know. "Mrs Pike, I wonder if you'd be good enough to tell me what's going on, please."

Joanna told herself she had plenty of work to do, and therefore would leave Louisa and go back into the office five minutes early. While it was true that she was busy, she really wanted to see if Ben was still there. Not that she expected to spend any time with him, but it was enough to know he was nearby. He'd leave for the London office soon and in future, she'd be unlikely to catch more than a glimpse of him.

As she entered the office, Mrs Pike and Ben were deep in a conversation that stopped abruptly when the bell tinkled. Both faces turned towards her. Mrs Pike cleared her throat and reached for a pile of papers which she stood upright and tapped on the desk.

Ben rearranged his features into a business-like look. "Ah, Miss Marshall, there you are. Mrs Pike was just filling me in on the unpleasant letter you received before Christmas. I believe my father was going to deal with it. Unfortunately, he's running late so if you could come into my office, please, I'll handle this matter myself. I understand you have a receipt for your plot?"

"Er, yes, thank you." Joanna took off her coat and, still clutching her handbag, she followed Ben into his office. Her heart soared at the thought of a few stolen moments with him. Then it sank as she admitted the parting would be harder.

Ben sat at his desk and gestured for her to sit opposite him. She passed the envelope to him, and he took out the contents. After unfolding the sheet of paper, he peered back inside the envelope, holding the edges apart.

He looked at her questioningly. "This isn't a receipt. It's a sales leaflet."

Joanna stared at him blankly. She'd been studying his face, not noting what he'd been doing, but as she looked at the paper he held out, her heart skipped a beat. He was correct; it wasn't the receipt. It must have fallen out. But how did the leaflet get in there? She stared. It was one of the leaflets Mr Parker had given out to advertise the sale of Dunton plots.

Blood drained from her face. The receipt must be in

her bag. She opened it and rummaged inside. Should she pull everything out? Did he believe her?

"Perhaps you left it at home?" His voice was gentle. Concerned.

It couldn't be at home. She'd kept it safe in her canvas bag. One corner of the envelope had become damp when she'd been out in the storm. The sales leaflet also showed signs of dampness, so it had obviously been in the envelope since that night. But she hadn't put it there. The envelope had only contained the receipt.

"When was the last time you saw it?" Ben asked.

She was grateful he seemed to believe her. But, even if he did, suppose she couldn't find it?

"I ... I'm sure I haven't taken it out since I've been in Dunton."

Ben rose and came to her side of the desk, perching on one corner. He leaned towards her. So close, she could smell the spicy, woody notes that always accompanied him. It was hard to concentrate. Thoughts ricocheted around her mind.

"I ... I looked at it several times when I was at my aunt's house in London. And then I gave it to the man who brought me to Laindon to check the plot number."

"Is it possible he put the leaflet in the envelope?"

She swallowed again and nibbled the corner of her lip. "Possibly. That's the only time I've ever seen those leaflets, and Mr Parker definitely looked at the receipt."

"Do you remember seeing the receipt after that?"

Joanna shook her head. "Do you think he could have it?" Her voice was full of dread.

Ben's face clouded, and he sighed. "I've heard a lot about Jonas Parker and his sales trips. He's notoriously unscrupulous, so I wouldn't put it past him. Have you had further dealings with Parker?"

"Yes, I saw him a few weeks ago. He's asked me several times if I'd sell my plot, but I've always told him it wasn't for sale."

"And now you've had a letter from him?"

Joanna nodded. A lump was growing in her throat, and it was hard to speak. "If Mr Parker has the receipt, it means I don't have proof of ownership."

"Leave that to me," Ben said firmly. "I suspect he can be persuaded to hand the receipt back if he has it. I've heard he's tried to persuade a few people who live near you to sell. And he always offers much less than the land's worth. Someone told me one of his associates wants to buy a larger piece of land and Parker's been after ten consecutive plots. The only way he can fulfil that is if he buys back a few of the plots he's already sold. But one way or the other, we'll resolve it for you."

"Thank you so much." The lump in Joanna's throat still made it hard to speak.

She rose to leave, but he held out a restraining hand. "While you're here, I wanted to talk to you. Well ... more to apologise, really. I think I may have upset you and I'd like to clear the air. I believe I overstepped the mark somewhat at the Christmas Dance ..."

"Oh, no."

"But I obviously upset you. If I'd known you were there with someone else, I wouldn't have ..." He paused and looked up to the ceiling for inspiration. "That is, I wouldn't have ..." He stopped again.

"I wasn't with him. Not in the beginning. And I'm not sure even now ..." Joanna whispered.

"Then what did I do to upset you?"

"You didn't upset me. I ... I was embarrassed." She looked down at her handbag, her cheeks crimson.

"About what?"

"I suddenly noticed you looked horrified, and I ..." She shook her head and swallowed, but having started, she'd now have to finish, or she'd appear even more foolish. Well, why not just say it? He'd be gone soon, anyway. And she'd only be voicing what he already knew. "I ... I saw your face and I thought I revolted you."

He sat up straight, his eyes wide open. "Revolted me? That's impossible. Whatever gave you that idea?"

"It was the ... smell ... the mothballs."

"For a second, I thought you said *mothballs*." He half-smiled, half-frowned.

"I did. It was the stole Sheila lent me. It smelt of mothballs, but I didn't like to hurt her feelings by not wearing it."

"Joanna." His voice was low and deep.

A shiver went through her as she heard the raw emotion in his voice.

"I didn't notice what you smelt like, and if I had detected mothballs, I assure you, it wouldn't have made any difference to me. You could have filled your pockets with mothballs, and you'd still have been the most desirable woman at the dance. When I bring you to mind, I can smell summer meadows, flowers and rainbows."

She laughed. "Rainbows don't smell."

He echoed her smile. "They do to me and they're beautiful. But did you seriously believe I'd care about a smell?"

"When I saw your expression, I realised how different we are. Your family is rich. I'm just a working girl. We belong to different worlds. Yours is full of perfume and cologne. Mine's full of more basic smells. I live in a house with chickens in the garden. I have to walk through mud to get to work and where I come from, clothes have to be smothered in mothballs to keep them for years. I thought you'd suddenly realised how different our worlds were."

He shook his head. "No, you couldn't have been more wrong. If you saw distaste on my face, it was because I noticed my mother had sent Mrs Pike to take me away from you, and I was annoyed. But if I gave you the impression I found you revolting, I'm so sorry. And even more sorry that misunderstanding drove you to someone else." He crossed his arms over his chest and shook his head. "You say you're not sure you're with that man but he certainly wanted to be with you."

She shook her head. "I don't know. He's been so good to me, I wouldn't like to hurt his feelings, but we've never discussed being together. Since you and I are being honest with each other, can I ask, does it matter to you? There could never be anything between us. You're as good as engaged to Miss Bailey."

"That's what my parents want." He shook his head. "But it's not going to happen. I feel nothing for her. I don't believe she feels anything for me. Emily's looking for a rich husband and anyone will do. She's also very competitive and doesn't like to lose. But what I want ..." He leaned forward and took her hand. Before he could continue, the doorbell tinkled, and his father's voice boomed out a greeting to Mrs Pike. Ben dropped Joanna's hand and drew back.

The door to Ben's office opened. "Ah, Ben, I see you're dealing with Miss Mitchell's problem. Good, good. Well, I'll leave it in your hands, then."

"Thank you, Mr Richardson," Joanna said as she rose.

It wasn't clear which man she'd thanked as she left the office.

"Just look at the pair of you! Like a couple of Hollywood film stars!" Betty inspected her daughter and Joanna once they'd finished dressing for the New Year's Eve Dance. Louisa had altered the pink dress she'd worn to the Christmas Dance to fit Joanna, and together, they'd both finished her new blue gown that morning.

"You're going to dazzle your young men, that's for sure. And if Florrie Cavendish is right, your young man will more than dazzle *you* tonight, Joanna." Betty smiled a knowing smile.

Both girls looked at her.

"What have you heard?" Louisa asked.

Betty tapped the side of her nose with her finger. "Well, I wasn't sure you and Sam were still on, but let's just say he's been seen in one of them shops along the High Road, and I don't mean the hardware store."

"Not the jewellers?" Louisa asked.

"Could be ..." Betty looked delighted she'd given away a secret without having mentioned it.

Joanna's stomach sank. Surely, he hadn't bought an engagement ring? But that was what Betty was suggesting. It was too soon. She and Sam had been out to the cinema with Harry and Louisa on several evenings and even gone for a drink in the Laindon Hotel bar, but they didn't know each other – not well enough to marry.

Sam's van had broken down and he and Harry had arranged to meet them at the hall.

"Don't mind Mum," Louisa said when they'd left the florist. "Sometimes her imagination runs away with her. If he really was looking in Bartholomew's window, he could have been interested in a new watch for himself."

Sam had not been able to wait and had walked along the High Road towards the girls to meet them. Harry followed, grumbling about the cold, and pointing out they'd arranged to meet inside the hall. Nevertheless, he offered Louisa his arm as they walked. Sam put his arm around Joanna's shoulders. Why couldn't he simply offer her his arm? She steeled herself, wanting to throw him off, and he mistook her reaction for a shiver of cold and pulled her tighter.

"I'll keep you warm," he said. "I'll always look after you."

Her stomach twisted again. Suppose Betty was right? What would she say if he proposed? He'd look after her, she knew, but she felt as though she was being sucked into a pile of feathers – warm, soft and comforting, but ultimately, they'd smother her.

And worse, suppose he proposed in front of people? Would she be able to refuse him then, knowing how foolish he'd look? But she couldn't accept.

Was that fair? Perhaps she ought to consider it. Why was she hesitating? He clearly idolised her and would do what he could to make her happy, even if that meant she had to fit in with his plans. But wasn't that how marriage worked?

It certainly hadn't been how her parents had behaved, but with Pa so ill, that wasn't surprising. Neither was it how Sheila and Bill shared their lives, but Bill was so placid, he did whatever Sheila wanted. It appeared most women did as their husband demanded. Would it be so bad? So far, Sam had only shown her respect.

It wasn't as though she could ever be with Ben. She knew that with all certainty now. Yes, he had feelings for her as she did for him, but even if Emily Bailey wasn't in the picture, Joanna knew Ben's parents definitely were. He'd dropped her hand so abruptly when his father had entered the office, and that told her everything. Ben was ashamed of her, and his pretty words about not worrying about the smell of mothballs and the inequality in their class were just words. He was unlikely to accept her as an equal. And if he did, his parents certainly would not. She wouldn't be his mistress, although she doubted that was on his mind. But logically, that was the only option open to them. Their love would have to remain a secret, in a relationship that would satisfy no one.

"Joanna? Did you hear me? Shall I take your coat?" Sam looked at her quizzically.

"Oh yes, thank you." She'd been so deep in thought she'd been standing trance-like in the vestibule.

Well, it was too late to do anything about Sam now. She'd just have to let him down as gently as she could and hope that if he asked her, it would be in private.

As she stepped into the lively atmosphere of the hall, she felt more relaxed and optimistic. She wouldn't marry Sam if he asked. She didn't need to be with anyone. Once she had her cottage, and the ownership of the land had been determined once and for all – as it surely must – she'd save her money and live on her own. Surely, life would treat her more fairly in the coming year?

When she took off her coat, Sam surveyed her with open-mouthed admiration. "You are truly beautiful. The most stunning woman here."

She certainly felt more glamorous in Louisa's pink dress than she had the last time she'd been in the hall. Sam offered her his arm, and they walked through the excitement and gaiety onto the dance floor with Louisa and Harry.

Despite his size, Sam was a good dancer, and as the evening progressed, Joanna began to enjoy herself, wondering if Betty had been mistaken. Then, Sam suggested he fetch them drinks, and sit the next dance out. His face was radiant, like an excited boy, and foreboding filled her. They sat at a table in the corner away from everyone else, and Joanna breathed a sigh of relief there was no room for such a large man to get down on one knee. She prayed he'd simply been thirsty.

He fumbled in his pocket and brought out a small box, then pulled back the lid, revealing a ring. "Joanna, you must know how I feel about you." He paused, smiling at her as if she'd already accepted. "I want you to be my wife." He lifted the ring and reached for her hand.

Joanna froze. Before he could separate her fingers, ready to slip the ring on, she snatched it away.

He hadn't even asked her to marry him. He'd told her what he wanted and assumed she'd do as he wished. Again, he reached for her hand, as if he thought she'd misunderstood his intentions.

Joanna stood up. "Thank you, Sam. That's very kind of you, but I'm not ready to marry."

He looked at her uncomprehendingly. "Do you need more time? Is that it?"

It was on her lips to say yes. She'd just been taken by surprise and that she needed more time, but that would simply push the problem into the new year – the year she'd promised would be hers. No, she had to be clear and not leave him any hope that in the future, she'd marry him.

"I'm sorry, Sam. I'm afraid we won't be getting married. Not now, not later."

His face twisted into an expression she'd never seen before, and she involuntarily moved away from him –

her back against the wall. He stood up, knocking his chair over backwards, and, after placing his large hands on the tabletop, knocking over their drinks, he leaned towards her.

His voice was low and menacing. "You'll regret this. Stringing me along like that. Letting me believe you wanted to get married. What kind of girl are you?"

He strode from the hall, knocking people out of his way as he went. Louisa rushed over. "Heavens, darling! What happened?"

Tears welled up in Joanna's eyes, and she swallowed down the lump in her throat. "He proposed, and I turned him down."

Louisa gently shook her head. "For what it's worth, I think you did the right thing. I've been talking to Harry, and Sam isn't the right man for you. Harry says he's become more controlling than ever. Never mind, he's gone now and I'm sure you'll have lots of partners tonight."

She held out her hand for Joanna and pulled her out of the corner, handing her over to Harry so they could dance.

Louisa had been correct. Joanna had no end of men asking her to dance after Harry had gone back to Louisa and spent the rest of the evening with her. Gradually, the earlier unpleasantness was replaced by relief. The more she thought about it, the more she wondered how she could have been so compliant – submissive even. She hadn't wanted to hurt his feelings, but in being mindful of his needs or wants, she'd lost herself. During each of the evenings she'd spent with him, she'd been on edge, not knowing what to expect from him. Now, she was free to be herself and to please herself.

When the church bells rang out at midnight, the dancers cheered and sang, pouring out into the street. Optimism for the New Year flooded through Joanna. As she turned to go back inside to get her coat ready to return to Louisa's, she saw Sheila and Bill. They were craning their necks, looking through the crowds of revellers, with worried expressions on their faces. She rushed over to them and saw a dark smudge across Sheila's forehead, and her usually tidy hair was in disarray.

"Oh, lovey!" she wailed. "I'm so sorry. We have some bad news. We'd just got back from Florrie and Tom's and found your cottage on fire. Bill and I finally put it out, but there's not a lot left. I'm so sorry, lovey."

1931 – January 1st

Joanna woke late, her eyes swollen and red, the smell of charred wood in her nostrils. She'd insisted on going home with Sheila and Bill, despite them trying to persuade her to stay with Louisa as planned. The journey home had been silent; each lost in their own thoughts. When she'd arrived, she'd walked over the plot with a lantern; there hadn't been a great deal to see. Charred, wet wood steamed in the frosty night air; jagged black ruins ghostly in the starlight. The only reminder that her cottage had once had walls.

There'd been no source of fire nearby, but no one had voiced any thoughts about how the fire might have started. Joanna hadn't mentioned the proposal and Sam's parting comments that she'd regret turning him down. Was he capable of such a vindictive act? She didn't know. He appeared to be an intense, complicated person, and while she'd done as he wanted, he'd been besotted with her. But now she'd rejected him? Could he have taken back the work he'd done for her?

In the living room outside her bedroom door, several neighbours had gathered and were talking in hushed voices with Sheila and Bill.

"It's a crying shame. That's what it is. A crying shame." Florrie's voice was followed by murmurs of agreement.

"I bet your lad, Sam, will be devastated. All that hard work he'd put in. All gone. Just like that." Mrs Benson from the house opposite tutted her disapproval.

Joanna sat up in bed to listen for Florrie's reply. Mrs Benson's comment suggested Sam might not know.

"I 'spect so. I haven't seen him since last night. He

left a note to say he'd gone to visit my parents in Whitechapel. He's such a kind lad. But he'll be devastated when he gets back and finds out. Funny, I thought he'd have some good news for me this morning. But I 'spect he's biding his time."

"What d'you mean, Florrie?" someone asked.

"Never you mind."

"Well, that's not helping Joanna," Sheila said. "We need to pull together and help her out, poor girl. She don't deserve such bad luck."

Murmurs of agreement met Sheila's words, and the voices faded as everyone went outside, presumably to view the damage. The neighbours were now too far away for Joanna to hear their words. Their concern for her was touching, but somehow, although in the past her neighbours' kindness had given her a warm glow inside, on that morning, she might have been made of stone.

It was 1931. It was supposed to be her year. Yet she was no further forward in her life than she had been when she'd come to Plotlands. Then, she'd arrived believing she owned a cottage on a piece of land. Now, she wasn't even certain she could prove she owned the land on which a pile of wet ashes stood. And she'd angered Sam. So, he'd gone to visit his grandparents? If he had started the fire, how convenient if everyone believed he'd been in London. But people had seen him at the dance and would know he'd had sufficient time to get to her plot and then to London by morning.

What did it matter? If he was caught and punished, how would that help her?

There was a tap on her door. "Lovey, I've made you a nice cuppa. When you're ready, come out and I'll tell you how the neighbours are planning to help."

Chapter Seven

Frank O'Flanahan stood outside Green Haven. He felt sick.

In his arms, Jack pointed a podgy finger at the burnt ruins. Frank gently placed his fist over the tiny hand and enveloped it. Somehow, it didn't seem respectful to point, even if the tiny child knew no better. Frank turned away so Jack could no longer see the blackened remains and ash.

Beside him, Mary held on to Gracie's hand and pulled her away. "It's not right! Such a wicked thing to happen to Joanna. I went into town this morning and there's a whisper going around: it was the Cavendish lad. You know, the big, brooding bloke. I've always thought there was something suspicious about 'im."

"Hold yer tongue, woman! You're as bad as that Betty Russell, spreading rumours! I mean," he added more gently, "it don't do to condemn a man until he's had a chance to speak for himself."

Mary snorted. "If he'd hung around, he'd have had a chance to speak for himself. But he ain't here. Funny that ..."

Frank didn't reply and the O'Flanahan family returned to their home. As they walked up the path,

Frank looked at his cottage with fresh eyes. It was a fine house. Well, relatively speaking. It was nothing like the large houses in the district – such as Priory Hall – but in Plotlands, it was considered one of the finest. Not surprising because he'd been in the money for some time. He'd told Mary he'd had a large win on the horses, which was partially true. But 'large' could mean anything. He'd won enough to secure the land, but the other money Mary thought was winnings had come from a little side-line he had in London.

He was a decorator and builder, turning his hand to most things, and had been employed by Jonas Parker to refit one of his nightclubs in Soho. Frank had soon noticed the punters were drawn from London's underworld. He'd skirted the edges of the murky depths of the East End's criminal life until he'd met Mary. Since then, he'd kept himself out of trouble.

Until recently.

Parker didn't pay well for Frank's decorating skills, but from time to time, he'd asked him to run a small errand. Nothing too dodgy. Just delivering parcels. Frank didn't ask what he was carrying. He just took the extra money at the end of the week. And then, he'd foolishly joined a game of poker. It had taken him a while to work out how the game was rigged, but by that time, he'd lost a tidy sum. And that meant doing more little jobs for Parker. But the more he owed, the more he found himself caught in Parker's grimy web.

"I'm going up to London this evening." He glanced sideways and saw Mary purse her lips.

"Why can't you go to the local pub with the neighbours? We don't live up in London now."

"I'm not going drinking. I've got some business to attend to. It might be the last time I have to go to London."

She looked at him with pleading in her eyes. "Really? And you won't get involved in a game?"

"I won't be playing poker. I told you. I've given that up. It's a mug's game. It's strictly business."

Well, it was true he wouldn't play poker. That evening, he was going to a boxing match. He knew one of the fighters and he was going to place a big bet on him. If he won, he'd clear the debts he owed Jonas Parker and walk out of his world forever. If not ...

He couldn't afford to consider that outcome.

He had to win.

Then, he could set his life straight. No more lies to Mary. No more delivery jobs in London. And then there was the matter of the Marshall girl. He owed her. She'd helped his family, and he'd ranted at her. He'd been angry at himself for having lost money in a bent poker game, and when he'd thought she'd handed Jack over to a stranger to take back to Mary, he'd let rip at her.

She'd accepted his apology, but Frank O'Flanahan

always paid his debts. He intended to repay in full ... and to rid himself of Parker. But that depended on Growler Baines winning tonight in the boxing ring. If he lost, Frank would be more in trouble than ever and no nearer repaying his debt to the Marshall girl.

Cheers. Catcalls. Shrill whistles. Faces twisted with blood lust, anguish, despair. Inside the ring, two men circled each other, bare fists raised, lunging and retreating. Outside the ring, punching fists stabbed the smoky atmosphere, pumping with triumph, encouragement or anger.

Frank's nails bit into his palms as he jabbed the air, urging on the boxer who controlled his future. His voice was hoarse with shouting, as if he'd been gargling acid.

Veins stood out on his neck. Much more of this and something inside his head would burst. And if Growler Baines didn't win, it'd be a good thing if it did. Loss tonight would mean Frank would be in Jonas Parker's pocket for the rest of his life.

Frank pressed his knuckles to his mouth as Danny Spencer, the favourite to win, stabbed a fist towards his opponent and caught a glancing blow on his head. Baines staggered backwards against the ropes, and Frank sucked in a mouthful of smoky air into his lungs until they were fit to burst. Had the world slowed down? Baines' mouth slackened and his eyes lost focus.

He's going down. *You've lost everything. Everything...*

But instead of slithering to the floor, Baines sprang sideways, avoiding the next blow by the merest fraction of an inch. Spencer was caught off guard, believing – like Frank – that Baines was finished. Before he could swing again, a bell rang to end the round. The fighters were dragged apart.

Frank tipped his head back and stared at the ceiling, running his hands through his hair. That was close. The beat of his heart drowned out the roaring crowd. Baines appeared to have given all he had. But he'd survived that round. He was still in with a chance.

The slimmest of chances.

Both boxers slumped in their corners. Their seconds sponged them down and urged them on for the next round.

If only Frank had bet on Spencer, but he'd had a tip from a mate who'd assured him the smaller, wirier – but less experienced – Growler Baines would win, despite Danny Spencer appearing to have the advantage.

"Big stakes," his mate had said, "Don't bet small. Yer won't regret it."

Frank's breathing was ragged. What should he do in the likely event he lost all his money? He'd insured himself, so Mary and the children would be all right. But as for him, he'd take a walk down to the river later ...

The bell rang and a barrage of sound reverberated around the hall as the two men stood. Sweat dripped down Frank's forehead into his eyes. As he wiped the blurriness away with his sleeve, he heard a fist slam into flesh, then the crunch of bone. He blinked and momentarily, his vision cleared in time to see a body hit the floor with a thud. The crowd surged forward to the ropes, roaring approval ... or displeasure. Frank sank back into his seat, his chest heaving as if he was sobbing, but if any sound scraped across his raw throat, it couldn't be heard in the chaos. He held his head in his hands and watched as the bleeding fist of the winner was raised in the air. Growler Baines had won the fight, and Frank had won enough to buy his freedom. Tears ran down Frank's cheeks and dripped off his chin. He sat there slumped in his seat, weak with relief.

Frank picked up his winnings and tucked them inside his jacket. No celebratory drink for him – he had work to do, and he needed a clear head. He hurried through the dark streets, past drunks and people who had partied all night and were now on their way home. At Jonas Parker's nightclub in Soho, he took a deep breath and sauntered in. David Jarvis was at the door, and Frank waved a greeting.

"You're late tonight, O'Flanahan. Or are you early?"

"A bit of both," Frank said. "I'm supposed to be

decorating that new office. But 'e wants it started yesterday. I'm not sure I've got all the paint I need. I thought I'd get ahead while it's quiet. Make a list of everything and buy it in one go."

"Right." Jarvis's attention was caught by two drunks who were approaching the entrance. He stood up and barred their way. "Evenin' gents, I think you ought to be on yer way 'ome."

One man started a scuffle, and while Jarvis was occupied, Frank hurried away from the foyer and made his way upstairs. He'd come across a bunch of keys while he'd been decorating and had new ones cut from them, replacing them before anyone noticed. The door to Parker's office was locked, which meant he hadn't returned from his other club. Frank tried to steady his hand as he inserted the most likely looking key into the lock. Suppose none of them worked? There'd been no time to try them out. It turned freely. Frank let himself in after a glance up and down the corridor, then locked the door behind him. He selected several of the small keys and inserted them one after the other in the locks on the desk drawers until they opened.

But now, what to take? What would be most incriminating? He finally decided on some addresses and accounts. After putting them in a folder, he slipped it into the waistband of his trousers and did up his coat.

"That was quick. You finished decorating already?"

Jarvis laughed at his joke as Frank rushed past.

"Got me list," Frank said. Then, remembering his hands were empty, he tapped his head. "All noted up here. See you later."

"Not me, mate. I got a few days off." He stepped closer to Frank.

Did he suspect something? Frank held his breath.

"Keep it under yer 'at, but I got a new job. Silver Stephens offered me more. Personal bodyguard." He nodded proudly.

"Good luck," Frank said.

"Remember. Keep it to yerself until I'm gone."

"Will do." Frank walked quickly, keeping his ears open for the sound of anyone tailing him. It was impossible to believe he'd got away with it. He ducked into a doorway and waited in the shadow, but no one appeared. After glancing up and down the road, he slipped out of the doorway and, keeping to the shadows, hastened away from Soho.

Next to Whitechapel Estate Agents.

With all he'd witnessed and the documents he had, there was enough to incriminate Jonas Parker and put him away for a while. However, there was one piece of information he needed, and it would most likely be in the estate agent's office.

By the time he arrived at the office, the sun was cutting through the grey gloom that hung over London.

Frank had already done some repairs in the office and had a key to that, too. He let himself in. It was later than he'd liked. The woman who cleaned the office would arrive soon. He'd better hurry.

It took him fifteen minutes to find what he was looking for, but finally, he had the receipt. It was made out to Mrs Rose Marshall for plot number 18, Second Avenue in Dunton, Essex.

It wasn't worth the paper it was printed on. Frank knew Parker printed out documents to please himself, making them look official and fooling the unsuspecting. Nevertheless, it would provide more evidence against Parker. He grabbed a handful of other papers as well and let himself out of Whitechapel Estates. Next stop Fenchurch Street Station and home. And with any luck, he'd never need to come to London again.

After a few hours' sleep, Frank got up. He ignored Mary's disapproving glances. She obviously thought he'd been out gambling again, despite his promise to quit. Although, to be fair, he had been gambling. But not in the way she might have imagined.

No. It had been much worse.

And might still be even worse than that.

One day, he'd make it up to her and the kids. It remained to be seen how long that might take. Frank ate his breakfast in silence. There was nothing to talk about, but plenty to consider. What he did next would be just as dangerous as the risks he'd taken last night. He intended to go to the police. He'd bargain first, hinting at the information he had and trying to make sure he didn't dump himself in it. But one way or the other, he was going to bring Parker and his henchmen down with all the paperwork he'd stolen the previous evening and the details he'd remembered. He may not be the smartest bloke in the world, but he had an excellent memory, and he'd soaked up everything he could while he'd been on all of Parker's premises.

But first things first. He'd go to Priory Hall, hand over the girl's receipt, and let them know the fire had been Parker's work. Mary had told him the Cavendish boy was under suspicion. No point in anyone else having their life ruined. Someone had wanted to buy several plots together and Parker only had a few dotted about, still remaining for sale. If he'd chased the Marshall girl and a few other people off, he'd have made a tidy sum. So, he'd paid some of his men to torch it.

Frank had never deliberately hurt anyone, but in fetching and carrying for Parker, he might have inadvertently caused harm to someone else. Had he ever delivered guns, for example? Perhaps not. And in all likelihood, he'd never know, but going to the police might go a small way towards making amends. Whether the police would be satisfied with the information he gave them, and his explanation he'd merely conveyed messages and parcels to others without knowing what was inside, he had no idea. It was a gamble. But this was definitely the final one. He'd never risk his family again.

If he were allowed one more chance, he'd make a go of it.

When Frank O'Flanahan arrived at Priory Hall asking for Mr Richardson Sr, Ben was home alone. He explained his parents were both at church. His mother had been annoyed he'd refused to accompany them, deciding instead, to go riding on his own. She thought Emily would be at the service with her parents, but Ben knew better. Emily had told him she'd be staying overnight with Ian Padgett-Lane, and he'd deduced she wanted to make him jealous. His lack of interest had stung her, and she'd accused him of being less than a man. Well, what did he care?

He was about to leave for the stables when the maid rushed in and said a rough-looking man was at the door asking for Mr Richardson Sr.

"I told him Old Mr Richardson weren't here, and he said you'd do, sir." The maid hadn't been in Priory Hall long, and Ben suspected his mother wouldn't tolerate her much longer. She would find the maid's voice too shrill, her way of speaking too common, and her apron too dirty.

"Did you ask his name?"

"Frank O'Flanahan, sir. He's in your father's study."

Ben groaned. It was the angry man who'd been so unpleasant to Joanna and Sheila outside Laindon Station. How he could have imagined that man had fathered a child with Joanna, he didn't know, but then again, he had no notion how she could have become involved with Sam Cavendish. But realistically, what were Joanna's options? Most girls he knew thought of nothing but marriage. Who, of all the men Joanna might know in Laindon, would be suitable? The thought of her with anyone made him grind his teeth.

Let it go. She'll never be yours.

He was tempted to keep his boots on and go into his father's study to see the man. It would infuriate his mother. She'd liken him to a common farmer traipsing mud across the carpets. Not that his boots were muddy. Mother insisted all footwear was cleaned and polished as soon as anyone entered the house and took off their shoes or boots. In fact, it was probably that maid who'd just appeared in a dirty apron who'd last cleaned his boots.

So many petty rules in this house. So much to know before you could hope to fit in. He wondered if the maid recognised she was in danger of losing her job because her mistress considered her socially inferior.

Once again, Ben stared into the chasm between the

social ranks. He kicked the second boot off and once again, wondered why people focused on the differences. If two people loved each other, they should be able to overcome any obstacle, surely?

He loved Joanna. But that wasn't enough. He was now ready to defy everyone – even his parents. But if he brought Joanna into his world, she'd be under constant scrutiny. And constantly found wanting. That would ultimately make her unhappy.

So, don't bring Joanna to Priory Hall.

There are other places. Make your own life. Take a risk.

The thought brought him up short. Yes, why not? He had savings so he could afford to be independent.

Excitement prickled his skin. Of course! What was the matter with him? Why hadn't he thought of it before? The carefully erected walls that separated his life from Joanna's were only there because years of tradition propped them up – and he allowed them to. After the Great War, the world had begun to change. Society was no longer as rigid. Not that his parents would have noticed, and if they had, they'd have ignored it. But he needed to put all those years of rules and assumptions behind him.

Don't fit into other people's ideologies. Create your own.

He hurried along the entrance hall to his father's

study, taking in the details he normally didn't notice – the grandfather clock, the ornate mirror, the expensive vase, the telephone on one of the walnut hall tables. Of course, he couldn't have brought Joanna to the grandeur of Priory Hall. But if he owned a small house …

Ben opened the door to his father's study.

Later, after Frank O'Flanahan had gone, Ben tucked the receipt in his pocket. He'd ride over to Plotlands and put Joanna's mind at rest about ownership of her land. There would be more legal work to do before she had all the correct documentation, but he'd make sure it was done. If Frank O'Flanahan's plan worked, the world would be rid of at least one criminal for a few years, and that would mean that Joanna was safe from his swindling and cheating. He'd also tell her he loved her and that he'd give up everything for her.

Joanna picked up a length of timber. One end was charred, and she wondered whether there'd be enough wood left to be useful if it was cut off. She sighed. Her chest was numb, and her limbs felt heavy, as if all movement was an effort. But she had to rescue whatever was useful before she started again.

Start again.

How was she ever going to do that?

She wanted to kick the pile of recovered timber and send it spinning, but that would've served no one. Sam had come around to see her on several occasions and she was almost prepared to believe he hadn't started the fire. He'd been shocked. Stricken. Enraged, even, that his work had been destroyed.

But really, what did it matter who'd started the fire? Or whether it had simply been a freak accident. She'd poured her savings into this cottage and even the timber that had been stacked up ready to form the roof had been damaged. Most of her money literally gone up in smoke.

Sam had returned several times and offered to put some of his own money into rebuilding. She'd thanked him but firmly rejected his offer. Sam alarmed her. He was unpredictable, and she craved stability. She wouldn't give him an opportunity to make her feel beholden to him again.

The muffled thud of hoofs caught her attention, and she swung around. It was Ben, leading his horse. He stopped at the edge of her property and after handing her the receipt; he told her the good news. Briefly, he explained what Frank had done and how he'd asked Ben to convey that he hoped it would compensate a little for his unpleasant behaviour towards her.

Was there something wrong with her?

The land was hers. It was everything she'd hoped for, but she simply felt emotionless. The joy that should have burnt brightly was quashed by the thought of starting again. So much wasted money and effort. The weight bore down on her, making it hard to breathe. Even the sight of Ben didn't touch her, as if an invisible wall had come between them.

"That night, fires were started in two other properties along Second Avenue and damage was done to several others. If everyone had sold cheaply to Parker, he could have made a tidy sum. Unfortunately for you, yours was the only fire that caused so much destruction. Those other cases of arson only came to light when their owners returned from London to find the damage. But you can rebuild. Frank said your neighbours have made a collection to start you off. The weather will improve now, so I'm sure it'll go up in no time."

Go up in no time. Joanna wasn't sure she had the energy to consider starting again.

There must be something positive about the situation. "So, Sam Cavendish wasn't responsible?" she asked.

"No, Cavendish had nothing to do with it." Ben's smile dropped at the mention of Sam's name.

"Thank you for taking the time to tell me, and for bringing back my receipt." Joanna smiled at him. "Well, I don't want to keep you. I need to go to the Cavendishes to let them know." Had she been impolite? She hadn't invited Ben into Green Haven, nor had she been particularly friendly. He hadn't simply been passing or he wouldn't have had her receipt. But the heaviness that had lain on her since the fire had slowed her thinking, and now she could only think of Sam. She owed him an apology for believing he could have behaved so spitefully.

She'd tell him about Parker's involvement and apologise, then walk away. If he had any thoughts of rekindling their friendship, she'd make it clear there would never be anything between them. That would only be fair. But perhaps he no longer had any interest in her.

Already, there was too much ill-will in the neighbourhood. Sheila and Bill's friendship with Florrie and Tom had faltered while suspicion had hung over Sam. Neighbours had taken sides – mostly against Sam. And all because of her. Everything needed to be resolved as swiftly as possible.

Ben started to say something and then stopped. She turned away, keen to go to Speedwell and give the good news. There was nothing more to discuss with Ben.

His face at first had been happy and excited but now, he appeared resigned; his expression the one he wore at work when he met with clients – competent, formal. "The authorities will inform the Cavendishes, but I'm sure they'll be pleased to know immediately. Well, I'll bid you a good day."

As he turned and left, she thought she saw the mask slip, and pain reflected in his expression. She couldn't cope with anyone else's pain. There'd been too much of her own.

Joanna brushed the ashes and charred wood off her hands, and as she set off towards Speedwell, she wondered if he would walk alongside her for a while. But he didn't. He mounted his horse and set off in the opposite direction. She looked back several times, but Ben did not.

The worst thing about telling Sam was seeing the tears in his eyes. For such a private and seemingly strong man, it was shocking to witness.

How had everything come to this? Florrie and Tom were reserved, and although Florrie offered Joanna tea, she refused, saying she had to get back. There was so much to do. Florrie seemed relieved she hadn't wanted to stay.

Sam accompanied her to the gate and asked quietly, "Is there any chance for us, Joanna? I can see how it might look like I'd caused the fire." He hesitated for a second. "I sometimes act a bit wild, but I'd never harm you. I'll help you rebuild. I'll have it up again in no time." His eyes begged her, and she was glad of the detachment that had overtaken her. At least she wasn't tempted to please him.

"Thank you, Sam. That's very kind under the circumstances. But I have to say no."

His eyes narrowed, and he turned away and strode

into the house without a backwards glance. The door slammed behind him.

Joanna slowly walked to Green Haven. She'd touched so many lives. When she'd first arrived, people had been welcoming and generous. And she'd brought unhappiness to so many of them.

She'd fallen in love with Ben. A man who could never be hers. Then she'd unintentionally drifted into a one-sided relationship with Sam. If only she'd followed her instincts and acted decisively in the beginning, she wouldn't have hurt him so much.

And then there was Sheila and Bill's friendship with Florrie and Tom. That was in jeopardy. All because of her. Everything she'd touched had gone wrong.

Ben had promised he'd get the correct paperwork to show that plot 18 belonged to her, but now, in her mind's eye, she couldn't see her cosy cottage on it. She couldn't see past the images of the burnt-out shell of what should've been her house. As she approached Green Haven, she fancied the smell of burnt wood still hung in the air like a malevolent lingering ghost.

Perhaps she ought to sell up and start again somewhere else? It would take a while before she had enough money, but she'd save hard and sell her land – once she had proof of ownership. She'd go far from Plotlands and its memories.

But where to go?

Why not Brighton to be near Uncle John? That was as good a place as any. When she got back to Sheila's, she'd search for Uncle John's address.

Uncle John's address had to be in Joanna's canvas bag. She hadn't used it since she'd arrived in Plotlands when the rain had soaked it during the storm – she'd merely dried it out and put it away. It reminded her of Ma. It also brought unpleasant memories of Aunt Ivy who'd stolen Ma's velvet, beaded evening bags, but rejected the plain canvas one.

Joanna found the bag at the bottom of a drawer and tipped the contents onto her bed. Out fell a few items she'd forgotten about; a small comb, a pencil, and the key to her parents' house in Wimbledon. Joanna sank to her knees next to the bed and held the key tightly in her fist. It seemed so long ago since she'd been home with Ma and Pa. What would they think of her now? They'd understand she'd meant no harm to anyone.

Why did you leave me? I need you. I can't manage alone. See what a mess I've made of things.

How many times had Ma and Pa used this key? Tears filled her eyes, as it bit into her palm. She squeezed harder, trying to draw comfort from gripping something they'd once held. So small, yet so vital. Without it, there was no entry. Why couldn't she find the key to unlock a new life? She relaxed her grip, the imprint of the metal remaining deep in her hand. Her parents would never again communicate with her and at the realisation, she wanted to throw the key down in childish, impotent anger. Instead, she placed it gently on the bed. This was one of the few things she had left to remind her of her parents.

Joanna must accept she was alone. Protesting at the unfairness of it wouldn't help her. She peered inside the bag for Uncle John's address. It wasn't there. It had been in there, she was certain. She'd thought of writing to him on several occasions but had wanted to wait until her cottage was built so she could tell him about it. He'd have been worried to know she'd arrived in Dunton to find an empty plot of land. Raking through the bag, she discovered it was empty. Empty? If she hadn't already been on her knees, she'd have sunk to the floor.

Well, wasn't that typical? Having decided to leave, she now had nowhere to go.

A spark of defiance flared inside her. Simply accepting everything life threw at her wasn't helping. She must stop being so feeble.

She turned the bag inside out in case it had slipped into a hole in the lining.

It must be here.

She stood up angrily and shook it. Nothing could fall out of a bag that was inside out, but it was good to use some of the pent-up fury. If Ma hadn't made it, she'd have hurled it across the room, or ripped it in two. Her eye was drawn to the base of the bag where the lining seemed to have come apart and something was poking out. It was the slip of paper on which Uncle John's address was written. Thank goodness.

But had something else worked its way through the hole? She investigated, slipping her fingers inside, between the lining and outer canvas. It seemed Ma had used something to stiffen the bottom, but as Joanna's fingers closed over its edge, it pulled free. Of course, the stiffening – perhaps cardboard – would have become wet in the storm. But as she pulled, something separated from the rest and came away. Her jaw dropped open when she saw it was a banknote. Five pounds. Ma must have hidden it from Aunt Ivy, and luckily, it had survived its soaking. Joanna inserted her fingers again and gently eased out the rest of the paper. More five-pound notes. Hairs stood up on the back of her neck as she smoothed out each banknote until in front of her, on the bed, was the huge sum of fifty pounds. Presumably, the money that had remained after Ma had sold the furniture and her rings.

It was a fortune.

Her body had been rigid with anger, but now, her muscles trembled with fatigue, and she laid her head on the counterpane next to the bank notes. Her parents had provided for her after all, and finally, something was going her way.

Why didn't she leave as soon as possible? She'd be able to pay Sheila an extra sum on top of her rent to compensate for any trouble she'd caused. And she'd travel to Brighton to find Uncle John. If he wasn't there or not in a position to help her, she had enough money to find a room. Once she had a job, she'd be able to save and since her needs were few, she'd easily find somewhere to live. Perhaps not her own cottage – just a flat. But who needed a cottage in the country?

On Monday morning, Joanna went into work. She'd been dreading the moment since she'd decided to leave Dunton. There was so much to do in the office and things were about to get busier, so she was reluctant to leave Mrs Pike alone to deal with it.

But the sooner she made the break, the better. She'd overheard Sheila tell Bill that Dolly and Ray wanted to come and stay. That would mean five adults and a baby would be crammed into Green Haven.

No, she needed to leave so everyone could get on with their lives. Mrs Pike would soon find someone from the Black & Snowden Employment Agency who'd be suitable. There'd be no shortage of help and Mrs Pike would soon acquaint them with her office procedure. Joanna's mouth was dry as she entered the office.

Mrs Pike felt one of her nervous headaches coming on. It was lucky she'd arrived at work early that morning to receive Mr Richardson Sr's telephone call. She knew there'd be an increase in the workload she and Miss Marshall had to get through the next few weeks, but she hadn't foreseen an outbreak of influenza in the London office. Apparently, a third of their employees were away sick. And at such a busy time. Thank goodness the two offices were separated by miles. Mr Richardson Sr had told her that until further notice, the two sets of staff would be kept apart, and his son wouldn't be going into London as planned until the influenza outbreak had run its course.

He'd said it might even be necessary to close the London office completely, although the next few days would tell. So, it was important they all work as hard as they could and that he'd be very grateful for all she could do.

Mrs Pike massaged her temples. It was hard to see how she and Miss Marshall could work any harder. Her efficient management of the office and Miss Marshall's energy ensured they always met their targets.

But work harder?

Thank goodness for Miss Marshall. She was young and fast, and, as Mrs Pike admitted to herself, a pleasure to work with. Not like some flighty girls she'd had the misfortune to have managed in the past. She'd been doubtful at first, assuming Miss Marshall's youth and attractive face meant she'd be as dizzy as the others, so it had been a pleasant surprise to find otherwise. Until the epidemic was over, Miss Marshall would definitely be an asset.

It was regrettable that since Young Mr Richardson wouldn't be going to London, he and Miss Marshall would be in the office together – and would be for the foreseeable future. However, there would surely be insufficient time for either of them to become distracted.

She'd seen their glances. As soon as their eyes met, they immediately looked away. But Mrs Pike was aware of them watching each other.

One thing was certain, it would end in heartache. Indeed, she suspected it may already have done so after the Laindon Christmas Dance. A romance between them simply wouldn't work. Or, more accurately – it wouldn't be allowed to work. Mrs Richardson would ensure that. Mrs Pike knew she shouldn't think ill of her employer's wife but really, it was hard to warm to such a cold woman. And it was a puzzle how she'd managed to raise such a fine son.

Mrs Pike had done her best to warn Miss Marshall, but she expected her advice had been ignored. She winced as a sharp pain shot through her temple. That boded ill on such a busy day.

Unfortunately, Miss Marshall seemed to be slow getting started that morning. Usually, she took off her coat and hat, sat down and began to work, but today she opened and closed her handbag repeatedly, in a distracted manner. Could she already know Young Mr Richardson was coming in? No, that wasn't possible. She'd only just found out herself and the decision hadn't long been taken.

So, if not that, what was amiss? She looked up as Joanna stopped in front of her desk, holding a letter.

What now?

"Yes?" she said, making it clear she didn't want to know.

"I'm so sorry, Mrs Pike. Please believe me that this is the last thing I wanted, but I ... I must hand in my notice."

Pain stabbed at Mrs Pike's temples and grew in intensity as her entire head throbbed. She stood up slowly, placed her knuckles on the desk, leaned forward and said slowly and deliberately, "You will do nothing of the sort, Miss Marshall. Put that letter away and go back to your work."

She then explained about the influenza outbreak in London and how they would be extremely busy. There was no time to engage anyone else, and it was unlikely Mr Richardson Sr would agree to take on anyone from their usual employment agency which was situated in London – the centre of the epidemic.

"I'm sorry, Miss Marshall, but if you expect a good reference after leaving the company while it's in such trouble, you must think again."

Mrs Pike couldn't make eye contact with the girl. Threatening her with a poor reference was a low blow. But really! This was extremely poor timing. If she wanted to leave, she'd have to wait until things were more settled.

Mrs Pike's head was throbbing fit to explode, but it wasn't as if she'd be able to go home and rest. She'd carry on.

"Well?" Mrs Pike stood up and crossed her arms over her chest. "Don't just stand there, Miss Marshall. We have work to do. Go and make tea I have one of my headaches."

Miss Marshall's mouth opened as if to say something. Then it closed, and placing the letter back in her handbag, she went into the kitchen. Seconds later, Mrs Pike heard the rattle of cups and saucers.

Yes, she'd been heavy-handed but needs must, and thankfully, the girl had backed down. She massaged her temples, then took two tablets from the bottle in her drawer and when the tea arrived, she took them. Hopefully, the pain would be gone soon.

Later, when the headache had subsided, and in softer tones, she asked Miss Marshall what had prompted her resignation. There was no time to chat, but briefly, Miss Marshall explained how she believed she'd caused problems for the Guylers, their friends and the intense young man with whom she'd spent much of the Christmas Dance.

"So, the fire and your suspicions about the young man ruined a perfectly good romance?" she asked. There wasn't really time for all this chat, but it was part of Miss Marshall's decision to leave and therefore important.

"No, it wasn't a perfectly good romance. And in a way, it's a relief. The young man in question felt more for me than I felt for him, and ... Well, it's just better we know where we stand. But he's still hurt, and that was my fault."

"Nonsense. No point in being with someone just because they like you. It's a good thing you're no longer with him in my estimation, Miss Marshall." Her tone was sharper than she'd intended. "And am I correct in thinking there is someone else in your thoughts?"

Miss Marshall blushed but said nothing.

"There's no need to explain to me. I can see that it is indeed the case, but there's no need for more detail. It's really none of my business. It is, however, my business whether you finish that work." She pointed towards a pile of papers. Miss Marshall sat at her desk and continued typing.

So, it was probably as Mrs Pike had suspected. There were still feelings for Young Mr Richardson.

What a shame.

Mrs Pike opened her drawer and rummaged at the back. She pulled forward a small, framed photograph, which she left concealed from Miss Marshall. She never displayed it on her desk. It was too painful. Inside the frame, a young man gazed back at her, a slight smile on his lips, and hope in his eyes. Like so many British Tommies, Philip had gone to France during the Great War, full of patriotism and a desire to do his duty. She gently eased the photograph to the back of her drawer, feeling the familiar stab of pain in her heart, even after so many years.

And now, here in front of her, a young woman's heart was being torn apart, just as hers had been. Not because of the war this time, but society and its inflexibility. That was ironic, since the Great War had disrupted the class structure, but obviously not enough to help Miss Marshall. On the other hand, Miss Marshall hadn't specified that she was interested in Young Mr Richardson. Perhaps she had her eyes on another? No, surely not. She wasn't that kind of girl. Throwing longing glances towards Mr Richardson, but with another young man in mind? Mrs Pike knew enough about Miss Marshall to be certain that wasn't the case.

However, it didn't matter what she felt if Young Mr Richardson didn't return her feelings. His glances said he did, but then he was a man. And Miss Marshall was a pretty, young woman. No, this wasn't lust, she'd been around long enough to know what was what. So, what to do? Perhaps, for the sake of peace – not to mention productivity – in the office of Richardson, Bailey & Cole, Mrs Pike must take things into her own hands

Clack, clack, clack.

Mrs Pike checked the clock, and after clearing her throat to attract Miss Marshall's attention, she announced it was time for lunch. The typing stopped, and the young woman flexed her fingers and curled them into fists, relaxing her hands after a busy morning.

After putting on her hat and coat, Miss Marshall went next door to the florists to eat lunch with her friend.

Mrs Pike's headache had almost gone, although the odd twinge confirmed it hadn't quite relinquished its grip. It was understandable. Too much worry. She'd had so much to do, she hadn't been able to give much thought to the conversation she must now have. No time to prepare. But perhaps that was just as well. Maybe it would be better if she simply came out with it.

Rising slowly, she tried to assemble a few thoughts. Suppose her imagination had clouded her judgement and incorrectly filled in the many blanks?

She thought back to when Miss Marshall had stood up to go to lunch a few minutes ago. She'd glanced towards Young Mr Richardson's office and had immediately looked away. To Mrs Pike, that said that he'd heard the scrape of her chair and had looked up and intercepted her gaze. Evidence they were both interested in each other. But that was supposition. Had she been reading something into nothing?

Mrs Pike took a deep breath. She was about to solve several problems at once, or to make a fool of herself – not to mention anger one of her bosses.

Well, this was it. Knowing how conscientious Miss Marshall was, she'd be back before her lunchtime had finished, so if Mrs Pike intended to carry out her plans, she must do it now. After a deep breath, she pulled back her shoulders, patted her bun to check her hair was tidy and tapped firmly on Young Mr Richardson's door.

"Come in."

Mrs Pike entered and stood, feet apart, hands behind her back in front of his desk, refusing his invitation to sit. She might as well get it over with. This would not be a cosy chat.

"Mrs Pike, what can I do for you?" His eyes lingered on the document he'd been reading. He was busy today, too.

"Mr Richardson," she said in a crisp, business-like voice, "I apologise in advance for what I'm about to say and hope I don't cause offence. However, I believe it must be said for reasons that will soon become apparent."

His attention was completely on her now. "Is something wrong, Mrs Pike? I realise the workload has increased significantly but—"

She held up her hand to stop him. "What I have to say is only partially to do with work, as you will see. It is more of a ... a personal nature."

"Ah, I see." He relaxed slightly. "Well, I hope you know you can talk to me. I assure you anything you tell me will be held in the strictest confidence."

"That is most kind, however, it's not my personal life I wish to discuss. It's yours."

Deep furrows appeared between his eyes. "I see." His tone was now guarded.

"I'm not sure how to say this, so I will simply come out with it." She swallowed and gripped her hands tightly behind her back. "I have been reading between the lines for several weeks now and I've come to several conclusions. Of course, I may be wrong. However, I hope you will indulge me for a few moments while I discuss this delicate matter. Perhaps it will be best if I tell you what I've seen and what I have deduced. If I am completely wrong, then I hope you'll forgive me and agree neither of us will mention this conversation again. However, if I am correct ..." She paused.

"If you are correct?" He rolled his pen back and forth beneath a fingertip. It was a gesture she'd seen before. He was uncomfortable.

Well, so was she.

Mrs Pike swallowed, trying to moisten her mouth, which had suddenly gone dry. "Since Miss Marshall started working here, I have noticed a certain ..." She looked up for inspiration, and finding no more delicate way of saying it, she said, "... a certain attraction between you. Miss Marshall watches you while she thinks you are unaware. You watch her under the same circumstances. When your glances meet, you both immediately look away." Again, she paused to see if he'd deny it, but other than rolling his pen, he said nothing, simply stared at her. She continued, "Indeed, the attraction is almost palpable."

His eyebrows rose slightly in surprise.

"Not that anyone else would have noticed. But I spend a lot of time with you and Miss Marshall, so I, alone, have the opportunity to notice these things. And then at the Christmas Dance ..."

A shadow passed across his face and his Adam's apple bobbed as he swallowed.

She pressed on. "I saw how close you and Miss Marshall were. However, as you know, your mother was also aware."

He nodded and looked away.

"And then, after I delivered your mother's message, suddenly everything changed, and Miss Marshall spent the rest of the evening in the company of a tall, brooding young man who made it his business to look after her. I have since had it on good authority ..." Mrs Pike's cheeks coloured slightly at this, knowing that her source of information was Betty Russell. But gossip or not, she was usually correct. "That Mr Samuel Cavendish is a rather controlling young man. Definitely an unsuitable companion for Miss Marshall."

Now, Mr Richardson appeared confused. She must get to the point. "I expect you're wondering where this is leading?"

He nodded.

"Before I make that clear, I will just say that I notice you have not denied that you are attracted to Miss Marshall ..."

Still, he said nothing.

"And my guess is that Miss Marshall is still extremely drawn to you, despite Mr Cavendish. And now, the reason I mention all these things is that this morning Miss Marshall tried to hand me her resignation."

"What?" He sat up straight, alive, alert.

Ah, so he does care.

She held up her hands. "Of course, I did not accept her resignation. However, I am ashamed to say I threatened to withhold a good reference if she simply walked out. I thought this would give us time to change her mind."

"But why? Why does she want to leave? I thought she was happy here." His eyes were wide with alarm.

"She intends to go to Brighton."

"Brighton? Surely not"

Oh yes. Young Mr Richardson's face showed more than simple dismay at losing an excellent employee. He was horrified.

"Miss Marshall feels – incorrectly, in my opinion – that she has disrupted people's lives. That odious criminal, Parker, robbed her of more than her house when he ordered it to be burnt. Now, she feels she's in the Guylers' way and is preventing their daughter from staying, thus depriving them of not only their daughter's company but also of their grandson. And then there's the matter of Mr Cavendish. She feels guilty she suspected him of arson. Not ..." Mrs Pike looked over the top of her glasses at him. "Not that she is attached in any way to the young man. But he seemed to have formed an attachment to her, and she knows she's hurt him. Good riddance to him, I say, but that's by the by."

On hearing Miss Marshall wasn't involved with the Cavendish man, Mr Richardson's face had softened. So far, so good. Her assumptions had been quite correct.

"I deduce from your reaction you wouldn't like Miss Marshall to leave the company, nor Laindon. But I'm wondering what you're prepared to do in order to prevent those things from happening. I'm also keen to know you have her interest at heart. Arguably, this is none of my business, but I have formed a liking for the girl and having precipitated something, I wouldn't like to think that my meddling resulted in her heartache."

"Mrs Pike ..." He paused as if considering how to proceed, then taking a deep breath, he finally added, "I believe from what you've said that you've correctly interpreted the situation and I appreciate your sensitivity. Please let me assure you I have nothing but Miss Marshall's best interests at heart. I believed she and Mr Cavendish were together and I had therefore tried to put aside my feelings. However, I'm slightly at a disadvantage since I don't know how Miss Marshall feels about me now. Do you think there's still hope?"

"I'm afraid I don't know, Mr Richardson. Miss Marshall is hardly likely to confide in me."

He nodded sadly. "But you mentioned earlier, you thought it possible to change her mind?"

"Yes." Her voice was slow and deliberate, wondering how he'd react to her idea. It was certainly going to take a lot of organising. But at least she now knew Mr Richardson's position on matters.

She explained her plan.

He leaned back in his seat and smiled. "Do you think it'll be possible?"

"I will need a little help, but I don't anticipate any problems."

As she left Young Mr Richardson's office, her head was spinning with all the things she needed to arrange, but strangely, her headache had completely gone.

She sat down at her desk and opened the drawer, then checking to ensure no one was observing her, she withdrew the framed photograph. She sighed as she gazed at the figure proudly staring back at her. Philip Pike. Her Philip. The man who'd proposed to her on the eve of his departure for France during the Great War. The man who'd arrived home a few months later unable to walk and with disfiguring wounds. And the man who promised to marry her – if she was still willing – as soon as he was able to walk down the aisle. That future wedding had given him something to aim for. She dabbed her eyes as his image grew hazy through the tears, remembering how hard he'd worked to walk. The shrapnel wounds had caused more damage than had been suspected. Philip had never walked again, and he'd died a few weeks after his return from France. At his funeral, she'd decided to leave her village and start again in London. How could she possibly live among so many reminders of their love? On arriving in the capital, she'd introduced herself as Mrs Mabel Pike. A few more weeks and it would have been true – she would have married Philip. But she'd refused to allow a matter of a few weeks to rob her of the name she'd most wanted to bear. It was all she had of her beloved Philip – and who was to say she wasn't worthy to have it?

Now, two young people were on parallel tracks, travelling in the same direction at the same time – but never together. If one of them needed a nudge so they could join the other and travel side by side, then she had nudges aplenty.

Chapter Eight

While Joanna had been at work, Bill and several other Plotlanders had cleared her land. Shortly after, it had snowed. A thick, sparkling layer of white covered the earth, smothering all evidence of the fire, as if it had never been. Each time it looked as though it might thaw, more snow fell, creating a glittering, magical world.

Everyone did their best to clear the pathways to allow easier access, but ruts in the avenues that had been created by cars and vans were concrete-hard. Walking was treacherous because of the ice and the uneven ground beneath the snow. Joanna wore her rubber boots to work as did everyone else and there was an array of boots in the kitchen of Richardson, Bailey & Cole lined up on newspaper, keeping warm for the return journey at night.

Joanna was glad Mrs Pike hadn't accepted her resignation. She'd written to Uncle John at his cousin's address but hadn't received a reply. If she'd known his cousin's name, she'd have written directly to her to ask where he was. If Uncle John wasn't there, no one would open a letter addressed to him. A snowstorm had hit Brighton, causing havoc. She knew because Harry had returned to Hastings, and had written to Louisa, describing the bitter conditions. Combing a strange town for accommodation and a job without Uncle John's help in such atrocious weather was an unpleasant prospect. There was no choice. She must wait until it was convenient for her to leave work and by that time, surely the weather would have improved.

At least she could forget the fire, since all evidence was beautifully draped in crisp snow. From time to time, footprints appeared in the fresh snow, and she assumed Bill was keeping an eye on things for her. Dolly didn't want to risk coming down to Laindon with young Billy, who had a cold, so Joanna didn't feel awkward about sleeping in Sheila's spare bedroom. And the awkwardness between the Guylers and the Cavendishes had eased, although Joanna didn't accompany Sheila and Bill when they visited Speedwell.

The snow took several days to melt, leaving puddles and mud everywhere across Plotlands. It was still cold, but the heavy frosts that shimmered in the moonlight each night gradually became less intense. As snow thawed on roofs, huge icicles hung from eaves and dripped during the day when the temperatures rose.

The number of influenza cases had fallen. The London office was now fully manned, and Joanna expected the workload would begin to decrease in Laindon. It would shortly be time to consider her move.

Sheila had offered to spread the word amongst the neighbours to see if anyone wanted to buy the land. She knew so many people – many of whom had families who still lived in the East End. If anyone could find a buyer, Sheila could. However, Joanna was saddened by the enthusiasm with which Sheila assumed the role of her estate agent. It was surely a sign she wanted to be rid of her guest.

Despite her many connections, after several days, Sheila hadn't found a buyer. Perhaps the bad weather was putting people off considering buying land in frozen Essex. However, it would soon be spring and that would be a good time for people to think about moving.

Ben had gone into the London office on two days the previous week, and Joanna expected he'd soon be there permanently.

Permanence. Such a comforting word. How wonderful it would be to know she had a place in which she'd always belong. When she'd first arrived in Laindon, she'd thought she'd found that place …

"Miss Marshall!" Joanna looked up and realised she'd been staring at her typewriter keys, dreaming.

"Yes, Mrs Pike." She looked across the room with what she hoped was an enthusiastic expression.

"Have you finished the documents for Silverman Brothers yet?"

"Nearly. I've one more to type."

"Excellent. I'll need them for next Friday. Mr Silverman is coming over a few days earlier. He's bringing his wife to London for a brief holiday, or as he says, 'vacation'. I hear it's even worse weather in New York than here, so at least it won't be too much of a shock. Such a nuisance, though."

"Nuisance?"

"Yes. I don't mind going to London for the day, but I certainly didn't want to stay the night. Mr Richardson Sr said he wouldn't dream of allowing me to come home so late on the train, so now I'll have to stay. And it's all well and good giving me the name of a nearby café where I can eat lunch but, really, how am I supposed to know when they've finished their meal? They'll be in a smart restaurant a few streets away." Mrs Pike moved paper from one pile to another and back again. "I simply must remember to pack indigestion tablets." The prospect of the trip to London was disturbing her.

"And if that wasn't bad enough, after lunch, I'll have to take notes at the business meeting. Although, that will be easy. But afterwards, the gentlemen will go to Mr Richardson's club, and until they return, it'll be my job to ensure Mrs Silverman has whatever she needs. Who knows what that might be? But hopefully, the gentlemen will finish early and come back to take Mrs Silverman to dinner. Then I'll be free."

For once, Mrs Pike seemed remarkably talkative. She

was a woman of habit, and Joanna could see how such a change from her usual routine might well make her anxious.

But how exciting it would be to go to London and glimpse such a grand world – even if only for one day.

On Friday morning, Mrs Pike arrived at work with a bag packed, ready for her night in London. Rather than the excited expression Joanna had expected to see, Mrs Pike's brow was furrowed, and her mouth set in a hard line.

Joanna knew she had tablets for her headaches in the top drawer of her desk, but she was usually very secretive about taking them, holding the bottle in her lap, and quickly transferring the pills to her mouth. That morning, however, she placed it on her desk in full view. After shaking it and rattling the tablets to get at them, she asked Joanna to bring her a glass of water. Her head obviously hurt more than usual. And what a day to have a headache. She'd have to set off for London shortly.

"Should I ask Dr Nichols to call, Mrs Pike?"

The elder woman looked up sharply. "You are employed as a typist, Miss Marshall, not a nurse. Thank you. I shall carry on."

Mrs Pike repeatedly checked the clock, and Joanna assumed she was dreading the time when she'd had to leave. Perhaps her tablets would work before then.

At a quarter to eleven, Mrs Pike groaned and massaged her temples. Joanna was alarmed. The headache hadn't improved after taking her tablets. Indeed, Mrs Pike seemed much worse.

Was it time to suggest calling Dr Nichol again? Joanna hesitated. Mrs Pike was a private woman who hated a fuss. She'd deal with the condition herself.

Assembling a notebook, pencils, pens, and paper, Mrs Pike tucked them in a folder. She groaned again and sat down heavily.

"I'm so sorry, Miss Marshall, but I don't think I'm well enough to go to London today." She shook her head sadly. "But I can't countenance the idea of letting the company down. I wonder if I could persuade you to take my place? I'm sure once you are no longer needed to take notes, Mr Richardson will ensure you get home safely since you don't have your washing things and a change of clothes. Mrs Silverman will manage quite well, I'm sure." Her eyes, normally so guarded, now appeared feverishly intent as her gaze bored into Joanna.

Go to London?

Well, why not? She was perfectly capable of taking notes in shorthand. Hopefully, that would persuade Mr Richardson to look upon her favourably when she finally handed in her notice. A good reference and perhaps a recommendation would help her find a new job. And it wasn't as if she had plans for that evening. Louisa had invited her to the picture theatre, but she'd cancelled the previous day.

"Yes, of course, I'll go."

Mrs Pike sank back into her chair, her hand on her chest. She heaved a sigh of relief. "Thank you, Miss Marshall. I appreciate it." Her voice had gathered in strength.

"Well, chop, chop." She held out the folder she'd just filled with stationery. "No time like the present." It was almost as if the pain had halved after knowing she didn't have to go to London.

Joanna put on her hat and coat. "I need to let Sheila know I might be late—"

"I'll do that. Leave it to me."

To Joanna's surprise, Mrs Pike put on her hat and coat and held the door open for her. Then she followed Joanna out onto the snowy pavement and walked towards a parked car. Opening the door to the passenger seat, she bent over and leaned in to speak to the driver, then indicated that Joanna should get in.

"I thought you said you were going by train, Mrs Pike."

"I planned to go by train, but this trip to London is so important Mr Richardson sent a car."

As Joanna got in, she saw the driver was not a uniformed chauffeur.

It was Ben.

"Good morning, Miss Marshall," he smiled. "What a lovely surprise."

"I ... I'm so sorry. Mrs Pike isn't well. She's asked if I'd go instead."

"Excellent." Ben pulled away, along the High Road.

"I hope your father won't mind me taking Mrs Pike's place."

Ben shook his head. "I'm sure he won't mind at all."

Mrs Pike's skipping days were long past, and anyway, the pavement was too icy for such nonsense, but inside, she was skipping. She walked briskly into Rosie's Posies, where Mrs Guyler, Mrs and Miss Russell were peering through the glass door.

"Well done," said Mrs Guyler. "She's been so down recently, I wasn't sure she'd go. But I brought all her personal items and underwear, as you instructed."

"I packed the dress she wore on New Year's Eve, and the suitcase is in the car," Miss Russell added.

"Well, that's our part done successfully. It's now up to the pair of them," Mrs Pike said.

"That calls for tea." Mrs Russell turned the sign on the door to 'Back Soon'.

Chapter Nine

Ben fought the urge to reach out and take Joanna's hand and hold it in a reassuring clasp. Repeatedly, she tucked hair behind her ear, smoothed the front of her jacket, straightened her sleeves, and checked her buttons.

Of course. He should have realised she'd feel uncomfortable eating lunch in this expensive restaurant. If he were to stand a chance of winning her over, he'd have to try harder to see things from her perspective. It was a shame they'd already ordered, or he might have suggested leaving and finding somewhere less ostentatious.

Well, it was too late now. He must find a way to put her at ease. It wasn't beyond him – he'd done it on the journey from Laindon to London. At first, she'd been apologetic, believing she was a poor substitute for trusted Mrs Pike. He'd almost owned up then and told her she was part of a carefully laid plan to get her into London to give them both time to spend together. Of course, at any point, if she expressed the wish to go home, he'd immediately take her. But he was desperately hoping she'd give him a chance to declare his love and to reveal if she felt the same.

He leaned towards her. "Have I mentioned you're

the most beautiful woman in this restaurant?"

She blushed deeply and after looking shocked; he thought he saw the glimmer of pleasure. "That's not a very business-like thing to say."

"But we're not at work now. And I know it's probably something men say to women to flatter them, but in this instance, I was merely stating the truth."

The colour in Joanna's cheeks heightened, but at least his comment, as clichéd as it had been, was accurate and truthful. One of the few honest comments today so far ...

When she found out the truth, would she feel foolish she'd been deceived, and refuse to listen to his explanation?

Mrs Pike had been responsible for thinking up the scheme. Without her and the other women in Joanna's life, it would have been impossible to organise. But how would Joanna receive the news that Sheila Guyler had packed her a bag so she could stay in London overnight? That her friend, Louisa, had lent her an evening dress, and that Mrs Pike had feigned sickness so Joanna could be there with him? Would she be angry with them, too? It was true she'd be required to take shorthand notes at the meeting later that afternoon with Mr Silverman. However, now the 'flu epidemic was over, and the company was fully staffed once again, any of the girls who could take down shorthand would have been suitable. There'd certainly been no need to bring someone from the Laindon office.

And then, there'd been the lie that Ben would take the Silvermans to a dinner and dance in the Savoy that evening. Not true. After they'd concluded their business, Mr Silverman intended to travel to his visit his sister and brother-in-law on their estate in Surrey, where his wife was waiting for him. Mrs Pike had booked a table for two in the Savoy, for Joanna and Ben.

Exactly why Mrs Pike was keen to play matchmaker wasn't clear. She evidently liked Joanna and didn't want her to leave the company. But these were rather extreme measures merely to keep an employee. She'd used her outstanding organisational skills in masterminding this scheme, but ultimately, would her methods prove too heavy-handed?

A waiter served the food and Ben saw Joanna frown as she watched which knife and fork he picked up. She selected the same. If he hadn't known her so well, he wouldn't have noticed the brief hesitation. Why had he put her through this? He was now so nervous on her behalf, he'd lost his appetite. How much better it would have been to go to a small teashop or café.

As the meal progressed, he made her laugh and, hopefully; it was keeping her mind off the other diners. Certainly, her eyes didn't roam from his. That was a good sign, wasn't it?

Only time would tell.

Joanna had forgotten how busy the streets of London were compared to the relative calm of Essex. After leaving the restaurant, she didn't have to battle through the crowds and dodge between cars as she crossed the congested streets. Ben drove them to the London offices of Richardson, Bailey & Cole. The building was smaller than the one that housed the Tredegar, Murchison & Franklin offices about a mile away, but they were just as grand. People walked purposefully across the large, marble entrance hall, their footsteps and voices echoing.

This must have been a silent place when the 'flu epidemic was at its worst, but now, there were people everywhere and, as they opened doors, Joanna caught glimpses of the typing pool, the offices and the meeting rooms beyond. Surely, they had enough people here to take notes? Perhaps not. It was puzzling why Mr Richardson had insisted Mrs Pike come. But perhaps he trusted her more than the employees in London.

Ben led her up the stairs to an office. He made sure she was comfortable and had everything she needed. Shortly after, a woman knocked at the door and ushered a grey-haired gentleman with a silver-topped cane into the room. Ben stood and shook the man's hand, then invited him to sit. So, this was the elder of the Silverman Brothers, who ran a chain of clothes and furrier shops in

New York and Boston.

Joanna expected Mr Richardson Sr to appear and was surprised when Ben asked her to take notes.

The meeting was underway.

When Mrs Pike had said 'Mr Richardson', Joanna had assumed she'd meant Ben's father, but that didn't seem to be the case.

Mr Silverman had come to London to buy a new clothing factory and several shops for Silverman Bros. and had chosen Richardson Bailey & Cole as solicitors to act on his behalf when he returned to New York.

The immaculately dressed Mr Silverman spoke clearly, although with an accent, and Joanna found it easy to record everything in shorthand. At the end of the meeting, Mr Silverman shook Ben's hand and excused himself, saying he was keen to join his wife at his brother-in-law's house in Surrey. The two men walked towards the door and briefly carried on with their conversation.

Joanna sighed and was surprised to realise it wasn't a sigh of relief, but one of disappointment. Mrs Silverman had obviously changed her plans, and Joanna's unexpected and exciting day was about to finish.

If Ben wanted her to type the minutes now, she'd stay until she'd finished them. If not, presumably, he'd allow her to leave for the railway station to travel back home to Laindon.

She thought back over the day which had passed so quickly. It had only been a few hours ago that panic had numbed her when Mrs Pike had asked her to go to London. Now, she saw her fears of inadequacy had been unfounded. The shorthand notes she'd taken were perfect. Perhaps if she'd travelled to London by train, she'd have had time to think about it, and she might have calmed down. But Mrs Pike had rushed her out of the office and hurried her into Ben's car. That had been a shock. When she realised she'd be driving to London with Ben, she'd almost refused to go. But how could she have explained to Mrs Pike, who was relying on her? And how rude to refuse to go with Ben.

She could hardly have explained her reluctance was partly due to a lack of confidence, but mostly because she'd, unwisely, fallen in love with her boss. Well, it was no one's fault but her own. And hardly justification for letting people down.

So, she'd got into the car, dreading what looked as though it would be an excruciatingly embarrassing and silent journey. However, Ben had been a perfect gentleman. Amusing, attentive and kind. She'd relaxed so much, she was disappointed when she realised they were in the East End, rapidly approaching the City.

And as for lunch in that elegant restaurant ... That had been nerve-wracking, but Ben had been such marvellous company. After a while, it had been as if they were the only two people in the restaurant. He hadn't treated her like an employee but as an equal and she'd forgotten how out of place, she looked among the well-dressed women. His gaze had been so admiring, she might have been wearing the finest, most fashionable clothes. And it hadn't been simply her appearance. He'd talked to her and listened as if he truly wanted to hear her opinions.

It was as if they'd both been acting a part in a play. In pretending they were sweethearts, she'd experienced what it might have been like, had that really been true. Ben had not been formal and reserved, as perhaps he should have been as her boss. Instead, he'd been attentive and admiring. Simply perfect.

He must have seen how disconcerted she'd been earlier, and he'd put her at ease. If only they weren't playing parts, and they really were walking out together. But of course, that was impossible. They both recognised it. And, she knew, after he'd declared his love that day in his office, he'd moved on.

Once in the London office, with Mr Silverman, they'd resumed their roles of boss and employee. Now, business had been concluded, assuming Ben didn't want her to type up the minutes. Her stomach sank at the thought of going home. It had been a wonderful day, but now she'd served her purpose, it was over. She congratulated herself on keeping her emotions in check. If she was rational and behaved in a grown-up manner, then it was perfectly possible to hide her feelings. Soon, she'd be in Brighton, and she'd never see Ben again. Her stomach sank further.

The conversation finally finished and, with a glance over his shoulder at her, Ben escorted Mr Silverman to the entrance. Joanna put her notebook and pencil back into the folder and fetched her coat and hat. If Ben wanted her to type up the notes, she'd have to go to an office with a typewriter, so she needed to be ready when he returned. Walking to the tall windows, she looked out at the street below and orientated herself. She'd noted where they were as they'd driven through the streets, and she knew how to get to Fenchurch Street Station.

When Ben entered the room, she turned and looked at him expectantly. Would he want her to stay or go? Now she'd got used to the idea her day in London was over, she was keen to get on the train. It would be dark by the time she got back to Laindon.

He pinched his lower lip between finger and thumb and looked down at the floor. Was he uncomfortable about asking her to carry on working? Well, he'd been so kind to her, she'd make it easy for him.

"Would you like me to type this up now?"

"No!" He looked up, startled. "That is, thank you, but no."

"Then, please, may I go?" She started to put her coat on.

"No! I ... that is ... I wonder if I could persuade you to accompany me to the dinner and dance at the Savoy Hotel? Now Mr and Mrs Silverman have other arrangements ..."

Joanna looked down at her suit. "I'm afraid I'm not dressed for anything so grand. But thank you for asking me." Well, she certainly hadn't expected that! But still, he looked troubled.

He ran his fingers through his fringe. "Please sit down, Joanna. I have something to tell you."

That sounded serious. Had she behaved incorrectly in front of Mr Silverman? She was sure she hadn't. She hadn't spoken. She'd merely taken notes, and Ben hadn't seen those to judge them.

"Please believe this came from a place of kindness and affection." He sat down next to her. "And for my part, more than mere affection. Please don't be angry. No one was trying to make a fool of you."

Joanna stared at him. A fool? Did he think her a fool? Nothing made sense.

"It's just ... this day isn't what you think it is."

She frowned. "Then what ...?"

"The truth is Mr Silverman and his wife weren't invited to lunch nor to attend the dinner this evening. Mrs Silverman didn't change her plans at the last minute. She came to England to spend a week with her sister-in-law in the country. The only part of today that was scheduled was that meeting with Mr Silverman and as you probably saw, there are plenty of women working here who could have taken the minutes for us."

"Then why ...?" Was this some elaborate joke? But if so, it made no sense.

"Because I want to spend time with you." He reached out as if to reassure her, then let his hand drop. "Please understand, the second you say you want to go home; I will take you and I wouldn't try to persuade you otherwise."

"But how can that be? Mrs Pike should have been here. It was only that she was ill ..." Joanna stopped, remembering the exaggerated rattling and displaying of the pill bottle that was usually so carefully concealed. Mrs Pike's groans. Usually, she suffered in silence and certainly never drew attention to her malady. "So, Mrs Pike was in on this scheme?" Her voice was incredulous.

He nodded.

"But why?"

"That, I don't know. She's very fond of you. She told me she'd noticed there's something between us and thought that given an opportunity, things might develop." He reached out once again to take her hand, and then, thinking better of it, curled his fingers into a fist, and let it drop into his lap.

"I must admit, I wanted to give things an opportunity to develop too—"

She drew back and shook her head.

"Joanna, you can't deny there's something between us."

"I don't deny it. But it doesn't matter. We've talked about this before. It's madness. You know we can never be together. It's going to be hard enough when I leave, but you're making it harder."

"Then don't leave. Stay and let us sort something out together."

"No. The last time I allowed myself to believe we stood a chance, your father came into the office, and I saw your face. You leapt away from me as though I might scald you. I don't want to shame you. Trust me, you'd always be embarrassed. I wasn't even sure which knives and forks to use in the restaurant today ..."

He hung his head and was silent. "I don't care about cutlery. And the reason I moved away from you that day was because we were at work. Yes, I know my father will raise objections to us being together. He's old-fashioned. Proud. I'd need to take my time in telling him, and I know he wouldn't accept it immediately. But if he'd come across us in the office, he'd never have taken us seriously. He'd simply have assumed we were having an affair. But ashamed of you? Never! I promise you, Joanna, if you'll have me, that will never happen again … It's no excuse, but I've had a lifetime of obeying my parents, of doing what they wanted and fitting in – but no more. I have enough saved to go my own way, and I'm quite prepared to do that if I must."

She slowly shook her head. "It'll never work." It was so tempting to believe him, but she knew they could never overcome such binding social restrictions. He needed someone like Emily Bailey. And if not her, then some other society girl who'd fit into his world.

"Let me prove to you it can work. We've never spent time together and just enjoyed each other. The closest we've got to that was in the car earlier and at lunch today. Please come with me tonight—" He held up his hand to stop her refusal. "Before you say you can't go dressed as you are, then please don't be angry, but Sheila and Louisa packed a suitcase for you in case you agreed to go to the dance and wanted to stay overnight."

She wasn't sure which surprised her most – that anyone might expect her to stay overnight in London or that Sheila and Louisa had known and packed her bag.

He placed his hand over his heart. "And before you decide, please allow me to say I promise my intentions are entirely honourable. Mrs Pike suggested you stay in the company's apartment. Your suitcase is waiting for you there, and she booked a room for me in a hotel. In the morning, I'll drive you home. Please …" His eyes were filled with hope.

It was as if she was soaring in the sky, only to discover the earth was no longer below. It was to one side and however she tried to right herself, everything was in the wrong place.

"Please," he said again, his voice filled with anguish. He reached out a hand, his fingers stretching towards her.

Why not? Everything was out of kilter. There was nothing she could do about it. And he'd been right. She had enjoyed being alone with him earlier. Soon she'd be on her own in Brighton. Why not take this one opportunity to be with him before they parted forever? "Yes," she whispered. "Yes, please."

"I'll change your mind about us being together by the end of the evening," he said, his face now alight with joy.

He stood up and held out his arm to her. "Well, if you'd like to go to the apartment to change, please allow me to take you there. I must pick up my clothes before I check into the hotel, and I'll come back later to escort you to the Savoy."

The distinctive velvety scent of Guerlain's Shalimar wafted out of the suitcase when Joanna opened it. The perfume had undoubtedly been Louisa's doing. Joanna had told her about the smell of mothballs and her friend had wanted to ensure nothing like that happened again.

Joanna's breath caught in her throat as she pulled

out each item, lovingly packed by her friends. Underwear, stockings, shoes and even a pair of brand-new evening gloves, still in the bag that showed it had been purchased in Prescott's dress shop in Laindon.

The pink dress that Louisa had lent her at New Year was wrapped in tissue paper and she carefully unfolded it and hung it up, ready to put on after taking a bath.

She'd expected the apartment to be tasteful but hadn't been prepared for such luxury. Lofty ceilings, ornate fireplaces and surprisingly modern lamps, mirrors and artwork. Chairs with gracefully curved arms and upholstery covered in printed swirls and arcs. Ben said he'd given the maid the evening off – presumably aware that Joanna would find her presence disturbing. He'd been so thoughtful. It was tempting to imagine this might be her life from now on. But of course, it wouldn't. It would be best not to think about tomorrow. Concentrate on today. Pretend she belonged in this world of opulence. Well, why not? It wouldn't hurt for one night.

Joanna stood in front of the oval cheval mirror and observed her reflection critically. She'd done a reasonable job of pinning up her hair and, for once, the curls remained in place. Louisa's pink dress fit Joanna perfectly, hugging her slim waist and hips, then flaring out to fall in soft folds to her ankles. Louisa had made a small cape that fastened at her neck, draping over her shoulders and upper arms to make the gown even more sophisticated. Although the gloves had been bought in Laindon, they were wonderfully delicate and fit her perfectly. She turned around and viewed herself over her shoulder.

She'd never looked so elegant. If people didn't observe her too closely, she might appear to belong with Ben.

Well, she was as ready as she'd ever be.

"Joanna, you're absolutely stunning."

She blushed under his rapt gaze, embarrassed at such a reaction yet basking in its warmth. He held out his arm, and she took it. Tonight, she'd be someone else. Not the shy, awkward woman she really was, but someone who Ben deserved. Confident. A woman who knew her own mind, not the mousy office girl. And if she could be that self-assured woman for one evening, at least he'd have wonderful memories of her once she'd gone.

It was even easier than she'd thought to conceal she wasn't Lady This or the Honourable Miss That. In the subdued lighting of the restaurant, the only obvious difference between her and the other women was her lack of expensive jewellery. Louisa's Dralon dress looked as though it was real silk, and she allowed herself to believe she belonged in Ben's arms when they danced.

She pushed the memory of the embarrassment of the Laindon Christmas Dance from her mind and told herself she now smelt of Guerlain's Shalimar – not mothballs. And there was no one in the restaurant they knew. No one observing or judging. Just her and Ben. His body against hers, his breath on her cheek. If she closed her eyes, she could almost imagine they were alone, enfolded in the music.

With his arms around her and his heart beating against her chest, it was almost possible to believe they could have a future together. Well, why not? They made each other happy. No one else should be allowed to keep them apart. But there was so much to consider. Ever since she'd known him, she'd see-sawed between hope and despair. For an instant, she would believe they had a future, then she'd return to long periods where she experienced the pain of reality.

She checked her watch nervously. The hours were speeding past. Soon he'd take her back to the apartment and leave her. In the morning he'd drive her home. She wanted this evening to last forever. How exciting to know while they were dancing, they belonged only to each other. She didn't want it to stop.

A thought crept into her mind. Why should they stop? What if they could seize a few more hours in this private world they'd created? When they got to the apartment, she knew Ben would leave immediately. So, why shouldn't she suggest he remain with her that night? Most of his belongings were in the master bedroom, anyway. He'd only taken a few essentials to the hotel nearby.

Dare she?

Yes. She must. Because this would be the last time she'd ever spend with him. He'd talked about persuading her they had a life together. But if anything, she could see the possibility was more remote than ever. She was pretending to be someone she wasn't, and away from everyone's scrutiny, she was succeeding. But tomorrow ...?

Tonight would be the last time she'd spend with Ben, so why not be a night of firsts too? Not her first kiss. Sadly, that had been shared with Sam. But it would be the first kiss that meant anything, because it would be with the man she loved.

And it would be the first time she'd lain naked in a man's arms. She shivered at the thought of Ben's hands caressing her. His skin against hers. Longing burnt deep inside her.

"Are you all right?" he whispered in her ear. "Are you cold?"

She smiled up at him. That face would be the first thing she saw when she woke in the morning and excitement bubbled up like the champagne they'd shared with their meal. Not cheap fizzy wine like Jonas

Parker had served a few months before on his sales trip. This had been French champagne, and she now recognised the feelings of elation and excitement a glass brought. But this sensation had nothing to do with bubbly alcohol.

"Everything is perfect," she whispered.

Gradually, the crowd thinned, and the music slowed. The earlier sparkle in Ben's eyes had gone. "Well, it had to finish sometime, I suppose." He gazed at her hungrily, as if trying to drink in every detail.

"Daahling!"

The loud voice made both Joanna and Ben jump. She felt Ben stiffen in her arms, but it took her a second longer to recognise Emily Bailey with a partner, standing nearby.

"Emily. Padgett-Lane," Ben said, acknowledging the couple with a nod.

"Richardson," the man replied, gently tugging on Emily's arm to pull her away. But she had no intention of leaving.

"Benny, daahling! What a surprise! And fancy! You're with the little office girl. You naughty boy! Honestly, I didn't think you had it in you. But I suppose you're a man like any other."

The man Ben had called Padgett-Lane pulled her arm again, and she shook him off. "Stop being so tiresome, Ian. I can say hello to an old friend, can't I?"

Ian Padgett-Lane, standing behind Emily, winced as he gestured to Ben with his hand to show Emily had drunk too much. "Well, you've said hello, now, Emsy. Let's leave them to it," he said.

"Of course. I was merely expressing my surprise, that's all." She pulled her arm away from Ian, who'd taken it again, and stepped closer to Joanna. "Well, I must hand it to him. You're a pretty little thing when you make an effort. But don't get your hopes up, daahling. You're far too unrefined for our Benny."

Before Joanna could react, Emily had reached forward and seized the cape of Louisa's dress. She slipped the fabric back and forth between thumb and forefinger, sampling its quality.

"I thought so," Emily said, with a disparaging look. "Cheap and artificial. Some people might be fooled into thinking you're wearing silk. But not those in the know. Quality will always out. And you, my dear, are as cheap and artificial as this rag." She tugged at the cape, pulling it askew.

Ben stepped between Emily and Joanna. "Joanna is worth twenty of you, Emily. You're a nasty-minded, spoiled snob."

"Ooh! Careful, daahling! That isn't very kind at all. I might have to chat with your mama. She wouldn't appreciate you calling me names. She adores me."

"My mother has yet to see through your act. But eventually, she'll find out about your lies."

Emily put a finger against his lips. "Hush, daahling. Isn't that the pot calling the kettle black? I know women aren't supposed to have fun, but this is a new decade. Times are changing. Even your little trollop must be having a bit of fun. You've been inseparable all evening."

Ben pushed her hand to one side and took hold of Joanna's arm to steer her away.

"Oh, and if anyone at home should find out anything they shouldn't know about me, I'll know who told them. And don't think I won't fill your parents in on all the dirty details about you and the office girl."

The lump in Joanna's throat grew until it felt as though it was choking her.

And there it was. She hadn't even fooled people for one evening into believing she was worthy of Ben. She'd felt safe that evening. Free from prying, judging eyes, but she'd been wrong. She could only ever cause Ben embarrassment and trouble with his family. He'd talked about moving away, but she couldn't allow him to give up everything for her. In the end, he'd realise what a price he'd paid. Family mattered. Perhaps only someone who had lost theirs would realise how much. But in time, Ben would resent her for separating him from all he'd ever known.

She glanced up at Ben. His jaw was clenched. With

humiliation? Fury? Perhaps both.

It had taken Emily's spite to point out the truth. Joanna was too common for Ben.

Chapter Ten

Ben clung to Joanna in the taxicab on the way home, and she held on to him. He hadn't believed her when she'd spoken about this being their last evening together. But now he knew it was.

He'd hoped to persuade her they could do anything – be anything – so long as they were together, but Emily Bailey had destroyed any chance of that happening. He screwed his eyes tightly shut and felt every muscle in his body tense when he remembered Emily's sneer as she moved the fabric of Joanna's cape between finger and thumb. Jealousy. Sheer jealousy.

His chances of talking Joanna around now were negligible. She'd been humiliated. Could he really ask her to face that sort of behaviour from his parents and friends again? In all likelihood, it would happen over and over.

He'd happily move away – anywhere. Earlier that day, Mr Silverman had hinted if Ben should move to New York, he'd have plenty of business he could put his way. That would solve the problem. But would Joanna agree to uproot and move to another country where she knew no one? She'd already lost her family. Could he ask her to go somewhere completely new and start again? It was worth asking ...

The cab driver drew up at the entrance to the grand Victorian mansion where the company's apartment was situated, and Ben helped Joanna out. He had minutes to put his suggestion to her. Once in the lift, the attendant would prevent such a conversation, so he had to tell her of his idea now. Before he could begin, she took him by surprise. She'd also obviously been deep in thought on their way home.

She stopped inside the entrance hall and while they waited for the lift to arrive; she looped her arms around his neck. "I was wondering ..." she broke eye contact and bit her lower lip. "It's just that we've only got a few hours left alone. I don't want to sleep. I want to be close to you. Please don't go back to your hotel. Stay with me until it's time to leave in the morning?"

"Are you sure?"

She nodded.

"I promise I'll be on my best behaviour," he said, kissing the tip of her nose. He wanted nothing more than to hold her tightly, but he didn't want her to worry he might take advantage of her. Her last memories of him would be ones she'd cherish.

The colour in her cheeks heightened. "I was rather hoping you might not be on your best behaviour," she whispered.

The operator opened the doors to the lift and there

was no opportunity to carry on the surprising conversation. Had she misunderstood? Had he?

They got out of the lift, and when the doors closed, she took his hand. "I've been thinking about everything since we left the restaurant. If this is all the time we have, then I want to spend it with you. I want to share everything with you."

"Joanna, of course, I'll stay. There's nothing I want more than to spend time with you, but ..." This was not a conversation he'd foreseen having. He'd been so careful to show he wouldn't take advantage of her. Everything they did had to be what she wanted. He'd have driven her home immediately had she expressed the wish. If it hadn't been for her obvious embarrassment, he'd have assumed her comment about sharing everything had been an unfortunate choice of words. He knew she was inexperienced.

She smiled up at him shyly. "Please don't look shocked. I don't suppose it's the same for you, but I won't ever love anyone like this again. And if this night is all we have, then I want to remember it for the rest of my life."

He unlocked the apartment door and led her in. Without switching the light on, he took her in his arms. "I'll never love anyone like this again either, and I want to remember this for the rest of my life, too. But it must be for the right reasons. I don't want us to do anything you'll regret."

"I would never regret making love to you ... There, I've shocked you again." Her eyes pleaded with him to approve her suggestion. "Is there something wrong with me?" Now, her eyes were filled with dread.

He pulled her close and whispered in her ear, "You're perfect. And I long to make love to you, but I don't want to take advantage."

"But I want this. I may never see you again ... Unless ..."

"Unless?"

She bit her lower lip. "Unless we meet in secret. If you spend most of your time in London, I could get a room and a job here."

"No!" His voice was harsher than he'd intended, and she flinched. "Joanna, there's nothing I'd like more than to plan a life together – but not like that. I don't want people to think I'm ashamed of you. I'm proud to be seen with you. You deserve better than to be hidden away like a guilty secret."

There were tears on her lashes now as she looked up at him. "Then please make love to me this evening." She reached up and, standing on tiptoe, brushed his lips with hers. It was as though someone had turned the lights on. He loved this woman and if she wanted him to make love to her, he would. But she was wrong, assuming this was the last time they'd be together. Determination coursed through him. He'd win her over if he had to leave his family and move away – even as far as New York. There must be somewhere in this world where they could belong to each other without opposition and disapproval. This would not be the only night they'd spend together – it would be the first of many.

He kissed her more passionately and felt her shiver in his arms. Cold? Fear? He didn't know. The room certainly was chilly. He picked her up in his arms and carried her into the living room, to the low sofa in front of the fireplace.

"Please help me," she said. He could tell she was afraid.

"We'll take everything slowly," he said. "Slip your coat off and I'll be back." He hurried into his bedroom and pulled the quilt off the bed, then carrying it into the living room, he placed it over her on the sofa and tucked her in.

Next, the fire. He took off his jacket and added more coal to the glowing embers to make a blaze.

She watched with wide eyes; the quilt pulled up to her chin.

"I expect you assumed I wouldn't know how to do that," he said, pushing the coal scuttle to one side. He would show her she was more important to him than anything, and he was willing to do anything to be with her.

He turned towards her. "And the last, but possibly the most important step, is this ..."

Her eyes widened further as he approached her, but he continued walking into the kitchen and came back a few minutes later with two mugs of hot cocoa.

Joanna laughed. "This wasn't how I thought it would be when ..." She tailed off.

At last, she was relaxing. He smiled in mock indignation. "Are you laughing at my methods of seduction?"

She giggled, and he slid under the quilt next to her while they sipped their cocoa.

When they'd finished, he took her mug and placed it on the coffee table.

"Now what?" she whispered.

"Now," he said, "I put my arm around you and hold you tight and we can tell each other about our dreams."

"You don't want to ..."

"I do want to ... more than you'll ever know. I ache for you. But this is not our last night together. And I'll wait until the time is right. Then, it'll be perfect."

Sheila's face lit up when she saw Joanna at the door. Her expression asking, 'Well? What happened? Did all go well?'

At the sight of Joanna's tear-filled eyes, her face softened, and she sighed deeply. "I take it you two didn't work things out?"

Joanna couldn't speak. She swallowed the lump in her throat and shook her head.

"Right, you sit down, lovey, and I'll make a nice pot of tea. No need for details. But if I can help at all. I'm here."

Joanna wiped the tears away bitterly. It should have been so simple. She loved Ben.

He loved her.

In an ideal world, they'd have been happy together. Of course, no one was perfectly content all the time, but they'd have dealt with problems together.

When they'd woken in the morning, still dressed in their evening clothes, cuddling up beneath the quilt, he'd tried to persuade her again. He'd assured her they'd win everyone over, eventually. But she'd seen the spiteful look in Emily Bailey's eyes the previous night. Why should Ben have to put up with that? And how much could she take? It had been humiliating. Could their love survive constant snubs and insults? Ma had loved Pa with every ounce of her being, but once he'd come home from the Great War a broken man, their love had changed. They'd had years together on which to build a solid foundation. What chance would she and Ben stand?

He'd suggested they both go to New York and start again there, where no one knew them. But it would be such a big change. Suppose they didn't like America? Suppose they met the same prejudices out there?

Suppose his love for her died? Suppose, suppose …

At night, bathed in firelight, she'd seen a possibility of them being together. But as the insipid dawn light had stolen into the room, she'd known it was impossible.

"Here, lovey, get that inside you." Sheila placed a mug of tea in front of Joanna and sat down. "I hope you didn't mind me packing your bag like that. We all thought it might give you both a chance to get to know each other."

"No, it was really kind of you, Sheila. But I realised it wouldn't work."

"D'you love him?"

Joanna bit her lip to stop it from trembling and nodded.

Sheila shook her head sadly and sighed. "Well then, I suppose you'll be off to Brighton as soon as you sell the land?" She was close to tears.

Joanna hesitated. "No. Actually, I've had second thoughts about leaving. Ben and I talked about the possibility of both leaving. But it made me see I couldn't bear another move away from everyone I know. That's all I seem to have done since Pa died. Please could I stay with you and Bill for a few more weeks until the cottage is built? Then I'll get out of your way. You didn't find anyone to buy the land, did you?"

"Of course not, lovey. You don't think I was actually trying to sell it, do you? Your plot of land being up for sale was the world's best-kept secret! I hoped you'd change your mind before you found out." Sheila laughed so hard she spilt her tea.

"But I thought you'd be happy to be rid of me. I've surely outstayed my welcome."

"Get away with you! Whatever gave you that idea? Bill and I have loved having you here! You're like another daughter to us. But now you've found your mum's money, you could have a really posh house built. Get proper plans drawn up and everything."

That certainly made sense. Joanna would stay in Dunton. Ben would stay in London. He'd made it plain he didn't want her as a mistress. But she wouldn't allow him to give up his family, home, and job for her.

At least if she remained in Dunton, she'd have her friends around her. And since she now had Ma's money, she could afford to have a proper house built, not just a wooden structure. A solid home. Somewhere she belonged.

The news that Harry had proposed to Louisa was, of course, wonderful. Joanna was so pleased for her friend. Harry had found a job at a boat-building yard in Leigh-on-Sea, at the mouth of the Thames, and the couple would live with Betty, above Rosie's Posies, until they could afford a home of their own.

However, Louisa's happiness merely underlined how alone Joanna was. It was probably a good thing, she reflected, that she'd had to face the knowledge she was on her own. Each day, as Louisa bubbled over with excitement at the coming ceremony, Joanna's acute pain subsided to a dull throb – constant and distressing. But in time, she expected, it would become so familiar, she'd get used to it – always in the background but only breaking through into her consciousness from time to time.

She'd moved into the flat above the florist's shop to help with the dressmaking and other wedding arrangements. Once Louisa and Harry were married, there'd be no room for her, but by that time, she'd have the excitement of moving into her own home. The plans for her house had been drawn up, and while she was staying in Laindon, Bill was overseeing the work. He'd engaged the services of Fanshawe & Sons, the best builders in the area, and had even negotiated a reasonable price. The house would have a living room, kitchen and two bedrooms like Green Haven, but it would be brick-built – with provision for extending, should she wish. She knew she wouldn't ever want more room. The house was large enough for her. But Bill had argued it was wise to remain flexible. Finally, Joanna had agreed. After all, it was only allowing for the possibility of extending – not the certainty.

"Bill's having the time of his life," Sheila told Joanna on one of her trips back to Dunton to visit. "Thank goodness! It's been so wet, he hasn't been able to do much in the garden, but now, he's gone to Wickford looking for building supplies. Thank heavens! At least he's out from under my feet!"

Very little had been done on Joanna's plot, and the trenches dug for the foundations were waterlogged, their sides collapsing. Work had been abandoned before all the digging had been completed, and it was impossible to see an outline of the house. Bill had taken the plans with him, so Joanna couldn't consult them and work out where each room would be. It had been disappointing. But Sheila assured her that after Louisa was married and Joanna had to move out of Betty's flat, she'd be welcomed back at Green Haven. Once the weather improved, the men would begin work in earnest, and by the time she visited again, the progress would be noticeable.

"Bill says once they start laying the bricks, it'll go up in no time. You'll see, lovey, you'll be in there before you know it."

Sheila was probably right. And in the meantime, there was so much to do for Louisa's June wedding. Betty had the flowers under control and after many hours of poring over catalogues and fashion magazines, Louisa had decided on a wedding dress and the bridesmaid dresses for Joanna and her two young cousins.

Louisa had ordered the dress patterns, and she and

Joanna had scoured Mrs Waverley's shop for suitable fabric. Joanna had turned away and pretended to inspect the rolls of lace when Mrs Waverley had pulled down several bolts of white and pink Dralon for Louisa to inspect. Joanna had never told her friend what Emily Bailey had said on that fateful evening. It had been Louisa's dress that had been ridiculed. Or more specifically, the fabric, and Joanna didn't want her to suspect that someone might look down on it.

Harry and Louisa were saving every penny for their own home and hoped before long to buy a plot in Dunton. They might soon be her neighbours. So, it made little sense for Louisa to pay a fortune for real silk. Wasn't it more important she married the man she loved? A bitter taste rose into Joanna's throat, and she swallowed it down. This wedding would be perfect. Silk, Dralon or canvas. What did it matter? At least the bride and groom would belong in each other's worlds.

One Sunday morning, two weeks before the wedding, Joanna got up early without disturbing Louisa or Betty, to walk to Dunton. Whenever Bill or Sheila came into Laindon, they dropped into the office to update Joanna about the progress on her cottage. Since her evening in London, Mrs Pike hadn't mentioned her part in the scheme. Neither had she referred to Joanna's earlier attempt to hand in her notice. There had been a slight softening in the usual brisk starchiness. Not that Joanna intended to take advantage of it, but whereas before, she'd have expected Mrs Pike to show displeasure at Bill's frequent visits and updates, now she didn't appear to notice. The reports, however, were rushed and therefore brief and rather vague. The previous day, Bill had told her the builder had a few queries and he needed to speak to her in person. Could she be at the site the following morning at ten o'clock?

Joanna was glad she'd risen early. She hadn't realised how much she'd missed the openness of Plotlands. The smell of mown grass, coffee and frying bacon accompanied her as she walked along the avenues, and the sounds of alarm clocks, whistling kettles, and the scrape of cutlery against crockery seemed to welcome her home.

Land that had lain empty and neglected since she'd first arrived was now under new ownership, and properties were springing up. If Jonas Parker hadn't been in prison awaiting trial, he'd probably have been highly delighted at the number of sales. But according to Frank O'Flanahan, it was unlikely he'd be free to wander the avenues of Dunton or to enjoy any profit for many years. The police had uncovered so many illegal activities attached to his name; he was facing a lengthy stay in prison. And thankfully for Mary, who was livid with her husband, Frank had got off with a warning.

Joanna breathed in deeply again. So fresh. Soon she'd be back, living amongst her friends. Well, as soon as her cottage was built. The last time she'd visited, she'd been disappointed to see so few changes. Bill explained the builders had been called away on another job but said she shouldn't worry. Work had been done on things that weren't immediately obvious.

When she'd asked what sort of things, Bill had waved his arms vaguely and replied, "Oh, marking out, measuring, digging, ordering. That sort of thing."

There'd been little evidence of digging and marking out, but perhaps the measuring and ordering were taking time. If Bill was happy about it, then so was she. He even seemed satisfied with the position of the building, which appeared, to Joanna, to be slightly off-centre. But Bill said it had all been measured and when everything was complete, it would look right. She took his word for it. But the delays had been disappointing.

"Reg Fanshawe's in demand. He has to juggle jobs to keep everyone happy," Bill had told her. "But he's the most popular builder around these parts. He'll do you proud. You'll see."

Before Joanna turned the corner onto Second Avenue, she looked up to check Bill's flagpole. The green flag, which now hung limply in the early morning sunlight, was a welcome signal the Guylers were home. It had also come to symbolise friendship and kindness.

Ben had told her when he'd first visited Green Haven, he'd assumed Sheila was her mother. That was simply because they were living in the same house. Although no one could replace Ma and Pa, Sheila and Bill had become as close to parents as it was possible to be. How fortunate she was to have them in her life.

Ben. Sharp pain stabbed her. She'd expected the agony to have subsided slightly by now, but it still hit her afresh whenever she thought of him. Well, she must forget him and concentrate on her cottage. That would give her plenty to think about.

The rhythmic rasp of saws slicing through wood and the beat of hammers rang out in the still air. The sound intensified, and she smiled. At last, the builders were working on her house. She tried to guess how far they'd got, deliberately downplaying the image in her mind in case she was disappointed.

When she arrived at Green Haven, she saw there was even less completed than she'd allowed herself to imagine. When were they ever going to finish? There were so many builders there, it was hard to believe they'd achieved so little. Her heart sank. But if Mr Fanshawe wanted to talk to her, well, she wanted to talk to him – and she wanted some explanations.

Mr Fanshawe's trilby hat marked him out among his flat-capped men – that, and his clipboard and loud voice. He strode from one group of men to another, shouting instructions and waving the clipboard.

She wouldn't be intimidated. She was paying him to work and so far, he'd done very little.

"Mr Fanshawe." She congratulated herself on sounding confident and assertive. Qualities she definitely didn't feel with so many male eyes on her.

He looked up from inspecting his list with a scowl. "Miss Marshall, is it? Good, you're earlier than I expected."

"Yes. I wonder if you could explain why so little has been done and when you will be finished?"

"And I wonder, Miss Marshall, if you could make up your mind. I'll be able to tell you when we'll be finished as soon as you let me know what *you've* decided."

Bill rushed out of Green Haven, hastily tucking his shirt into his trousers. "Now, Joanna, there are a few things you need to know." He smiled at Mr Fanshawe and took her elbow, steering her towards his cottage.

"There've been a few ... er ... complications. Or perhaps I should call them developments."

"Developments?"

Bill's frown wasn't reassuring.

"The land next to yours has been sold and the owner ... well, let's say the owner has plans and there have been, err ... suggestions about your cottage."

"Suggestions? Do you mean complaints? Is the new owner objecting to my cottage?" This was outrageous.

Joanna knew owners were supposed to comply with building regulations, but in practice, very few people bothered to find out what they were, much less abide by them. Her cottage wouldn't be obtrusive – if it ever got built. How could anyone object?

"No, not objecting as such." Bill's expression was vague and innocent – the same one he wore when Sheila asked him if he'd been to the pub, and he didn't want to admit he had. "Come and have a cuppa. Sheila's put the kettle on. We weren't expecting you till a bit later or ..." He paused.

"Or?" Joanna tried to catch his eye, but he was looking anywhere but at her.

"Tea. That's what's needed. Tea. This'll soon be sorted out ... One way or another," he added under his breath.

Before Joanna could question him further, Sheila was at the door. "Come in, lovey. Tea's up."

While they drank tea, Sheila chattered nonstop, talking about her grandson and how clever he was. As soon as Joanna tried to steer the conversation back to the building work, Sheila thought of a funny story she had to recount. Meanwhile, Bill gazed out of the window, his attention completely on the builders. Joanna wondered if he felt responsible for the lack of progress, and awkward at having recommended them.

"Right," said Bill, standing up abruptly. "Time to

get things sorted out good and proper."

Joanna expected Sheila to appear as baffled as she was, but she jumped up too, hands fluttering. "Well, best you go out with Bill, lovey."

Mr Fanshawe was standing in the avenue with a group of his men. They were holding the four corners of some plans, and leaning over to inspect it, along with a smartly dressed man who had his back to her. Was he the architect? Was there a problem with the plans? But as Mr Fanshawe looked up and spotted her, everyone turned around.

The smartly dressed man was Ben.

Mr Fanshawe indicated to his men they should let go of the drawings, which immediately rolled up, and he handed them to Ben.

"I'd be obliged if you'd come to some sort of arrangement as soon as you can, Mr Richardson. Time's money. I don't s'pose I need to remind you." Then, in a quieter voice, he added, "I'm sure you can persuade the little lady to see sense."

See sense? Joanna bristled at the builder's tone. It was as if she'd been obstructive, and he was blaming her. If Mr Fanshawe had brought in a solicitor, it must be something serious. Something legal. And undoubtedly, something to her disadvantage. She didn't return Ben's smile as he walked towards her. They might as well get the bad news – whatever it was – over with, so she knew what she had to deal with.

"I'm sorry to keep you waiting, Joanna. I didn't realise you'd be so early. I dropped by Rosie's Posies to see if we could come here together, and I'd have explained. But you'd already left."

"Well, perhaps you'd explain now. I'm sure you'll be able to persuade me to see sense, as Mr Fanshawe said." Her voice was harsh. It was painful to see him again. To stand so close. To savour the faint spicy smell that teased her nostrils as it came and went. And it was even harder to recognise he was about to cause problems for her and disrupt her dreams of owning a cottage.

"Well," he said, his voice still friendly but now more formal. "It's like this. I've bought the piece of land next to yours—"

"You? Why?" Rage bubbled up inside Joanna. The merest thought of him was torture, but to live next to him and see him often …

Ben held up his hand. "Please wait and hear me out, Joanna. Have you changed your mind about me?"

"What difference does that make? We can't be together. Living next door will just make things harder—"

"No, it won't. I know it would be hard for you to live in my world. We've already seen that. But I've just come back from New York. I went to see Mr Silverman. While I was there, I wanted to see if we could make a life for ourselves far from my family. New York is an incredible city, so energetic and full of people from so many parts of the world. I knew I could live there—"

"Are you saying you want me to go to New York?"

"No. I could live there but I realised how much you'd have to give up. All your friends are here. And then I knew what to do. You can't easily live in my world, but I can live in yours. Your friends accept me. And, if you think about it, Plotlands is also full of people who've arrived here from different places. Everyone who settles here is accepted."

The breath caught in her throat. It sounded so simple. Could it work?

"But your parents won't like you living here."

"They won't. But either they get used to that or they lose me to America. I'm not worried about what they think. I'm only concerned about what you think."

"So, we'll be next-door neighbours?"

"Ah, well, that's the thing. Not exactly. The reason Mr Fanshawe is so agitated is that there are two sets of plans. Bill told me which architect you'd engaged, and I went to see him."

He rolled out the plans and held them out for her to see. "This one shows the first idea, with my cottage being identical to yours." He allowed the drawings to roll up and then pulled out the one from underneath and unrolled that. "But this plan shows how we can put our

334

two pieces of land together and then, with the foundations that have already been dug on your land and more foundations on mine, we could have a much larger house for us both."

"One large house." Joanna stared at the new drawings, trying to imagine what it would look like. "But Ben—"

"Of course, we wouldn't want to do that unless we got married first."

Joanna closed her eyes. Could this be true? Her own home with the man she loved away from the scrutiny of his friends and family. With the support of her friends, they could do it …

"Joanna, please say something! If you don't want this, I promise I'll sell the land."

Joanna flung her arms around his neck. "I want this more than anything!"

The builders cheered and waved their caps in the air, and Mr Fanshawe strode towards them and slid the drawings out from between them.

"Right, let's get cracking then, lads," he shouted as the men cheered louder and whistled while Joanna and Ben carried on their kiss.

Joanna looked back over Ben's shoulder at the group of friends standing in the light of their lanterns at the gate. She was in his arms and when he reached the door to their new cottage, he'd carry her over the threshold and into their new life together.

The noisy crowd at the gate cheered and threw more rice. Not an enormous number of guests for a wedding, but they included everyone she loved. Sheila standing next to Bill, who'd given Joanna away. Their eyes glinting with pride in the lamplight, as if she had been their daughter. Mary next to Frank holding Jack in his arms, with Gracie, who'd been Joanna's bridesmaid, in front of them. Louisa and Harry, just back from their honeymoon and thrilled at the developments while they'd been away, shouted encouragement for their first night together, and Louisa blew kisses. Betty waved and, with finger and thumb in her mouth, produced a whistle a docker would have been proud of. She'd provided all the flowers and the bouquet that – much to everyone's amusement – Mrs Pike had caught. And slightly to one side, Mrs Pike, holding the bouquet, watched quietly. Was Joanna being fanciful in imagining she saw tears in her eyes, reflected in the lantern light?

Ben's parents had unexpectedly turned up for the ceremony but had declined the offer of a party in Green Haven. Thank heavens for that. Who could possibly have enjoyed the celebration with Mrs Richardson there? The recognition that Joanna was now also called Mrs Richardson made her giggle.

Ben looked down at her and smiled. The love shining

in his expression took her breath away. He'd been so right. Thrusting her into his social circle would have ended in unhappiness for them both. But everyone had taken to Ben immediately. No judgement. No prejudice. People's attitude seemed to be that if Ben lived on Plotlands, he was a Plotlander and, therefore, one of their own.

"Well, Mrs Richardson, what's making you smile?" he asked.

"I was just thinking I couldn't be any happier."

He frowned, feigning dismay. "I was hoping I might make you a little happier as soon as we close the doors."

She kissed his cheek, her heart beating faster at the thought of making love to him. Excitement and fear. So far, they'd only kissed, despite her suggesting they take things further on their night in London. But since he'd come to the building site that day and proposed a new joint house – and life, they hadn't been alone together.

There'd been so much to do to make the house ready and to arrange a wedding. They heard the voices drift away in the darkness to Sheila's. The lively chatter, now muted, continued and Harry struck up a lively fiddle tune. For the first time since they'd been in London, Joanna and Ben were alone. A oil lamp glowed in the corner of the room – thoughtfully lit by Sheila. Ben gently lowered Joanna's feet to the floor. Their floor. And one that was much larger than the floor she'd once dreamt about. She kept her arms wrapped around his neck and he slid his around her waist, pulling her tight.

This hadn't been how she'd imagined their first night together. She could see them together in their new bed, arms and legs entwined in the heat of passion, but not this awkward stage where they both knew what was going to happen but neither wanted to rush straight into things. Perhaps she should take his hand and lead him into the bedroom? But that seemed too cold. Too contrived. Like a duty. Perhaps she simply ought to change out of her wedding dress and into the lacy nightie Louisa had ordered for her.

"Shall I go and get out of my dress?" she whispered, wondering if this was actually what making love was like – impersonal and detached.

"No. Let me do that," he whispered and nibbled her ear, sending shivers of pleasure through her. Turning her around, he opened each pearl button down her back and placed a kiss on her skin until the dress slipped to the floor. He unpinned her hair and gently eased it out until it hung around her shoulders.

Taking a cue from him, she undid his shirt buttons and kissed each piece of naked skin as she exposed it, running her hand through the soft hairs on his chest, and breathing in the sweet smell of his skin.

Sweeping her up in his arms again, he carried her into the bedroom and gently laid her on the bed. He knelt next to her and continued to undress her slowly, his fingers feather-brushing her skin as he explored her body. Each kiss and caress adding to her mounting pleasure.

Later, as they lay in each other's arms, she remembered her earlier worries that she might feel detached and unresponsive when they made love, but the opposite had been true. Ben had taken things slowly, and she'd clung to him, poised on the edge of ecstasy for so long, she'd lost all sense of herself and her inhibitions, moaning with soft longing.

So, that was what it meant to become one.

Joanna awoke early the following morning. Ben's face was inches from hers, his breath deep and even. She lay studying his face, longing to stroke his cheek, to touch the tiny scar above his eye and to trace the outline of his lips; but feared she'd wake him.

It was unbelievable that only yesterday, they'd committed their lives to each other. She was Ben's wife. Mrs Richardson. She smiled at the thought. How long would it be before she felt she owned that name and didn't immediately think of Ben's mother?

His eyes moved back and forth beneath his eyelids as if he was searching for something and he smiled. What was he dreaming about? During the last few weeks, she'd learnt so much about him – his childhood and his hopes of one day farming the land. And now, they had the rest of their lives to live their dreams – together.

Ben sighed and stirred. His eyes opened and when they'd focused, he smiled. "Good morning, Mrs Richardson." He stroked her cheek.

"And good morning to you, Mr Richardson." She moved as if to wriggle out from under his arm.

"Where are you going?" he asked, playfully pulling her back.

"I thought I'd better prepare something for breakfast." She was now a wife and Ben would expect a certain standard of living.

"I must admit, I am rather hungry," he said, sliding his arm around her waist, before adding, "but only for you." He nibbled her ear, sending ripples of delight through her.

"But don't you expect me to—"

"I don't expect you to do anything, Joanna." He tenderly ran a fingertip down her neck and chest, planting kisses in its tingling wake. "What would you *like* to do?"

"Oh, this. Oh, definitely this ..." The breath caught in her throat as his finger traced a line down her body and his mouth followed, his stubble gently scratching her skin.

"I'm hungry for food now," Ben said, laying back on

his pillow with a satisfied sigh after they'd finished making love. "What shall we make for breakfast ... or is it time for lunch?"

"We? What shall *we* make?"

"Of course, *we*. Do you doubt I can cook?"

"Well ..."

"You're probably right!" He smiled mischievously. "So, you'll have to be patient with me."

"But don't you want me to do all the cooking and housework?"

"Not unless you want to. I didn't marry you to do the cleaning. I intend to help."

"But is that how it's usually done?"

"That's just the thing," Ben said, winding a lock of her hair around his finger. "It doesn't matter what's usually done. We'll do what suits us. The world's changing. We can do as we please."

How thoughtful he was. This man who'd given up his place in his family and social world for her. How lucky she was.

He tucked the hair behind her ear. "Before I forget, you'll need this." He leaned over to his bedside table. He held up two keys. "One for you and one for me."

Her own key! To her own cottage. A cottage she shared with Ben. She thought back to Aunt Ivy's house. Prim, fussy and cold. Her home would be full of love and warmth. And Ben.

"Well, I suppose I might as well learn how to boil an egg now as any time." He reached for his gown.

She sat up. "Are you serious, Ben?"

"Of course. Now, how do we get the eggs out of the chicken?" He got up and started for the door.

For a second, she thought he was serious, then she saw his body shake with laughter.

There had never been happiness such as this, such a lightness inside, she might almost have been floating.

Once, she'd wondered if birds were overawed by so much freedom when they first learnt to fly. There were no limits, no warning signs, no markers at all. Just a sky full of emptiness. Now, she knew Ben had set her free to soar, and that his love would always be her haven. Her Plotland haven.

At last, she was home.

END

Dawn would be thrilled if you would consider leaving a review for this book on Amazon and Goodreads, thank you.

If you'd like to know more about her books, please sign up for her newsletter on her website:

https://dawnknox.com

About the Author

Dawn spent much of her childhood making up stories filled with romance, drama and excitement. She loved fairy tales, although if she cast herself as a character, she'd more likely have played the part of the Court Jester than the Princess. She didn't recognise it at the time, but she was searching for the emotional depth in the stories she read. It wasn't enough to be told the Prince loved the Princess, she wanted to know how he felt and to see him declare his love. She wanted to see the wedding. And so, she'd furnish her stories with those details.

Nowadays, she hopes to write books that will engage readers' passions. From poignant stories set during the First World War to the zany antics of the inhabitants of the fictitious town of Basilwade; and from historical romances, to the fantasy adventures of a group of anthropomorphic animals led by a chicken with delusions of grandeur, she explores the richness and depth of human emotion.

A book by Dawn will offer laughter or tears – or anything in between, but if she touches your soul, she'll consider her job well done.

If you'd like to keep in touch, please sign up to her newsletter on her blog and receive a welcome gift, containing an exclusive prequel to The Duchess of Sydney, three short humorous stories and two photo-stories from the Great War.

Following Dawn

Blog: https://dawnknox.com

Amazon Author Central:

mybook.to/DawnKnox

Facebook:

https://www.facebook.com/DawnKnoxWriter

Twitter:

https://twitter.com/SunriseCalls

Instagram:

https://www.instagram.com/sunrisecalls/

YouTube:

https://tinyurl.com/mtcpdyms

The Duchess of Sydney

The Lady Amelia Saga – Book One

Betrayed by her family and convicted of a crime she did not commit, Georgiana is sent halfway around the world to the penal colony of Sydney, New South Wales. Aboard the transport ship, the Lady Amelia, Lieutenant Francis Brooks, the ship's agent becomes her protector, taking her as his "sea-wife" – not because he has any interest in her but because he has been tasked with the duty.

Despite their mutual distrust, the attraction between them grows. But life has not played fair with Georgiana. She is bound by family secrets and lies. Will she ever be free again – free to be herself and free to love?

Order from Amazon:

mybook.to/TheDuchessOfSydney

Paperback: ISBN: 9798814373588

eBook: ASIN: B09Z8LN4G9

The Finding of Eden

The Lady Amelia Saga – Book Two

1782 – the final year of the Bonner family's good fortune. Eva, the eldest child of a respectable London watchmaker becomes guardian to her sister, Keziah, and brother, Henry. Barely more than a child herself, she tries to steer a course through a side of London she hadn't known existed. But her attempts are not enough to keep the family together and she is wrongfully accused of a crime she didn't commit and transported to the penal colony of Sydney, New South Wales on the Lady Amelia.

Treated as a virtual slave, she loses hope. Little wonder that when she meets Adam Trevelyan, a fellow convict, she refuses to believe they can find love.

Order from Amazon:
https://mybook.to/TheFindingOfEden
Paperback: ISBN: 979-8832880396
eBook: ASIN: B0B2WFD279

The Other Place

The Lady Amelia Saga – Book Three

1790 – the year Keziah Bonner and her younger brother, Henry, exchange one nightmare for another. Eva is transported to the far side of the world for a crime she hadn't committed. Keziah and Henry are sent to a London workhouse where they'd been separated but when the prospect of work and a home in the countryside is on offer, both Keziah and Henry leap at the chance.

But the promised job in the cotton mill is relentless, backbreaking work and Keziah is full of regret that her wilfulness has led to such a downturn in her family's fortune.

Then, when it seems she may have discovered a way to escape the drudgery, the charismatic nephew of the mill owner shows his interest in Keziah. But Matthew Gregory's attempts to demonstrate his feelings – invariably result in trouble for Keziah. Is Matthew yet another of Keziah's poor choices or a triumph?

Order from Amazon:

https://mybook.to/TheOtherPlace

Paperback: ISBN: 979-8839521766

eBook: ASIN: B0B5VPLHGQ

THE DOLPHIN'S KISS

The Lady Amelia Saga – Book Four

Born 1790; in Sydney, New South Wales, to wealthy parents, Abigail Moran is attractive and intelligent, and other than a birthmark on her hand that her mother loathes, she has everything she could desire. Soon, she'll marry handsome, witty, Hugh Hanville. Abigail's life is perfect. Or is it?

A chance meeting with a shopgirl, Lottie Jackson, sets in motion a chain of events that finds Abigail in the remote reaches of the Hawkesbury River with sea captain, Christopher Randall. He has inadvertently stumbled across the secret that binds Abigail and Lottie. Will he be able to help Abigail come to terms with the secret or will Fate keep them apart?

Order from Amazon:
https://mybook.to/TheDolphinsKiss
Paperback: ISBN: 979-8842582969
eBook: ASIN: B0B85JX9BD

The Pearl of Aphrodite

The Lady Amelia Saga – Book Five

In 1790, three-year-old Charlotte Jackson is transported with her convict mother from London to Sydney. Twenty-one years later, Charlotte is offered the chance of a new life in London by the mysterious and brash Ruth Bellamy. Charlotte yearns to belong. A new start in a new country might be just what she needs.

On the perilous voyage, she falls for handsome Alexander Melford, also seeking betterment in London.

Fate throws them together. But the deceit of those they trust threatens to tear them apart. Will they ever escape the lies and finally be free to love?

Order from Amazon:

https://mybook.to/ThePearlOfAphrodite

Paperback: ISBN: 979-8356843648

eBook: ASIN: B0BKSPC93Z

The Wooden Tokens

The Lady Amelia Saga – Book Six

1768. Two children abandoned in the Foundling Hospital, London.

A boy. A girl.

Their material needs are met.

Their futures are organised.

Lacking a mother's love, they cling to each other. But their friendship is forbidden, and they're cruelly torn apart.

Now grown, their paths cross on the high seas.

Will their fragile childhood friendship blossom into something deeper?

Can they overcome a lifetime devoid of love? Now on the far side of the world... Will they create their own happy ending?

Coming in May 2023
Paperback: ISBN: 9798378855384

The Great War

100 Stories of 100 Words Honouring Those Who Lived And Died 100 Years Ago

One hundred short stories of ordinary men and women caught up in the extraordinary events of the Great War – a time of bloodshed, horror and heartache. One hundred stories, each told in exactly one hundred words, written one hundred years after they might have taken place. Life between the years of 1914 and 1918 presented a challenge for those fighting on the Front, as well as for those who were left at home—regardless of where that home might have been. These stories are an attempt to glimpse into the world of everyday people who were dealing with tragedies and life-changing events on such a scale that it was unprecedented in human history. In many of the stories, there is no mention of nationality, in a deliberate attempt to blur the lines between winners and losers, and to focus on the shared tragedies. This is a tribute to those who endured the Great War and its legacy, as well as a wish that future generations will forge such strong links of friendship that mankind will never again embark on such a destructive journey and will commit to peace between all nations.

"This is a book which everyone should read – the pure emotion which is portrayed in each and every story

brings the whole of their experiences - whether at the front or at home - incredibly to life. Some stories moved me to tears with their simplicity, faith and sheer human endeavour. " (Amazon)

Order from Amazon:

mybook.to/TheGreatWar100

Paperback: ISBN 978-1532961595
eBook: ASIN B01FFRN7FW
Hardcover: ISBN 979-8413029800

THE FUTURE BROKERS

Written as DN Knox with Colin Payn

It's 2050 and George Williams considers himself a lucky man. It's a year since he—like millions of others—was forced out of his job by Artificial Intelligence. And a year since his near-fatal accident. But now, George's prospects are on the way up. With a state-of-the-art prosthetic arm and his sight restored, he's head-hunted to join a secret Government department—George cannot believe his luck.

He is right not to believe it.

George's attraction to his beautiful boss, Serena, falters when he discovers her role in his sudden good fortune, and her intention to exploit the newly-acquired abilities he'd feared were the start of a mental breakdown.

But, it turns out both George and Serena are being twitched by a greater puppet master and ultimately, they must decide whose side they're on—those who want to combat Climate-Armageddon or the powerful leaders of the human race.

Order from Amazon: mybook.to/TheFutureBrokers
Paperback: ISBN 979-8723077676
eBook: ASIN B08Z9QYH5F

Printed in Great Britain
by Amazon

41741154R00195